RIVER OF LOVE

River of Love

Aimée Medina Carr

Homebound Publications
Ensuring that the mainstream isn't the only stream.

HOMEBOUND PUBLICATIONS
Ensuring the Mainstream Isn't the Only Stream | Since 2011
WWW.HOMEBOUNDPUBLICATIONS.COM

Quantity sales. Special discounts are available on quantity purchases by corporations, associations, bookstores and others. For details, contact the publisher or visit wholesalers such as Ingram or Baker & Taylor.

All places, characters and events are fictitious.
Any resemblance to actual places, persons or events is coincidental.

Published in 2019 by Homebound Publications
Cover & Interior Designed by Leslie M. Browning
Cover Illustration: Native Design by © Dimas Adi
Cover Illustration: River/Wave Design by © Meranna
Interior Illustration (Title Page) by © Meranna
Interior Illustration (Section Page) by © Transia Design
Rosary Illustration by © F-dor
ISBN 978-1-947003-49-1
First Edition Trade Paperback

10 9 8 7 6 5 4 3 2 1

Homebound Publications is committed to ecological stewardship. We greatly value the natural environment and invest in environmental conservation. Our books are printed on paper with chain of custody certification from the Forest Stewardship Council, Sustainable Forestry Initiative, and the Program for the Endorsement of Forest Certification.

DEDICATION

For Chris
first and forever
Christopher and Collin
Mi todo vida

RIVER OF LOVE

Rollin' on The River
Art of moving on
without letting go

River of Life

Trust the Spirit
Faith simply allows
Love to *flow in and out*

The Divine Dance
circle in–out–receive
Release fear and doubt
that stops and resists
the *One Flow of Love*

In The River
no need *to push it*
Relax–in God's current
carried by surprise

The River, the Flow, the Lover

Delicious ambiguity
Love–stronger than death
Love–who we are

Let the moment unfold into
what it is–
as it is

Just This...

Oh, I wish I had a river
I could skate away on
Oh, I wish I had a river so long
I would teach my feet to fly
Oh I wish I had a river
I could skate away on

—*River* by Joni Mitchell

PROLOGUE

Great Blue Heron

The measure of Love is
to Love without measure.
–St. Augustine

I SOAR INTO THE BLESSED, BRILLANTE, BLUEBIRD SKY, and bolt through thin, layers of silvery, mares' tail clouds. "Whew! My flying is rusty. I'm Juan de la Cruz (John of the Cross) Chávez, a wraith—a celestial being. I fly-by and drop in on my past life family to make sure all is *muy bueno*. It's a chance to see my granddaughter Rose Ramirez who's visiting her mother Alma, my daughter.

When Rose was in high school, this was a popular party spot on the Arkansas River. I watched over her, easily with a wingspan of six feet and a birds-eye view of all the activities. My camouflaged, blue-green color blended in with *The River*, rendering me almost invisible.

A strange word—*Arkansas,* pronounced Arkansaw, derived from the Quapaw Indian word akakaze meaning "land
of downriver people." *The River* carries the weight of the past.
Rose is drawn to *esta tierra encantada*—this enchanted land.

I met my wife Eugenia, at a community dance, in a small
town in *Nuevo Méjico.* I was eighteen; she was sixteen—*I'd
spend eternity Loving her.* Her father was a prominent lawyer,
and I was a poor shepherd's son. I tried unsuccessfully to convince him that I'd be a good provider. My father found me a
job at a large sheep ranch in Red Cañon, Colorado. The town
straddled the easterly flowing Arkansas River. We married in
secret and moved to our new life in the foothills of the majestic
Rocky Mountains.

I worked as a sheepherder for a ranch owned by the Ku
Klux Klan's Exalted Cyclops of the Klavern, allegedly, that's
why I'm murdered. The three angry and jealous ruffians from
Mexico couldn't stand that I had a happy family life and modest fortune. I helped them with a beat-up friend, as I dressed his
wounds, they slipped rat poison into my glass of wine. I was
the author of my misfortune, a victim of my kindheartedness.

I left behind my beautiful wife Eugenia with three, small
children to raise. We had eight grown children; four married
daughters with families and four sons, proudly, serving in the
armed forces during World War II.

A terrible time to disappear from *mi querida's*—my darling's life, with no savings to care for our daughters Alma, sev-
en, Adele, five, and youngest boy, John, three. I hovered for
over a year to ensure no harm came to them. I cursed the wicked murderers.

I fly west toward the Arkansas River where we lived off
River Street. Our *casita de la río vista*—the house with *The*

River view was a quick stroll on a rocky, ribbon path to the shimmery bluish-green water. A small, two-bedroom, brick house on a large lot with a garden for the big family. The softball diamond-sized side lot perfect for neighborhood games.

The house now is long gone, but tender memories transport me to happier times. The Chávez Ranchito bursts with children's squeals, lively laughter and loud conversations of family, friends, and neighbors. The coffee warming on *el fogón*—the old, wood burning stove, continuously stoked with *palillto's*—wood.

We always had room at the table especially during holidays the front porch double doors open wide welcoming with tamales, tortillas, *papas*—potatoes and *frijoles*—beans. Washed down with strong coffee while sharing *dichos y cuentos*—wisdom laced tales with Eugenia.

She'd lure them onto the edge of their seats while spinning supernatural yarns. Then curtly announced: "Time for midnight mass, grab your coats and jump in the truck." Tough as steel and delicate as a butterfly.

A lay member of the Carmelite Discalced Order of the Catholic Church, her life work was assisting those in need. A healer and midwife who used herbal concoctions.

Red Cañon was the headquarters of the Ku Klux Klan in the 1920s. The white supremacist terrorist group had a resurgence. A wave of anti-immigrant sentiment fueled by bigotry against Jews, Catholics, and Blacks. The Klan surfaced after the Roman Catholic Church announced plans to build an Abbey monastery. Their motive was to block the unwelcomed Catholics. The town's nickname was Klanyon City.

The Catholic Church enlisted a devout, Catholic gold miner as the front man to purchase the 90 acres of apple orchard land.

He took along seven monks and passed them off as his sons.

I sail over Sacred Heart School. Construction of the monastery began in 1924, and Sacred Heart School, a Benedictine boys parochial boarding college preparatory high school, opened in the fall of 1926. It was home to 90 monks and 250 students. The flowing fields of alfalfa for the horses and Gymkhana program replaced now with a winery. I dip and swirl past the gargoyles on the west side of the monastery, admiring their ageless beauty.

I've one more stop. I must peek in on *qué linda*—my beautiful daughter Alma. After my death, *pobrecita* was the Loving heart that held *la familia* together. Her youngest daughter Rose is the mirror image of my gorgeous Eugenia and *Loves as fiercely*.

Sitting at Alma's side, I close my eyes and listen to her long, deep conversation on the telephone, almost unknown today. Her voice sounds like it's smiling with a lilting laugh. The moment slows down, and I drink it in.

It's wrong to assume we're gone permanently when we die. We flit from Heaven instantly when our Loved ones are in need. To hold them and wipe their tears, and give *pésame*—sympathy during desperate, lonely hours. It doesn't have to be sad or scary; we can be here anytime. Almost everyone in Heaven has someone on earth they watch. Love transcends space and time, *even death*.

Alma tells Rae, her oldest daughter of the Prince Albert tobacco she smells while praying to the large, blue-robed Mother Mary statue in her bedroom. A naughty vice Eugenia and I, deliciously shared; she rolled them better than I did.

Spirits are Heaven's serendipity calling cards. We're the

hawk or deer companion on the morning walk. We appear as surprises, or as a new development, voices heard in the shower, a soft tap on the shoulder. That barely audible whisper right before falling asleep. We're in the origins of your Love. *The Alpha and Omega*, in the air around you, swirling through your thoughts. The unexplained breeze weaving *Love* from Heaven to the in-between and Earth.

I blast straight up two-hundred feet and shoot westward over Main Street where it's no longer allowed to *"drag the gut."* A four-block strip of downtown, where bored teenagers in souped-up cars with loud mufflers, cruised up and down searching for excitement. *A sacrosanct place of connection.*

I pass over Chautauqua Park, where fun times echo with Fourth of July picnics and the many Chávez family reunions. I spot my oldest son, Julian's house, one block from the park. His strong-minded daughter, Chavela and Alma's audacious daughter, Rose raised like sisters wore down a one-mile path between houses, distinguishable from other rocky and tangled trails. One mile west forged through the side of a mountain is Tunnel Drive, another teenage party spot, a four-mile, man-made road with two tunnels.

I get a tug—it's almost time to return. Three miles north is Star Watcher Mountain where a star-crazed, Indian princess lost her life. The mountain silhouette is a perfect profile of a woman lying down. We'd tell our children this tragic, Indian legend and end with; *"Happy counting, Star Watcher."*

Directly across as the crow flies is Skyview Drive a scenic, touristy spot. A one-way highway built on a razorback ridge by Colorado State prisoners in 1903. It's 500 feet high with a spectacular view and a road that whips like a roller coaster.

Red Cañon's referred to as "prison alley," because of its nine, state and four, federal prisons and penitentiaries.

My blue yonder exit portal—I don't know when or if I'll return. *I leave overwhelmed with gratitude,* savoring every second in Red Cañon. In the flicker of an instant, I vanish.

La Familia

1965 - 1975

A place belongs forever to whoever claims it hardest,
remembers it most obsessively, wrenches it from itself,
shapes it, renders it, loves it so radically that
he remakes it in his own image.
–Joan Didion

There is no past, no future;
everything flows in an eternal present.
–James Joyce

Red Cañon River People

The only time you should ever look back
is to see how far you've come.
–Anonymous

M Y NAME IS ROSE RAMIREZ—*this story is my glory.* Summer of 1965, our family moved from Colorado City to the rural town of Red Cañon. My father, Blaze cut hair in Colorado City. We relocated so he could open a barbershop in Red Cañon. The really real reason: Dad got busted having an affair—and she'd given birth to a baby boy. He didn't know if the baby was his, and wasn't sticking around to find out.

When my mother found his girlfriend's prescription bottle in the car, he had to end it. Mom was to never know about the prostitute he met at a beer joint next door to where he worked. When confronted by my mother, Dad fiercely denied it.

We saw the result of the Lover's argument; she used a church key to slice open the right side of his face, from the sideburn to the bottom of his chin. It left a nasty scar and a permanent mark of the indiscretion. I was too young to understand, but as an adult, my older sister explained during a discussion of our parent's hot mess of a marriage.

My mother was eager to take her children out of Colorado City which included me, Rae my sister, and brother Essé. My siblings ran with the neighborhood riffraff. A next-door neighbor and best friend Eddie busied me with playdates and escorted me to school every day.

Eddie's mother bellowed over the fence for him to come home in the evenings for dinner: *"Eddiiieee!"* He yelled back: *"WHATTEEE?"* Heartbroken to move away from my first, best friend my ethnically diverse school in Colorado City was not the situation in Red Cañon where there were few minorities.

My mother's sister Lucy, brother Julian, and my father's parents, Grandma Grace, and Grandpa Frank lived in Red Cañon. It took two, overflowing pickup loads to move our belongings. She was relieved to see Colorado City in the rearview mirror of Dad's silver, 1957, Chevy. Looking forward through the big windshield to what's ahead, was vastly more important than what's left behind.

Shortly, after we moved to Red Cañon, my mother got pregnant. It could've been an honest slip, being Catholic, but it appeared to be an attempt to hold onto the marriage. I was mommy's little helper with baby Mangas, (Coloradas after the Apache leader) who we called Gus. She went to work as a teacher's aide at Head Start when Gus turned three years old. She took him to work, returned home exhausted and delegated the night duties to me. I can't imagine life without my first cousin, Chavela a.k.a. Cha Cha—Uncle Julian's daughter. I was introduced to my cousins during the summer, the only saving grace of that painful first year at an unaccepting, all-white elementary school in Red Cañon.

Mom adored her oldest brother Julian; he was a carbon copy of her father, Juan. I delighted in Uncle Julian's modest white house; it even had a flagpole! I ran up and wrapped my body around it like a tetherball and chanted a lively rendition of *Ring Around the Rosie*. Cha Cha (named after the legendary Mexican singer Chavela Vargas) was a standoffish tomboy that lived in cutoffs, and T-shirts with a wild dark Indian mane in contrast to my frilly dresses, patent leather shoes, and short prim haircut. Adept at running and playing sports with her five siblings, I kept close to Mom, coloring, reading, and playacting alone indoors. Years later, Chavela teased me—all the cousins thought I was mentally challenged.

Uncle Julian was a gifted gardener and good provider with quiet gravitas. Unlike my father, he worked a regular job and came home every night. My Aunt Lily's tamales were the highlight of the holidays, the vittles top-notch. I never left her house without eating.

I fought back fears of the unknown living in this new place. The house wasn't cockroach infested like other rentals we'd lived in. Dad had an exciting new business and was on his best behavior and Cha Cha was becoming my best friend.

Blessed Day

Gratitude is not only the greatest of virtues,
but the parent of all the others.
—Cicero

B LAZE'S BARBERSHOP WENT BELLY-UP within the year.
He drank up the profits while the *borracho*–boozehound
friends scared off the paying customers. A call from the county
jail seized my mother with panic or a cruel disappearing act
propelled her into a tailspin of worry.

Thankfully, she got a job at Head Start. Aunt Lucy came by
with the life-changing news.

"Alma, sit down." She readies the younger sister for opportunity knocking.

"What is it, Sis? Hope it's good news, I sure need some."

"I met with the board of the Head Start Program and starting Monday you are their new teacher's aide with Gus enrolled
in your class." It's only part-time and low paying but a foot in
the door and *she'd blast it wide open.*

"What a blessed day, thank you, Lucy." Before my mother
got her job, we'd been on welfare, food stamps, and received
commodities. *Commodity day was a day of celebration.* We
picked up the box of government-issued food: blocks of orange
processed cheese and Spam-like meat, a large can of honey and

peanut butter, a ten-pound bag of rice, and boxes of powdered milk, and oatmeal.

She rounded out meals by purchasing a hundred-pound bag of *frijoles*–beans, and a hundred-pound bags of *papas*–potatoes, and flour. She kept a freezer full of roasted Pueblo and New Mexico green chili, bought by the bushel. Solid staples in poor Chicano families' pantries and the Holy Trinity of Mexican cuisine: *hot green chili, pinto beans, and tortillas.* Blaze and his two brothers hunted and provided deer and elk meat.

Mom's efficient with every cent and paid her bills on time. She taught her children frugality and responsibility in living within your means and *to never owe anything to anyone.* Her motto, "If you can't pay for it in cash, you don't need it."

Thanks to Aunt Lucy's string pulling we all had after school part-time CETA (Comprehensive Employment and Training Act) jobs, a government student work program for low-income families.

A bank held a contest to win the installation and yearlong cost of a residential telephone. My sister Rae opened a savings account and filled out the entry slip. She mentioned it to Mom and forgot about it, till they sent a letter that she'd won.

Mom ran through the house shouting and genuflecting, "Thank you, Mother Mary, Santo Niño, and Holy Family for performing this small but powerful miracle!" It opened new doors for us, and we never go without a phone again. It became the main source of my mother's solace, entertainment, and primary social outlet. She had the misfortune of Loving a man who cared only for his next drink, but her children, each in their small way made efforts to compensate.

Little Mama Cha Cha

A single rose can be my garden
a single friend my world.
—Leo Buscaglia

C HAVELA, A.K.A. CHA CHA IS A WILD GIRL with *colossal cojones*. Full of fire and sass, *"a live wire"* who carries Tortilla Flats, the projects and the *rez* in her veins, and poetry in her heart. Her mind snaps like a whip with clever *cuentos* that spark wisdom and wit. Her brilliance burns too bright for the simpletons in this town. I'm frightened by her fearlessness. She never gives a flying fart–*petho* what others think of her, I envy that.

We grow up inseparable, in this small, all-white conservative town. Flash forward to the summer before our freshman year of high school, Cha Cha's already fifteen precisely six months older and will forever celebrate the big birthdays first.

She's at my house on a hot and sticky August afternoon. We watch four, good-looking Chicano boys, play catch football in the next-door neighbor's backyard. Later we find out they're from San Francisco, California, on a family visit with their Uncle George.

"Who do you think they are?" I ponder while peering through the lace curtains. We joked that we couldn't date Chicano boys because they were either relatives or scuzzy lowlifes our parents wouldn't approve of.

"What the hell–*let's go introduce ourselves.*" Cha Cha blurts, jaw set with dauntless nerve as she dashes out the door. A seminal moment that changes her life forever. The oldest one Sam latches like a leech onto her from that instant. Sexually active for over a year and not using birth control she naïvely believes *she can't get pregnant.* In the backseat of a green metallic, 1969, Ford Thunderbird at the Skyview Drive-In while Clint Eastwood shoots up San Francisco—*a son's conceived,* and her childhood ends.

¡*Que pinche lástima!*

She moves to San Francisco with Sam. On a bright shimmery spring day, Cha Cha comes to say goodbye. Mom cries, and Rae takes a pitiful Polaroid of the three of us standing outside in front of the brick house. Cha Cha wears a flowery hippie shift that hides her protruding belly.

Summer begins, and *Now I have no one,* nada. I devise a routine to compete in the cheerleading try-outs for Red Cañon High School. I pick Steely Dan's song *Reeling in the Years* for the audition. I start the first week in June working on my routine with try-outs in August. I practiced diligently every day until I could do the routine in my sleep, so no matter the outcome, it wouldn't be from lack of effort.

I am stunned when I don't make the squad but proud of myself. I receive a telephone call from Ms. Frey, the cheerleading sponsor. "Rose, I want to offer you a position on the cheerleading squad. The totals were so close after the judges left, I re-tallied them and found an error in your favor. Congratulations, I hope you'll accept my offer, and I sincerely apologize for the mix-up." She said in her measured, stiff tone.

Score one for the boss-ass brown girls–Boo-yah!

Bonfire

I'M CHATTING ON THE PHONE with Paul Rosas; we're discussing the upcoming 40-year high school reunion at Sacred Heart School in Red Cañon, Colorado. I'm scheduling a time to interview him for my book about mutual high school friends and experiences that happened in the early 1970s.

"Hey, comadre, how did you meet that *pendejo*, Jack Dillon?" Paul, a District Attorney from New Mexico, and my high school boyfriend, Jack Dillon attended the private, parochial Catholic college prep high school in my hometown. Paul was a super shy, Spanish speaking, wiry pipsqueak from Santa Fe. The last guy in his senior class to get stoned.

"You got that much time, *vato? It's a Long and Winding Road."* I trilled. "It's taken two months of emailing and texting to connect I don't want to waste time with the nonessentials."

"Yeah Rosie, for you I'll make the time. Tell me how you met Jack," he pleads.

Just hearing his name sent a stab through my heart. I spent a lifetime chasing a ghost memory and haunted by this *Old Love.* Finally, I'm free of years of sad illusions, truth born out of pain, beauty spawned by neglect. The Great Spirit's quivering arrows guided my life in the right direction and saved me from myself. *If only he'd been a better man.*

Infinite Love draws us toward the fullness of our being; it's at our core—don't fight, resist or deny it. *Love will always win.* I aimed for reason, but no matter what my brain thinks, the heart is its own master. Peering back on the road not taken is a seesaw of senseless misery. A constant battle—*a war between remembering and forgetting.*

"Ready to shoot the nostalgic whitewater rapids of *Lost Love?*" I quip.

"I'm buckled up Buttercup." Paul laughs.

"It was Homecoming weekend in the fall of 1972; excitement riffled through the crowd. Many new faces: the incoming, *"fresh meat"* freshmen, attend the festivities for the first time. I was a cheerleader; the squad marched in front of the Lions High School band at the beginning of the Homecoming parade." The faces sling past my mind's eye.

Starting on Main Street, the entire town attended the parade of the marching band, a busload of the junior and varsity football teams and the Homecoming Royalty. The King and Queen glide by on top of a sporty red convertible. The high school students clasp hands and *"snake dance"* down Main Street. Boys tugged at the girls, some refusing to hold hands, jumping, herky-jerky, going too fast, and others holding back.

We convene at the high school for an old-fashioned bonfire, every year it's built too roaring big and hot. Gray smoke billowed from the giant fire. The cheerleaders cough and frantically fan through the thick haze.

The squad of six line up in front of the bonfire, working the crowd into a *Lions' frenzy.* The lion mascot entertained with high backflips and round-offs ginning up more excitement. I see a face that I don't recognize. He is *really checking me out*. I'm surprised, being a Chicana that this new student's interested.

We yell: "What ya gonna do? *Beat the Panthers!*" We jump and kick—endorphins pumping. A large log on the bonfire slips and almost falls on top of us. We dart away, I seize the opportunity and dash to where my admirer is standing.

"Hey, that was close!" He shouts and flicks ashes off my gold and ivory uniform and ponytail, our eyes meet.

"Thanks, I'm Rose Ramirez, are you a new student?" My heart is thumping fast—I've never acted so forward *especially, toward a gabacho*—a white guy.

"No, I go to Sacred Heart School," he beams a wide smile. He knows I singled him out. We're showered with more ashes from the log avalanche. Burnt soot whooshes in the soft breeze, mixed with the hoppy, beer breath of the band members. The loud music booms in our ears. The jazzy, pep song *"Lion's Rag"* blares behind us.

"Shhh! Not so loud—do you want your head stomped in by all these goat ropers? This is Red Cañon High School's territory, just admitting you're from that school will get you a beating. What are you doing here?" I ask.

"We were just looking for something to do," he leans back and introduces his hunky friend, Caleb King. A tall boy with a halo of blond curls, he smiles, and waves. I case the crowd to see if anyone's watching us.

Frowning now, I say, "*You need to leave* before these boneheads figure out who you are and there's a brawl." I grab his grooming hand and squeeze it tight. I look longingly, at the glossy, chestnut brown hair, and imagine combing my fingers through the silky mane. *His hair is his crowning glory.* I take stock of their effortless ease and raffish, preppy demeanor. Talking with a cheerleader put them in the crosshairs of danger.

"I'm Jack Dillon, do you like football?" He asks.

"I prefer basketball, but it's OK." I shrug.

"Do you want to come on Tuesday, to watch my intramural football team, *the Gonads* play?" He asks.

The drill sergeant cheerleading sponsor, Mrs. Frey barks: "Rose Ramirez, please, get in formation, *NOW!*" I lean in and whisper in his ear; "I'd love to see your Gonads." I bite my lip. He laughs and elbows his sidekick. "Let's get going."

The wind flutters—*Joy.* Whipped up with the smoke and fire—*Excitement.* Hovering above the havoc, here and in-between everything, tenderly slips in—*Love.* The Spirit is and will always be *unmerited Grace.*

Jack and Caleb were unaware that boys from their school followed them. The group is the Mexican clique. Their leader is Fernando Fernandez, a serpentine fellow from Taos, New Mexico. A natural leader, his macho manner driven by pride and ego, beneath it all he's terrified and clueless.

Paul snorts, "I remember that douchebag. He harassed both of you. So, what happened between you and Jack?" He asks.

"Now, happily married and with a family, I couldn't connect the dots till looking backward. A dark gravity field of a wounded past held me hostage for decades. My focus was on the daily routine, afraid of the rich, mysterious inner world. What held me back; fear of failure and insecurity? Neediness and security overruled my deepest desires. *La cola mueve al perro*—the tail wagging the dog.

Recently, on a golden Indian summer afternoon while on a visit to Red Cañon I went for a run on the trail of the crystalline Arkansas River. Daydreaming along the wide riverbank, I reviewed the jigsaw jumble of my life. *Jackpot!* It was as if someone had ripped off the ceiling and showed me the sky. Not getting what you want is a wonderful stroke of luck. Simply, some Love is ill-timed. I let go of what wasn't meant to be including the negative storyline that defined me. My nightmare twenties made me who I am. Messy mistakes are portals of discovery. I bloomed from the wound that once bled.

The late afternoon sun danced off the tumbling waves creating intense twinkling light. I looked upstream and was soothed by a sinuous bend in *The River,* the rushing, Rubicon healing water of this timeless place. The powerful epiphanic jolt filled me with gratitude.

"Paul, I know you feel this with your oldest and dearest friends from Sacred Heart School, after forty years—our attachments are invisible threads that run from our hearts and reach through dimensions of time and space. We are held in place by what links us. *Separation is an illusion.*

"No, shit when I see these guys we are like kids on the playground, wrestling and fighting with each other. *We're all still so tight.* They know you know who they are which is their quintessential selves. We are the same bro's we were in high school. Friends are the family you choose," He said warmly.

"At fifty-nine, I'm the same Chicana that pines for more beyond my reach. Unappeasable hunger—an inherited genetic congruence. *Creating problems that don't exist.* I grapple with the ego and how it frames life in *expectation* and comparison. The gap between what I want and have is the origin of my dissatisfaction. I rely on grace to shower light on appreciating what's here, instead of longing for what isn't.

I'm still that young girl, watered by my own tears. *Life longing for itself.* I grew in rich, riverbed soil along a path of roses that guided my way. I sprang from *sacred ground* the homeland of my Apache, Diné, and Ute ancestors who hunted and nurtured families with blood, sweat, tears, and Love. Always— *Love is what we're made for, and Love is who we are.* Our ancestors work through us we are all walking family trees. I am the result of the *Love* of thousands.

The journey between who I once was and who I am becoming *is where the dance of life takes place.* The dark and light together is the heart of Wisdom and Love. It's easy to let go of the past, once I realized that no matter how different it might've gone down, *I couldn't be more Loved than I am now.* I'm right where I'm supposed to be—just a tiny flicker of a much larger flame that is Life itself."

"Amen, *sistah.* The Love we experienced back then is still a thriving, powerful, force connecting the bright-eyed brimming with magic teenagers to the present life-weary adults." Paul said.

"It was *something of a gorgeous time,*" I recall wistfully.

"Do you think Jack will come to the reunion?" Paul asks.

"I sent a letter inviting him, but I haven't received an answer. I'd like to reconnect." There was a long silent pause.

"*Now,* I really have to boogie, I've got a deposition to prepare, thank you for your patience and for not thinking what a *pinche cabrón* I am. See you Memorial Weekend in Red Cañon *mujer;* it's going to be Crazytown!" Paul signs off with "God bless you and your family, take care, *Love You.*"

Sacred Heart School Glory Days

THE RIVER REFUGE

1971 - 1975

—————— ☥ ——————

*Where there is great Love
there are always miracles.*
–Willa Cather

*The only things that are important in life
are the things you remember*
–Jean Renoir

The Gonads

*Love is a fruit in season at all times
and within the reach of every hand.*
—Mother Teresa

CHA CHA RETURNED TO RED CAÑON before the ink faded on the Polaroid. The romance soured as soon as baby Julian was born and both would be back living with her parents with Cha Cha re-enrolled in high school. She embraced the suck and moved the fuck forward. *She is one tough Chingona.*

Cha Cha and I ride our bikes along the frontage road on the outskirts of town to the Sacred Heart School campus. Jack saunters up, "Hey, you made it! The *Gonads* are raring to go. We're playing the *Nutsbe Chaffin'* team—a bunch of baby stoners that we'll easily cream. I'll catch up with you after the game." He turns and runs toward the football field.

During the fall, Tuesday is Intramural football game day at Sacred Heart School the Benedictine college preparatory high school and monastery located 3 miles east of the sleepy, prison town. The Benedictines came to Colorado in the late 1880's seeking relief from tuberculosis. The main building housed the administration offices and the Abbots living quarters. The Tudor Gothic Abbey church and the monastery were home for 90 monks with 200 residential and 50-day students.

We sit crossed-legged on the grassy sidelines, breathing in the tingly air of boundary-free wild youth. Dust blew off U.S. Highway 50, which ran in front of the school.

"Who's that?" Cha Cha pointed at a demure, birdlike bespectacled boy downfield, standing with another awkward looking student.

"That's Oliver, a friend of Jack's. *I really like him.* He's super friendly. He came by my house to make sure I'd be at the game. He's gay and so open about it, it's refreshing." I think of my older sister still *"in the closet"* not able to come out to our strict Catholic parents.

"The petite Mexican guy with the John Lennon glasses is Gomez 'Gonzo' Gallegos. They're roommates and best friends." I wave at them they're discussing us at the same time. Shielding her eyes with her hand from the late afternoon sun: "Hmmm...Who's to be my next victim?" She contemplated, trying not to laugh, tapping her fingers on her thigh.

"See the blond, curly-haired, teddy bear looking guy, *isn't he adorable?"* I point at a boy standing near Oliver. After the game, when she's introduced to Mac, his smoke blue eyes lit up, "Hey, Sexy Mexy." He said. A sweet addition to Jack's gang and Cha Cha, *who steals his heart.*

There were sixteen buildings on 250 acres. The Notre Dame like vesper bells chime hourly from the cathedral's tower. It's the second largest employer in town; the state and federal prisons are number one. The own another Catholic boarding high school—Scholastico Academy (sister school).

The barns housed the herd of 45 horses for the Vaquero Riding Club, which hosted Gymkhana's—rodeo competitions with local schools. Extracurricular activities included a full varsity sports program. Also, a Glee Club Choir that toured the states, a theater arts program, skiing, tennis courts, and an outdoor pool. Twenty-six states and nine foreign countries were represented. The school through the years produced politicians, doctors, lawyers, musicians, artists, entrepreneurs and distinguished representatives in every profession.

Headmaster Rawleigh Rio described it as—*Caught between the Devil and the Gulf.* The Colorado Federal Prison on one end and the Royal Gorge, the world's highest suspension bridge at the other end.

I spot a group of dark-haired boys downfield. It's Fernando Fernandez & Company. He shadows Jack at all his activities and boasts that he's going to befriend Jack, to maneuver me away from him. All this energy focused on a girl he hasn't seen up close. It enrages him that a Mexican girl prefers a white dude.

The high jinks kick off; Jack hides the football under his shirt. The *Nutsbe Chaffins* dogpile him, and the football slips out. A rowdy performance for us, the boy's school doesn't receive many female visitors. All eyes are watching us.

Midfield, sophomore boys, cheer for the Junior team: *"GOOOO—NADS!!!"* Cracking each other up between yells, and ringing a loud, clanging cowbell. We roll our eyes and giggle.

We watch an elegant, white-haired, lady approaching.

"Well, look what I've found—*girls.* I'm Marie Noonan, I teach Humanities here." She waits for us to stand up.

"I'm Rose Ramirez, and this is Chavela Chávez, so nice to meet you. We're friends with Jack Dillon." I offer my hand to shake.

"This is such a pleasant surprise." She smiles warmly.

"Humanities, what's that?" Cha Cha asks.

"Right now, we're reading Joseph Campbell's, *Hero with a Thousand Faces*; he was a fascinating mythologist," Marie said. I flash a thousand-watt smile.

"Would you like to sit in on one of my classes?" She asks. Before we answer, she heads toward her parked car behind us.

"Ms. Noonan, I want to come to your next class, when is it?" I hustle to catch up with her.

"Oh, call me Marie, all the boys do. On Thursday at 3:30, Room 6, bring a notebook and pen, I look forward to seeing you." She placed her black leather purse and folded, New York Times newspaper on the front seat of the pristine blue, 1965, Chevy Nova. She slips in and drives away, waving her hand, nodding dismissively at me. A faint wisp of Jean Naté perfume lingers in the air with the puff of exhaust.

Cha Cha passes on the class; she has to take care of baby Julian. Usually, a straight-A student, she's held back a year and must work extra hard to make up classes missed while in California.

« —————•————— »

I'm a budding maverick with a beginner's mind. *I yearn for a large-deep-spacious life.* My parents try to hold me back; my mother warns, "be cautious." I want more of everything: art, books, movies, and music. I'm an adventurous seeker, an empty tablet primed for new words. *I crave radiance* and ache for transformation. I want a life *that is more* than Red Cañon.

Things that happen when you're young seem so much more important because *they're happening for the first time.* Choices made unknowingly, are so vital and profound. I'm a proud Colorado Chicana, with honey-brown skin, long, curly, black hair, big chocolate eyes, and a light-up-the-sky smile that I'm quick to flash.

Jack Dillon is whip-smart and well read, with boy-next-door good looks. I fall for his lively, eager, sky blue eyes that perk up when laser beamed at me. We have a strong mental connection that is more of a turn-on than any physical attraction. True Love fuses beyond sexuality. Our souls alight, align and dance in celebration.

He's enigmatic and retreats into himself with a sideways gravity. Gentle but heartlessly direct, after meeting my plump mother, he remarked: "Now there's a set of hips!" His laconic, cool grace and indifference renders him stuck up, but he is just shy and reserved. *He's the inverse of me.* Jack is genuine and honest with indifference to the rules. Tall and slender with a dry sense of humor, his introversion flows with slight distrust. A shock of thick, satiny, chestnut hair falls like a closed curtain over one side of his face shielding him from the world.

Everything is charged, vibrant, and alive when I'm with him. My life was one way until there was Jack... *Enormous. First. Permanent.*

Baptism by Boulder

We shall be changed in a moment,
in the twinkling of an eye.
–Corinthians 1:15

C HAVELA AND I CRUISE ON BIKES to El Martinez Mexican restaurant, a small adobe building, the perfect rendezvous place and only a mile from Sacred Heart School. We stash them in a storeroom; Mom's a childhood friend of the owner.

Jack and Caleb wait in the parking lot; they're excited to share a new discovery. It's the first time we're invited to *The River.* The crisp, elm and poplar leaves flutter red and yellow to the ground, swirling at our feet, on the blustery autumn day.

"How far is this place? Are we the first girls to see it?" Cha Cha asks. It's her first time meeting Caleb. She looks sharp in jeans that fit after losing all the baby weight. Her family took care of little Julian while she's at school or with friends.

"It's a half mile down this road which dead-ends at *The River.* Yes, you are the first non-Sacred Heart students to grace our new find," Jack confirms.

"It's a beautiful, peaceful spot. We can light up a joint and hang loose," Caleb adds, oozing charisma. He's tall and lanky, with a slight swagger, shoulders slouched with hips thrust forward: *A Keep on Truckin' lean.* His slit perpetual stoner eyes are framed by a mop of curly, shimmery blond hair and a blissful smile. He's from Santa Fe, New Mexico; Jack picked him as his best friend, a couple of hours after arriving at Sacred Heart School.

We skip and pretend hopscotch on the road, and moo at the Holstein cow audience kept in by an electric fence. "How did you find it?" I ask.

"Our squirrelly friend, Oliver Fellini got pissed at a jock for calling him a fag, stomped off campus *wandered down this road and stumbled into paradise,*" Jack explains as he kicks a rock down the middle of the road.

"He lit up a doobie, mellowed out and returned to campus. He pulled us aside and said, 'This weekend let's gather dope, booze, and snacks and spend the whole weekend at *The River*." Caleb said.

"Did you?" Cha Cha's curious if they had a far-out time.

"We got so wasted, Ollie whipped up a batch of wicked magic mushroom shakes and some nimrod fell into *The River!* We rushed him back to school before hypothermia set in. He's the druggie last year that dropped acid for 30 days straight after a devastating heartbreak." Caleb shakes his head in disbelief.

"This is our refuge, where we can be ourselves, howl like wolves, and skinny dip. We leave our worries at school. Moonlight is so intense and campfires are the best. Such an ideal location on a dead end road, no one comes back here. *No pigs, no parents, no priests, no hassles.*" Caleb chants the explorer's anthem in their new world.

We reach a thin, worn, deer trail at the end of the road.

"Watch that wire; it's an electric fence, it'll zap you. It's for cows but works the same on humans. Our friend, Don, whizzed on it and got the shock of his life." Caleb points to a thin, black wire that ran the length of the field, next to *The River*. The air changes and the temperature drops with a damp, mineral scent, which is brisk and cooler by the flowing water.

We meander down the lush path about fifty yards, then... *We feel it—it's like a force field.* A crossing over into sacredness. The lacy, cathedral canopy of cottonwood trees filtered with dabbled *"God light"* streamed through thick branches. The effulgence of magic wildness.

"At the still point of the turning world. Neither from nor towards; there the dance is, neither arrest nor movement," Jack recites T.S. Eliot. "I discovered him over the summer," he grins.

We all stand at *The River's* edge and watch the swift, powerful waves whisk by vibrating us with a roaring wall of sound. Transfixed by the shushing of the waves *flowing ~ flowing ~ flowing. "Let The River take you."* The mountain wind whistles through the sacred cottonwoods.

"Bombs away!" Cha Cha yells interrupting the reverie. She wings a huge rock into the rumbling Arkansas River. It makes a solid *tunk* sound and splashes up violently.

"To the Goddess Sulis who believed water can wash away sadness, pain, and suffering. She was a Celtic Sun Goddess, I just wrote a paper on Goddesses for an English class. I'm *loco*—crazy for them, research still fresh in the *ol' cabeza.*" She pokes her temple with an index finger.

Caleb is startled by her wildness.

"Baptism by boulder," he jokes.

"Imagine a religion called *Far Out-ism:* enter this moment without resistance or attempts at control in this mind-blowing inspiring cathedral. Experience the beauty and *know everything is a Miracle.* Nature eclipses words. The first Bible is the *Bible of Nature.* The Great One's power is all around us; our minds refuse to see it. I feel it here." Caleb's smooth, dreamy voice communicates in a slight, astonishing way.

"Whoa, cowboy, that's some heavy shit!" Cha Cha cries.

Jack gathers us together, "Let's keep this sacred ground secret and christen it ours." We bow our heads, Caleb said a quick prayer: "Please allow the earth and cosmic energy to flow through our body. May it be with the blessings of the Supreme Being, that we benefit in our spiritual growth, awareness, and understanding." He opens his eyes, surprised he remembered the bedtime childhood prayer. I chime in with, "A'Ho! Amen."

"Let's build with river rock a Labyrinth," Jack said while watching the crystal prisms dart off the bouncing water. We nod in agreement.

"We can start designing it immediately—*Ollie will go bonkers.*" He glances at me; we share a splash of happiness.

"Let's keep this place to ourselves, for now, we don't want loads of stoners crashing our spot," Jack said.

We gather stones to build a large fire ring close to *The River.* Next outing, we'll bring tools and finish it. We hear the cows mooing next door, it's milking time, the temperature drops and we're losing light. It's rapidly growing dusk.

"Let's gather ten, large boulders, that'll make a large fire ring," Jack said.

Cha Cha wanders over to the riverbed and hits the jackpot.

The two boys heave them up to the flattest open area. The

sunset's final orange slab fades into deep purple shadow, and the smoky air flows from nearby fired up wood stoves.

"Get going, you're going to be riding in the dark, we'll finish up here." Jack kisses me goodbye.

God's Garden

Love is repaid by Love alone.
–St. John of the Cross

O LIVER EXPERIENCED IT, the day he was drawn to *The River* for the first time. A line of a Rumi poem echoed in his thoughts: *"Let yourself be silently drawn by the strange pull of what you really Love."* He's pulled by an invisible thread of Love to *The River*. Deeply moved by his willingness, Love responds. We're all moved by it—trust, surrender and it accepts the invitation. *Only from a place of spirit does Love become visible and enable one to see clearly.*

It happens to anyone who crosses *The River* threshold, we enter into God's Garden—pure naked being, a springboard to the sacred. A way out of our heads and into the reality of non-dual thinking. A free-fall into the *boundless chasm of Love:* the bliss yielding, silver stranded, *Eternal Now.* Whether it's a townie or a trust fund preppy entering into the majestic heart of *The River,* the blindfold of the ego vanishes, and the possibilities unfold.

It's thrilling to share this new experience with friends; the first visible jolt—*their gaze changes.* The blinders removed, lenses cleaned, replaced by reverence, indescribable well-being, and awareness of the resplendent surroundings.

"Wow! What's happening?" Is their most common reaction.

"Relax, let go, let the sublime beauty wash over you. It's trippy at first, but once you open up, grace flows." I assure them, and hold their hands or lead them by the arm.

When the senses open up to the *Divine,* the veil of everyday ugliness is lifted. The wild danger of awareness is a glorious side effect when having an inner experience with the Supreme Being. There is no separation between the secular and the sacred. Regrettably it doesn't last, but as long as *The River* invites and opens up to us, we'll return for more.

I refer it to friends feeling bent out of shape, distraught or fearful. "Go to *The River* for a spark up, or *God shot at the mystery holding tank,*" I assure them of its healing qualities. Mind-altering substances help deal with the intense, alluring pull of the mystical elements and its emerging theater of undiscovered beauty. Smoking enhances the celebration of pure *delight, creativity, and Love* that radiates from this place.

Cynical students from Sacred Heart School make fun of the naïve, *"holy hippies"* that party with the Chola townies. They say we drink hobo wine, drop acid, and get stoned till we hallucinate a *mystical event.* They send Mark Dusk, Editor-in-Chief of the school newspaper—*The Bullsheet* to check it out. He's blown away by an encounter with the spirit of his father killed in Vietnam.

I meet Jack and Caleb on a sun-soaked October afternoon. We plop down on a limestone outcrop slopped to The River's edge. We're about to begin our ritual of tantric gazing at The Arkansas River when Mark Dusk startles us. He looks like a leprechaun with thick reddish-brown hair, twinkling eyes, and a stout body. He scuttles up, sits down, and nods at Caleb to fire up the joint he'd just put in his mouth.

They razz each other about a disastrous chemistry lab project with colorful commentary of the spaz teacher, when a robin flutters inches from Mark's face and then, perches beside him. Like the surprising shaft of God light beaming or the brief brush of a butterfly, we hold our breath and wait for the bird's next move. Tears trickle down Mark's round ruddy cheeks.

"The last encounter I had with a robin was the day everything changed." He said softly. "I was in my dorm room studying when a large robin flew kamikaze style smack into the dorm window. I looked up just as it's flattened torso shook the room. I jumped up to help it, but it was gone. Then, I heard a sudden knock on the door and was summoned to Headmaster Rio's office.

We watch the curious creature while listening to the lapping and soothing sounds of the water's waves. After the bird flew away, Mark pulls out a red bandanna from his back jean pocket and wipes his face. "Thank you; this means so much to me. I know now that my father is OK." He refused to let anyone ridicule our sacred space at the *River of Love*.

We surrender to the internal power flowing at *The River* and discern the difference between the ego operating system and radical connected belonging. *Grace flows underneath all that Love and stunning beauty.* There is no formula, only to live with God's Spirit that dwells within you, let go of feelings and become quiet and small, then The Great Spirit will be obvious in the very now of things.

The students from Sacred Heart School know religion domesticates God. Eliminate judgment, and the surroundings magically open up. Eliminate separation; add infinite acceptance, unlimited receptivity, and participation in something larger than yourself.

I don't hesitate at the doorways of the Divine and move toward what is expansive and truly alive—the rush of the soul longing to know itself. *It's an undeniable force.* This unity makes me question, all the nonsense about being separate or alone.

What if there was a greater reality? Jesus tried to unmask the lie in our belief of separateness. I feel a real, invisible power which is the source of all life. My future is in the hands of the Great Spirit who knows what's best—*The River* and Jack. A grateful consciousness opens us up *to Love and surrender.* In our *participative seeing,* we experience spaciousness, joy, and contentment.

I feel a shift in perception when looking at whatever it is before me, instead of filling it with personal meaning or interpretation, *I simply look at it, as it is.* I accept life as it occurs and as it speaks to me. Whenever believing is replaced with *inner sight* something changes. A new realm appears. *Stop thinking and just look.* Delve into the Gateway of the *Here and Now.* Presence, attentiveness, the "is-ness" and "here-ness." Seeing this way is why Mark Dusk's Spirit Robin didn't freak us out. Primal experience, the mind, mostly keeps us from that—it can also, get us there. I surrender and enter the present moment and what is right in front of me, fully—without resistance or attempts to control. The exact opposite of giving up, it is being given into.

The secret to the natural world: let go of names and all preconceptions of God. You cannot search for what you already have. Just be with Him, here, at *The River of Life*. Simply, receive the ever-benevolent gaze of The Presence, returning it in kind, mutually gazing. Prayer is not starting the conversation from scratch it's plugging into one that is always in progress.

Saint Teresa of Avila believed prayer was an intimate sharing between friends, not an exercise but an *encounter*, not a practice but a *presence*, can't control it but can create the climate for the unfolding—*meeting the Beloved.*

The longing and need are so great, and Grace fills the vacuum. I want to spend every free moment with Jack. I'm incredibly happy, how do we sustain this euphoria? I question if he feels the same way and ignore the nagging doubts. *Jack wouldn't hurt me, I can trust him;* my feeble mantra.

Jack's introversion, dry humor, and imposing vocabulary intimidate me. I carry a dictionary in my backpack and increase my reading volume. I conceal nervousness by projecting a confident and energetic personality. I'm pressured to be smart, witty, and exciting for fear he'll lose interest. My goal was continuous learning and and constant reaching intellectual heights.

Nobody Rides for Free

WE CAN'T WAIT TO TELL OUR FRIENDS about the cute guys at the private school on the edge of town. Scarlett and Sadie Morgan moved here over the summer. They're chic hippies with long, straight hair, stylish bell-bottom patched jeans with aromatic patchouli peasant shirts. Scarlett ties a thin, leather strap as a headband against her long, flowing cornsilk hair.

They bump into me between classes by the locker bays. "Where did you disappear to after school yesterday?" Sadie asks.

"*Oh-lah*, it was so trippy! We went to *The River* to check out this magical party place our friends from Sacred Heart School discovered." The twins look at each other puzzled and turn to go to class. I spur-of-the-moment blurt, "Hey, wanna check it out? We can catch a ride after school. Scarlett can bring her guitar; we'll make a fire, sing songs and get stoned." I offer.

"Wow, that sounds fun, let's meet in the front parking lot," Scarlett says, her moss green eyes widen with excitement.

"Cool, I'll arrange a ride." I amble to my next class and realize I broke the promise to Jack to keep *The River* secret. Ky Kerry's an old trusted friend whose jovial and robust hardiness and pickup get him invited. I scribble a note to him in third-period Semantics class:

Bro,
Wanna get high after school—need to bum a ride
for me and the Morgan twins, I'll take us to a beau-
tiful River hideaway. Do me a solid, por favor.

He sits in front of me. I poke him and hand the note under the desk. Ky writes on the note:

If it's primo weed and I can score a couple of bucks
for gas for the GMC. Ass, gas or grass, nobody
rides for free.

He reaches under the desk and hands it back to me.

We wait for the Morgan twins who are fresh new faces. Ky has a gleam in his eye. He's known me since second grade; I'm like a pesky, little sister to him. He's Irish/Italian; handsome with long, red auburn hair, burly with bearish muscles, lumpy arms, and big, doughy hands. A cherub in a Hulk body with sunshine in his pockets.

"Kinda stoked to meet these new, hot chicks, huh?" I tease. He grabs me to dole out noogies when his thick index finger accidentally, pokes me in the eye.

"Yeow! Don't blind me, crazy Ky!" I scream. He drapes his thick arm over my shoulder. Scarlett and Sadie rush up with the guitar and backpacks. We were too distracted to notice the Sacred Heart School van driving by.

Fernando Fernandez is sitting in the passenger seat of the van, "*Mira! Mira! Mira!* Oh, holy shit, some guy's hanging all over Jack's girlfriend!" He shouts while jumping up and down in the seat. The van's full of scared freshman clueless to why the Mexican dude is so frantic.

We pile into Ky's blue, 1968, GMC pickup, and tool down the road. He parks at the dead-end entrance of *The River*. Scarlett lugs the guitar and follows me down the path thick with bushes and reeds. "Geeze, you need a machete to get through here," she whined.

I'm anxious Jack and Caleb might appear but relieved to find Oliver alone at *The River*. He lounges by a cozy fire basking in the mellow, fall day. He excitedly runs up to us, "Hey, what a surprise. How did you know about this place?" I explain Jack and Caleb brought Cha Cha and me, swearing us to secrecy.

"So much for that!" I roll my eyes.

"No worries, the more Merry Pranksters, the better, let's get loaded." He cheered.

"You know the rap: '*No pigs, no parents, no priests, and no hassles!*" His high-pitched giggle echoes through the campsite.

Sadie pulled out a thick, fat joint. Morgan sisters come from a large bohemian, hippie family. Their mother is a free-spirited, gypsy divorcée. The fraternal twin girls are inseparable with different personalities. Scarlett's a petite, lively extrovert full of zing, a flaxen-haired mini Joni Mitchell. Sadie's thin, coltish, with long, thick chestnut brown hair, a sweet shy introvert. Both have magnificent moon-shaped eyes—Scarlett's green, Sadie's blue.

They're priestess of music that play guitar, piano, sing, and harmonize beautifully. Their presence at *The River* was as natural as the deer and stunning as the sparkling sacred cottonwoods growing along the banks.

Oliver fires up the joint, "Please play; it's so *far out to have music* in this blissful haven." Glee lights up his bird-like eyes. "I was so bummed out before you showed up. I suffer such a rash of shit from the jocks and stomps at my school. I come to *The River* to purge the negativity and replace it with *pure Love*." He tilts his head, closes his eyes and smiles.

Oliver stretches out his legs and pops his knuckles. "I came from a lesson in Headmaster Rio's Psychology class about how our negative and critical thoughts stick like Velcro; where the positive and joyful thoughts are like Teflon and slide away. We have to *deliberately choose* to hold onto positive thoughts and memories for at least fifteen seconds before they 'imprint' and store in our memory banks. Isn't that the coolest?" He bobs his head with an impish smile. We stare at him in stoned astonishment.

Sadie pulls out the guitar, tunes it and the sister's warm up their voices. They sing, *Go with The Snow,* an original song older sister Eve wrote after the death of their grandmother. A harmonious closeness permeates the group.

Everything's moving in slow motion; I'm paralyzed, until wait... *I'm just stoned.* Oliver leers at Ky—looking super butch in his green plaid, flannel shirt, and faded patched blue jeans. Ky's giant boy face with glacier blue eyes sweet with intent and gaiety. Oliver's burning gaze alerts Ky that he's *hot for some Italian Papa.*

Ky leans toward the singers and reels us back to earth.

"Hey, it's almost dark—hate to be a buzzkill, but Rosie and I have a pain-in-the-ass Semantics test tomorrow. *Time to va-moose.*" He cocks his head toward the path to the truck. Our squinty, bloodshot eyes blink us back to reality.

Later that night Jack calls, his voice is hesitant and halting with a cold, stilted quality.

"What's wrong?" I immediately ask.

"Someone told me while riding in the Sacred Heart School van this afternoon, they drove by the high school and saw you making out with a hippie guy."

"Oh, Jack, *are you serious?* Ky Kerry's an old grade school friend; we were waiting for the Morgan twins to take them to *The River.* He poked me in the eye while we were horsing around. Who made up such a blatant lie and why would you believe it?"

Coldness melting, he said, "I didn't say I believed it, just inquiring." His voice trails off.

"Whoever told you this, is not a friend. It might've looked like we were hugging from a distance. We left right after with the twins. Oliver met the girls, they sang songs and we had a blast." It angered me that such an innocent act got misinter-preted. One of Fernando Fernandez minions had reported the incident to Jack.

Go with the Snow

go with the snow

go with our Love
look at the sky
the white snow dove

think of the time
and the songs to be sung
in the cold of the winter
in the heat of the sun

fly with your soul

and take you some lovin'
it'll keep you as warm
as that old bakin' oven

think of the forest
the wind in the trees
just as sweet as you imagine
as kind as you please

Think of joy—joy
Think of joy—joy

–Eve Morgan

Something Extraordinary

I find ecstasy in living; the mere
sense of living is joy enough.
–Emily Dickinson

I ATTEND MARIE NOONAN'S HUMANITIES class on Thursday afternoons at 3:30 p.m. I ride the 3 miles on my burgundy, Batavus, ten-speed bike. I'm breaking an unwritten rule being the only girl at an all boy's school. Marie Noonan's a direct, no-nonsense teacher who makes the rules, if she takes a shine to a local, *"townie"* girl and wants her in class, *so be it*.

I arrive a few minutes early and thank Marie. "Please, stay after class so I can go over the material with you," she said curtly.

"Yes, ma'am." The bell rings, and the boys file into the last class of the day. They murmur in low tones that I can't hear. The small plain classroom has ten half-desk chairs arranged in a circle with Marie's wooden desk in the corner. A row of metal framed windows lines the outer wall facing the open quad where the Gonads play football.

Marie at seventy is an elegant and petite lady with a shock of white, wavy hair. She wears light-colored sweater sets with A-line skirts, plain low-heeled pumps, and a strand of pearls.

Her vibrant eyes are full of incessant curiosity and wonder. I sense she's thrilled to have me in her class.

"Our guest student is Rose Ramirez. Please, when appropriate, introduce yourself. Let's take out the handouts from yesterday; Joseph Campbell's *Hero with a Thousand Faces*. I'd like to go over a couple of the quotations. Rose, here's a copy." She hands me a mimeographed paper.

"The idea regarding the hero myth: he ventures forth from the world of common day into a region of supernatural wonder where fabulous forces encountered, and a decisive victory is won. He returns with power and the incarnation of God himself, and with the energies of eternity. This transcendent force lives in all, in all our profound obeisance," she reads the quote.

She dramatically pauses and they eagerly wait for her next sentence. "Campbell had a different take on spirituality than Carl Jung. We'll go deeper once we finish Joseph Campbell's book and move on to Carl Jung's teachings. I want you to finish the last chapter of *Hero with a Thousand Faces* and write a summary of modern-day heroes. This is due by next class." She returns previous homework assignments, commenting on the outstanding papers, the feedback is all positive.

Class ends, and the nine boys file out. I remain at my desk. Marie asks, "Did you understand what we discussed?" She sits down next to me.

"Yes, it was exhilarating. You don't talk down to your students," I said.

"No, but I don't assume they know what I do." She says while studying me, I'm uncomfortable and squirm in my chair. I hope Jack's outside waiting for me.

"How do you define yourself, dear?" She asks with little expression. I'm taken aback.

"I wish to live a creative life and grow into a well-rounded independent person." I stumble over my words. My blood shifts from a pound to a racing pulse.

"What are your passions? What's the first thing you think about in the morning and the last thing at night?" Her direct gaze puts me on the spot.

"He's a student here, Jack Dillon." My face lights up; I crack a smile.

Marie frowns. "Rose, *that's not acceptable*. Do you like to read? She picks up a magazine. Do you write?" She rolls a pen toward me. "I want you to start reading the New York Times, at least the Sunday edition. The public library has it."

She glides over to her desk and pulls out a leather journal and writes my name inside the cover and places it on my desk, "Please, start keeping a daily journal and write about anything—whatever comes to you. Stretch your mind and improve your analytical skills. Wake up and be aware, *lead a life of concentration*, rather than sleep-wading through *la Vida*." She sits down in the chair and releases a long, extended sigh.

"Girls rely too much on their looks and firm bodies—as they should. Do you realize, you're at the peak of your beauty? *You're at your best physically that you'll ever be!* But it fades, and wisdom prevails—engage the mind by reading and writing and live a rich, vibrant and exciting life. We all have a creative spirit at work pushing us to evolve, to become better, to make what is rare commonplace. The universe is full of creatures that continue to create and recreate. A Mother Spirit that nurtures through evolution.

"I'll wager what you learn in class, will *spark the emergence of something extraordinary* in you like our heroes. I didn't rely on beauty, I managed to raise two boys and teach. I'm thrilled when my students grasp a new idea and want to learn more. It's my drug, my *fix,* as you kids say. I see real possibilities in you, Rose, and hope we'll become great friends. Now go, it's a long ride home. I'll expect your best writing on the summary. See you next Thursday." She stood up and started packing up her things.

Outside of the red brick building, Jack's waiting for me. "How did it go?" he asks anxiously. I drop my backpack and grab his hand: "Yikes! *That was intense.* Marie wants to mentor me, I think... *possibly?* I'm overwhelmed by her interest and directness. A teacher hasn't ever paid this much attention to me." I said.

"She sees potential in you, all the smartest, most brilliant students take her classes. There's a waiting list every semester. I'm just psyched to see you every Thursday." He slips an arm around me. We walk past the classroom window and catch a glimpse of Marie and Headmaster Rio conversing in the hallway. We stop to watch their animated exchange.

Marie calls out to Headmaster Rio, whom she's fond of calling *"Esteemed Headmaster."* They're best of friends and have a high regard for each other. She has a way of treating him as an adult and a kid at the same time.

"How are you, Rawleigh? You look down in the dumps."

He'd just finished teaching a senior class on critical thinking. He tried to explain the anti-Nazi German, Lutheran Pastor, Dietrich Bonhoeffer's theory of no person existing simply in their own space in time: the past—we inherit, the future—we create it, and the present—is the vehicle we inhabit now.

"I explain this theory once again, and probe them with questions. It's clear; *they don't understand an iota* of what we covered this week." He cries discouraged. She looks at him quizzically. "My dear boy, when will you ever learn, all they're interested in, is sex!" She playfully slaps him on the back as they laugh together.

Womb to Tomb

Let the farthest, oldest, most ancient
ancestors speak to us!
And let us be listeners at last, humans
finally, able to hear.
–Listeners at Last by Rainer Maria Rilke

IT'S AN AUTUMN AFTERNOON with a stone-grey sky, the Aspen leaves have turned to liquid copper. Cha Cha needs soul sister time away from the frenetic activity of Red Cañon. She bursts through my bedroom door. "I need a River fix," she said.

I look up from my book, startled. "Oh yeah, what's up?"

"Blues Baby, I'm bummed out and *on the rag.* Let's blow this joint and go smoke one." She twitches toward the door.

We approach the deer path leading to *The River.* I pray no one is there. We're in no mood for stilted small talk or sharing our Scooby snacks. We desire time alone to get high and chill out. Then, return home for a bowl of savory frijoles and atomic-hot green chili. And... *The Holy Grail of Chicano chow down cuisine:* Mom's warm off-the-griddle, homemade tortillas fluffy with crusty crowns of brown bubbles slathered thick with butter. Our sister-friendship is effortless and everlasting; *Comadre, mi todo de Vida*—my friend, my everything.

"Cool, no one's here but us chickens." I pushed Cha Cha toward the fire ring.

"Cop a squat and spill the beans—I demand to know why you're bummed out." She selects a flat-topped boulder, brushes it off and plops down.

"It's a gnawing gut feeling of anxiety with low energy, like a *chinches'*—bedbug's stuck in my craw. *I'm throwing a major drag here.*" She smiles through the pain.

"*¡Ay, Chavela!* I raise my hands in the air and mock-choke her.

"Look around you—*where you live and breathe* check out this beautiful shrine we worship at. Our ancestors walked on this same spot. Do you think they had time to *bum out?* We build on the inherited wisdom traditions they laid the foundation for." I move to sit next to her and nudge her.

"I just read in a book for Marie Noonan's class: '*From womb to tomb we are related to others, past and present and by each crime and every kindness we give birth to our future life, rippling through eternity.*' Wrote, Carl Jung. We owe it to them to rip the doors off life, to be the most transcendent, smart and creative creatures." I reach and squeeze her hand.

"*Seriously, time to get twisted*, pull out that joint and spark 'er up." She demands. We take a few tokes off the joint; I stub it out on the rock I'm sitting on.

"*¿Quien eres tu?* Who are you and what have you done with mi goofy prima?" She jokes and the cloud lifts. I snap her out of the doldrums for now, but she'd deal with depression requiring medication for the rest of her life.

Cha Cha's slit eyes, squint at me, "Oye, this is some kick-ass mota." The plants and rocks pulsate with the roar of rushing water, the trees thrum with energy in front of us. *The Magnificent River*—so alive. We're vulnerable as our surroundings communicate with us. *Eternity whispers ever so gently...* The wake-the-hell-up sound of *The River* is completely still for a full beat. The high knock, knock, knock, of a nearby Redheaded Woodpecker startles and forces us to look up. The tinny rustling of the silvery cottonwood leaves showers us with glittery sweetness.

We see them standing at the footpath that spills onto the fire ring: *Indians!* They huddle together—five of them, in 1800's regalia. Two warriors, a Chief, an older Indian woman, and a beautiful, Indian princess, dressed in white, fringed, buckskin. She grasps a long, sacred Eagle Talking Feather in her delicate hands. The others are wrapped in buffalo hide blankets embellished with fringe and wooden beads. The Chief dons a large, feathered headdress. Their braided straight hair tied with beaded leather straps. They stare at us.

Their regalness stops time. All our heartbeats and tribal tones are in a rhythm called *"deep time,"* where the past, present, and future gathers into one holy eternal presence. *Love fiercely, give thanks and share our gifts with all who will listen.*

This joining of hands from one generation to another, impacting the future by connecting to the past. We're in harmony with the group standing before us. I'm ineffably stunned, afraid to move or to look away would break the rare spell. I glance at sheet white Cha Cha who's holding her breath. What seems like ten minutes is only about sixty seconds, and then, they vanish.

We scream simultaneously, "What the hell was that!" I stand and run to Cha Cha.

"Do you think I summoned them with the *'womb to tomb'* talk?" I'm overjoyed by their appearance.

"FREAK-a-delic!" Cha Cha squeals and stamps her feet, she's still shaking. We vow to tell no one, for fear of ending up in straight jackets and rubber rooms. *The River* full of mind-blowing communion, radiant splendor, and dazzling illumination on what began as a dreary and depressing afternoon.

At my house, I pull Cha Cha into my bedroom. "Do you know what we witnessed?" I'm like a tourist in my own history.

"Scary spooks haunting the hell out of us." She tries to make light of it.

"These are our ancestors passing the torch to us. We're the ancestors of an age to come-a collective spirit through the centuries push us forward, to make a difference, every generation has to move the boulder of good forward."

Cha Cha with those big, unwavering, black eyes, "How do you know all this?"

"Taking Marie Noonan's Humanities class about myths helps to connect the dots. I'd like to share this with her, but she wouldn't believe it."

That night I wrote in my journal—what did the ancestors think of Carlos Santana at the tender age of twenty-two, wailing on his guitar at Woodstock? Or, beautiful Joan Baez singing *We Shall Overcome,* at war protests? They must be proud of two-time Grammy Award winners Mary Youngblood and Rita Coolidge and Buffy Sainte-Marie's work in education and social activism.

How did they interpret the 1960s, a time of civic disaffection, speaking truth to power and religious idealism? I'm proud of Dad's brothers Bernie and Gill's involvement with the Brown Berets—Chicano Power activism. The Coors and grape boycott proved how solidarity through actions could force large union busting corporations to their knees.

César Chávez was the gutsy genius with the vision and foresight to engineer the boycott. An effective leader of El Movimiento who believed in peaceful protest. "¡Sí Se Puede!" ("Yes, we can!") A call to activism to inspire Mexican American workers to unionize and fight for civil liberties. Years later, the first black American president borrowed the slogan for his winning campaign.

Five years before César Chávez's death in 1993, he did a fast to end the use of pesticides in agriculture, he told his son, "I haven't done enough with my life. I will do this fast to bring attention to the cause." César Chávez and his wife Helen, awoke early, every day to say the Rosary on their knees, next to the bed.

Alongside César Chávez was Dolores Huerta, a Civil Rights activist and co-founder of the United Farm Workers of America. A rebel veteran of immigrant rights and the feminist movement. She suffered the harsh treatment of the macho and narrow-minded males of the union. The workers called her the *Madonna of the Fields*. The growers called her the Dragon Lady. When told she couldn't do in Arizona what was accomplished in California; *she coined* the brilliant MeXicana mantra, "¡Sí Se Puede!"

She strived on after César's death to found the Dolores Huerta Foundation for Community Organizing continuing to fight in her late-eighties, weaving together voter and immigrant rights, LGBT, feminist, environmental and labor activist issues. She inspires and leads by helping the downtrodden and diminished, the forgotten poor, and the outcasts. Those who don't have lobbyists in Washington to fight for them. "We can't let people drive wedges between us...because there's only one human race," writes Dolores Huerta.

In the same journal, I had a copy of Rodolfo "Corky" Gonzales famous poem; *I am Joaquín*, it described the economic, cultural, and political battles Chicanos face in this country.

If we stopped looking forward and backward, we would see the Kingdom of God right beneath our feet. Right under our noses. Everything is given to us. Rich beyond our dreams. What will my life contribute to the centuries, to the eternal concord?

Love is Color Blind

Love begets Love
Love knows no rules
—Virgil

J ACK CALLS ME EVERY NIGHT AROUND 10:30 P.M. or after the prefect of Hedley Hall goes to sleep. He slips quietly into the pay phone booth at the end of the hallway in the dorm. I keep the family phone with the extra, long cord in my bedroom. We visit for hours, some nights until 1:00 a.m. during the lively conversations, in his quiet and measured way, *he downright charms me.*

We discuss everything including Watergate, Vietnam, favorite music, and authors. I crave the confident sound of his voice and swell with contentment during the long hours courting on the telephone. I strive to be the best version of myself.

He speaks in a singsong cadence with short pauses, numbering points sucking in air, *ta-ta-ta tapping* the tongue on the roof of the mouth while calculating the next comment. "Hmmm" could be judgmental but mostly used as a stalling tactic. His crystal voice and golden laughter is pure joy. Calls begin formal and stiff until he relaxes and wades into the warm, conversational flow that opens him up.

We have similar views on most subjects, which was unusual considering our different backgrounds. *Jack has a temper.* During a disagreement, I said offhandedly, "The juice isn't worth the squeeze." He demanded to know what I meant. When I tried to explain, he got even more agitated. The eye-opening dust-ups point to his calculating and cold nature. He sees the world through a sharp analytical prism. Computer analytics is the perfect career choice as an adult. It's difficult for him to grasp complicated emotions, to feel deeply, and Love completely.

I always manage to smooth the ruffled feathers. His eloquent intelligence is his most attractive quality. *I fall in Love with his mind.* Women fall in Love with what they hear, and men fall in Love with what they see.

His father is an executive for a shipping company, and the family lived all over the world. They're living in New Zealand, the reason why Jack is at the college preparatory high school. He's a natural learner; a straight A student who made Honor Roll every semester. School is easy for him—*even stoned.*

We see each other on the sly—sneaking around town. My parents aren't aware that we're dating. They're strict, cradle to grave Catholics; girls, don't date until age eighteen. My curfew is 11:00 p.m. until I graduate from high school. I am the jewel of the family; they have big hopes for me. I'm to be the first to graduate from college, have a career, the first of my generation to lead a creative life and *break out of the poverty cycle.*

I'm Daddy's little princess: *la consentida, no one's going to be good enough for me.* I need excellent grades to get into college, distractions must be kept to a minimum.

Jack calls on a Friday night after I return from cheering at a football game.

"Wanna meet tomorrow?" He asks, first thing.

"Of course, where?" That's the big issue now. *The River's* so popular, going there involves partying with half of his class. "How about the softball field behind the high school? Let's meet at 1:00 p.m. That'll give you a chance to return for dinner." He agrees.

The following day, I ride my bike and lock it to the softball field fence. We meet at the baseball diamond on a pleasant, winter day. The bright, incandescent sky is warm when the clouds clear but cool when blocked by the sun. The field is empty except for us. We climb the metal bleachers, *tunk, tunk, tunk*. We eagerly hold hands. I pull out of my backpack a small, lap blanket, and lay it over our legs to keep warm.

I'm awed by how funny Jack is, his dry sense of humor catches me off guard. One hour into our visit, we see a car approaching the dirt road entrance. It's not just any car—a cherry red and white 1957, Ford Galaxy 500, one of kind. My tough, butch older sister Rae is about to bust our clandestine meeting.

We're trapped; there's no other way out. I stiffen and warn Jack. "This is my sister Rae, she's got a terrible temper and will be super pissed I'm here with you, don't argue with her. Please, don't hurt her."

Jack understands the gravity of the situation, "Will you be all right?"

"I'll be grounded for life, but she'll be more pissed that you're white. He leans over and tenderly kisses my cheek. I bite my lip, fear leaks out of me. I jiggle my leg, against the metal bleachers, it vibrates and makes a tinny, rattling sound.

Rae's beautiful, red and white car comes to a violent, abrupt stop—dust, dirt and small rocks spray in all directions. She's short, about 4'11, but built like a brick shithouse. Rae's the ultra-protective—*"I'm the boss of you"* older big sister by six years. We Love each other, *we just aren't friends*. She's the oldest of four kids, entitling her to feel responsible for me. Her angry, swirling Tasmanian Devil energy, hurls invisible punches. The squinted dagger-eyes look like she's caught a stranger molesting me. She explodes out of the car, leaving the door open.

"What the HELL are you doing here? Who the fuck are you?" She screams at Jack. He stands up nervously, then sits back down. Rae charges up the bleachers and throws a right cross blow hitting him on the cheek. He stands up with a jerk, steadies himself, hands me the lap blanket, and looks helplessly at me for direction.

"Leave him alone. *Jack get outta here now!*" I scream and shield him with my body. He stumbles down the loud, metal clanking bleachers.

Her head looks like Mount Vesuvius about to blow. To her, I'd always be the tiny, defenseless, four-year-old girl standing in front of our projects house in a Princess coat in the black and white photo taken of me years ago.

"Rae, it's not what you think. He's just a friend, *we were just talking.*" I slowly, make it down the bleachers, fighting off tears.

"Get in the car!" She yells, her black, bulldog eyes bulge with anger. The knife crease between her eyebrows deep. Her stiff body with fists clenched.

"I can't leave my bike!" I cry.

"Unlock it, and I'll throw it in the trunk." She growls.

I tremble while fumbling with the cheap padlock. My stomach churns, and heart races. I roll it to the car. She grabs it with one hand and shoves it in the trunk slamming the hood so hard on the bike tires, it bounces back up and almost hits her.

I jump in the backseat and slump down. Rae slides into the driver seat, puts the key in the ignition and pauses for a few seconds. Her breathing heavy, body surging with adrenaline. She turns around to face me. "What the hell are you doing with that white boy? Who is he? Do Mom and Dad know you're seeing him? Where are you supposed to be right now?" She feels so righteous catching me red-handed. *Mom and Dad's little darling.* A-1 favorite daughter, Miss Goody Two-shoes, cheerleader-prissy-face. The pretty one that everyone compares her to.

I'm sobbing hard now; she's going to wail on me—this eggs her on; the little sister's guilt unmasked. Rae jumps up onto her knees in the front seat, reaches over the backseat pummeling my face and head. I put up my hands to protect my face. "I Love him!" I shout in bold defiance.

"You can't Love a *gabacho, pinche* white boy!" Rae swings one, last hard blow. I put my hands down, "Yes, I can, *Love is color blind.*"

Rae slumps behind the steering wheel and peels out. "Mom and Dad are going to be so pissed at you. You've lied and sneaked around with that creep, for how long?" Her stabbing glare bounces off the rearview mirror. "If I hadn't had softball practice today, you'd still be deceiving your family and *yourself,*" she barks.

I hang my tear-streaked face out the window and search for Jack. I choke back retching sobs. I pooh-pooh Rae's accusations and explain that he was just a boy I ran into, an innocent chat that Rae misconstrued. To appease her, they ground me for a month, but while she's out of town at a volleyball tournament, they let me off the hook.

Happy Place

If you obey all the rules,
you miss all the fun.
—Katharine Hepburn

O LIVER AND I WRAP UP MAKING TORTILLAS in his dorm room, *which broke all the rules.* We wear frilly, flowered aprons; I caved into his *Leave it to Beaver*—June Cleaver fantasy. All but a few of the prefects are away at a weekend retreat. Jack's writing a paper for a history class.

Homey, toasted flour and yeasty aromas drift through the dorm hallway. It took two hours to roll out and prepare the fluffy, thick, tortillas. My friend is a quick study, rolling out round ovals of doughy perfection. His dark-framed glasses and tousled, messy hair evoke a mad scientist look. I watch the *comal* to flip the tort timing it perfect for bubble-induced browning.

I'm attracted to his alacrity and boldness. His curiosity is infectious and equally his flair for joyfulness. He's resourceful, passionate and fearless.

"Ollie, *there's nothing sexier* than a man cooking in the kitchen." I tease.

"Or better—two men cooking together!" His voice squeaks with nervous exhilaration.

The well-stocked mini-kitchen in the tiny, cinderblock room has drawerfuls of cooking supplies: flour, salt, baking soda, shortening, utensils, dishes for two, and a hotplate. I brought in my backpack a round, cast-iron, *comal*—flat skillet to cook the tortillas on. We make three dozen tortillas, enough to feed the entire floor of Oliver's dormitory.

"When we finish, let's go to *The River*, I want to sit in one of those willow huts and get super stoned. That area looks like the forest in the *Wizard of Oz*. Hmmm... let's call it Munchkin Land." He giggles, his Looney Tunes eyes full of eager excitement. After cleaning up, we're ready to blast outside, out of the hot, smoky and cramped dorm room.

"There's a new secret code word for *The River*." He wipes his hands on a towel.

"What is it?" I ask.

"We named it '*Art*' so if a priest overhears us they'll assume we're off to create."

"Hell yeah, we're off to see the wizard in our painting smocks." I pat my hideous apron.

Oliver's roommate Gonzo pokes his head in the door. "What's going on?" He spent the afternoon studying in the library, seeing me startles him.

"Let's mosey down to *The River;* you wanna come?" He's adorable with flour on his cheek, steamed up eyeglasses, and *masa* caked balls on his fingers, that he flicks at Gonzo.

My heart sinks: *I don't get Gonzo.* He wears a permanent scowl on his sad Eeyore face. A cloud hangs over him. His dark, sorrowful eyes are vapid and soulless. He doesn't like me:

I'm best friends with his best friend—suck it up. This brand of bullshit, girls deal with naturally.

The gray overcast day presages rain when we reach *The River*. The air is still and heavy. The huddled up cows make me uneasy. The four mounds of willow-like huts, line-up in a row, along *The River*. They emanate a strong power. The overgrown igloo-shaped willow shoots tangled and layered are the same size as Indian Sweat Lodges.

"Let's go inside—*down the rabbit hole.*" I flash Ollie a Cheshire cat grin.

He leads the way; his thin body snakes through the thick brush. A bright, red rain jacket protected him. Luckily, I dig out a windbreaker in my bike bag; I'll need it if it starts pouring.

Gonzo's quietness is uncomfortable. I know by the stiff way he watches me; he's judging me. I'm boisterous and friendly, the total opposite of him. I make myself miserable worrying what others think of me. It turns out; *he's just shy* and extremely introverted.

We stand before a gorgeous, round, stick hut. Holstein cows on one side, the pesky electric fence doing its job, with *The River* on the other side. A sturdy dam built by a family of beavers is in a swampy section next to the huts. The owners of the land come and knock the dam out. By their next visit to Munchkin Land, there's a bigger, more dynamic dam rebuilt. *Hoo Ha!*

We hear a rumble of thunder, heaven's bowling balls threaten our post-tortilla makin' celebration. The thick and layered willow shoots keep it dry inside. I inhale the fresh, mountain snow runoff swiftly flowing in the roaring water beside us. The resident Great Blue Heron perches near the water's edge. "He likes you, Rosie—I only see him when I'm with you." *Ollie, my Champion.*

The Great Blue Heron—*Ardea herodias* stands roughly four feet high with the wingspan the length of my outstretched arms. His slate blue-green feathers blend in with the rippling river. The stealth-like bird appears out of nowhere. The long, graceful neck stretches when surveying the area, the white underside of the body and head dotted with a dramatic black patch of feathers. While resting, he lays his head on his shoulders and sticks his formidable bill under his wing. I watch him fly above the water casting a shadow on its bottom. He's regarded as the Regal River mascot and our *mysterious, feathered guardian.*

We climb in the small stick hut, "It's so peaceful and perfect here." Oliver sighs. I close my eyes, and imagine I'm a Mayan princess. At birth, the doctor slapped my bottom and noticed a moon-shaped, blue birthmark on my left buttock, a known trait of the Mayans.

Damp leaf and amber wood muskiness fill the hut. Gonzo gasps for air.

"I'm claustrophobic," he whispers to Oliver, who whips out a joint and lights it. He knows when to ignore him.

"Rosie, you're going *to dig this Maui Wowie* it's outta sight!" Ollie smiles slyly.

"These huts look like Indian sweat lodges which are mystical shrines for spiritual cleansing. Have you ever been in one?" I ask. They both shake their heads no. "My dad goes to sweat lodges with his friends in the mountains."

Time for show and tell. I pull out a small, yellow, leather medicine pouch from my jean pocket. Its Thunderbird design has white feathers and red pony beads that dangle from the drawstring. Inside is a heart-shaped rock with sage a sacred talisman from my grandma for luck, protection, and strength. "When I die, it'll burn with my body," I said and hand it to Oliver with the instruction not to open it.

"SOOO cool! I feel its power." Oliver's eyes widen. He bounces and claps with childish excitement. Gonzo doesn't look up; *his heart closed to everything.*

"Did you know that Sweat lodges consist of willow shoots formed in huts, like what we're sitting in? The frame is covered with mats, blankets, or canvas. The floor carpeted with matting, grass, ferns, or fir boughs. The fir boughs are *strong medicine* and give strength. The Indians rub their bodies with them for power and scent. Small rocks heat in a brisk fire then placed in an opening of the lodge, piled high, sprinkled with cold water, creating a dense steam.

Due to the sweltering heat, five minute's is roughly the limit in the lodge. A dip in a pool/river follows a sweat. Warriors and hunters *sweat housed* before expeditions." Ollie hands me a joint.

"A Sweat Ceremony repairs damage done to spirit, mind, and body. A place to receive guidance by asking spiritual entities—Grandfather, Creator and Earth Mother for wisdom and power. The entrance of the Sweat lodge faces east, as does the sacred fire pit. Each day begins in the east with the rising of the Sun, the source of life and power. The *Dawn of Wisdom,* while the fire heating the rocks is the undying light of the world— *Eternity."* I take a toke off the joint.

"Dang, it's so far out these huts face east," Oliver gets giddier with each pass of the joint.

"Sweat Leader smudges all who enter with the smoke of burning sage, cedar or sweetgrass. *Smudging* is wafting the smoke over you with an eagle feather. They load the sacred peace pipe in prayer for all to know and speak the truth to Great Spirit and Earth Mother. Tobacco is offered to the sacred fire while saying a prayer or asking a question. The smoke from the tobacco carries the request to the Great Spirit."

"Can you bring an Indian pipe to the next River party to pass around?" Oliver asks.

"I can't borrow the sacred pipe, but I've got sage and an eagle feather for smudging. This is my dad's favorite part—Stone People spirits awaken by heating them in the sacred fire pit. Placed one at a time, in the shallow pit inside the sweat lodge. The first stone is to the west, the north, east, and south. In the center is Grandfather, more stones for Grandmother and The People. After the stones are in place, the Sweat Lodge Keeper, the fire tender, seals the entrance. The stones glow and illuminate the lodge. The Sweat leader sounds the Water Drum and calls for the spirit guides in prayer from the Four Directions. Sweat leader pours water on the raging hot stones producing large amounts of steam. One dipper each for the four directions or until instructed by the spirits to stop. They begin prayers, chants, and songs. It's a sacred place to steam the sorrow out.

Yikes! *Maui Wowie is tripping me out,* "Ollie, will you take care of me if I freak out?" I ask, fading. I lay flat on the grassy floor.

"Of course." He lightly strokes my head to reassure me. I wish Gonzo wasn't here. I fear he'll go back to school and spread horrible rumors about me.

"You turn paranoid when you smoke, mellow out and go to your happy place, Rosie dear." Oliver pats my hand.

"*I AM in my happy place, Ollie.*" I peek out of the hut and miraculously, splintered sunlight filters in. A golden beam lights up the darkness; the threat of rain has lifted.

He passes the joint to me one more time. I glance at Gonzo and imagine him as a skeleton and Oliver is a glittery, psychedelic, butterfly with horn-rimmed glasses.

It'd Love to spend the entire weekend on *The River* with Ollie in this flaming rainbow hut. We'd talk, get high, and stroll along the riverbed. I relate emotionally with Ollie. Gonzo is standoffish, and cynical, his fear has a distinct vibe. Some people you just can't win over.

Queen Alma's Pearls

Lord, take me where you want me to go;
let me meet who you want me to meet.
Tell me what you want me to say;
And keep me out of your way.
–Father Mychal Judge OFM

Q UEEN ALMA, MY MOTHER, holds court in her kitchen
every Friday night. We help with a large family dinner
at least once a week, usually on the weekends. Cha Cha spends
many nights at her Dad's younger sister's house. She brings
her son, Julian, who plays with our two dogs: King—a silver
German Shepherd and Chiquita—a squatty, black Pekinese/
Dachshund mix.

Cha Cha flops down in her favorite chair at the large,
round, butcher-block table. She bounces to the Stealers Wheel
song blasting on the radio: *"Clowns to the left of me, jokers to
the right, here I am stuck in the middle of you."*

My mother punctuates her stories and jokes at the table
with *"¡Ay, Chavelita!"* She Loves her like a daughter. The
three-bedroom, brick house magically swells to hefty welcome
size, when family and friends show up. Located on River Street,
smack dab in the heart of Red Cañon. Exactly, 3-miles west of
Sacred Heart School.

Cha Cha respects her Auntie Alma for working as a Head

Start teacher in the rural mountain town and attending college classes at night, while raising four kids.

Mom used this setting to slip in wisdom and hard-earned life lessons lecturing us while preparing dinner with *"dichos de Mi Madre"* or "As my mother would say" cautionary truisms handed down the generations. Her numero uno aphorism: "Education is *EVERYTHING!* Get educated, and no one can hold you down, and you'll always have a job." Mom is a feminist of the Modern Era. Grandmother Eugenia was a role model of an independent woman raising a family after my Grandfather Juan was murdered. Mom's antidotes reflected strength, independence, and self-reliance.

"You never want to depend on a man—they'll let you down." Mom is the primary wage earner, paid the bills, and fixer of the family problems. She has the *drive to thrive* and sets the bar high for her children. We're to *make a difference,* lead lives of value, go to college and land fulfilling jobs.

Cha Cha and I are a captive audience in the small, rented, cramped kitchen, listening and hanging onto every word. Our little bird mouths open with unassuaged hunger and ancestral desire. *Frijoles* boiled on the gas stove and *papas* fried in a large, cast iron skillet. A radio blared in the background. My family was into music, especially Mom, *she Loved to dance.* She doesn't drink or smoke, is a teetotaler and the *Belle of the Ball* at all the family parties, weddings, and celebrations.

My mother's table is her most sacred treasure. She believes that the kitchen is the heartbeat of the home and spends a small fortune on a round, beautiful, butcher-block wooden table with the extension it seats ten. *Pure duende*—magic blossomed at her intimate, wild Goddess kaffeeklatsch sessions. Naughty cuentos shared with prisoner wives' friends and Head Start mothers whose children she teaches.

Belly laughs echo through the neighborhood. A joyfulness that lightens the mood realigns the soul, lifts sadness, heartbrokenness, and anger. Sacred laughter women share when men aren't present; free to talk openly, without criticism, and from their *corazón*. They share off-color stories stirring the libido and lifting depression. Reaching deep into the psyche, releasing wild pleasure and healing energy: *soul evoking goodness*. So many of these women went long stretches without intimacy and Lovemaking; this helps fill the void.

My mother's biggest gift was her wicked wit and *sheer mischievousness*, quick to laugh at self-deprecating humor. Limitless curiosity keeps her sharp, well into old age. *Curiosity is the lust of the mind and the wellspring of creativity.* Her laser beam focus makes one feel *Loved and included.* Word spreads about these enlivened and uplifting gabfests. Homebound because she doesn't drive this naturally supplies a healthy stream of friendships.

On this Friday night, she shares colorful chestnuts with us. "You, young girls give it away too quick—why buy the cow when the cream is free?" Another jewel: "Lay down with dogs, and you'll get fleas," a cautionary warning—you're judged by association. This one imprints and hooks me with doubt: "A white boy wants to date a Spanish girl, for one thing... when given that, he'll drop you like a hot potato," she warns. My favorite, for the sheer absurdity: "A woman can run faster with her skirt around her waist, then a man can with his pants down." She nodded.

Her repertoire of adages—*pearls of wisdom* are available for any practical teaching moments. Losing her father at such a young age produced a fearful and cautious personality. Often, her bluntness embarrasses me, but Cha Cha doesn't mind. *She adores her auntie for not judging her* when she returned at fifteen, from California as an unwed mother. Cha Cha would graduate from college and become a writer and teacher like her aunt, making Mom so proud. She honors her spirit in poems and books for future generations.

My mother got a kick from preparing Defcon 1, *extremely hot,* green chili to scorch the taste buds of her dinner guests. *"It's not too hot...is it?"* she'd ask innocently while giggling with tears streaming down her cheeks.

"Come, *mi'jita* and turn the pilot light on the gas stove. She hands the box of wooden stick matches to Cha Cha. "Right there on the bottom rack of the oven, drop the match—there." Cha Cha leans down and drops it exactly where she pointed. *"WOOOF"* the gas flames whip up with a soft, sonic boom that singes Cha Cha's eyelashes, eyebrows and hair framing her face. Burnt hair and gas fumes fill the small kitchen.

"Damn, that's a wicked oven, Auntie!" Cha Cha shakes her head, wondering why she always falls for that prank. I roll on the floor laughing; *"¡Qué mala!* Stop, I'm going to pee my pants!" I squeal.

The chili is ready; a tortilla cooks on the comal, rising beautifully dotted with toasted brown bubbles. A towering pile accumulates on the stove wrapped in a large tea towel to keep warm. The cozy kitchen smells of sublime, spicy pork chili and yeasty flour weaving through the small house.

"The potatoes need mashing," Mom says. Rae storms in from the living room.

"That's my job." She mashes violently, adding butter, milk, salt, and pepper. She whips them into a frothy, heavenly heap.

"Dinner's ready—come get yer vittles!" hollered Cha Cha.

Go-to Girl

Life shrinks or expands in
proportion to one's courage.
–Anaïs Nin

IT'S ABHORRENT TO LIE TO MY PARENTS, but it's the
only way to be with Jack. I'm guilty and torn with a split
personality: one urged to follow the strict Catholic rules, the
other questioned a universe that manifests Jack and *The River,*
just to take it all away?

Cha Cha and I are hunkered down in my room, scheming
how to pull off a night of camping at *The River* that weekend.

"You've got a sleepover, pajama party with the head-up-
their-asses, hoochie cheerleaders." Cha Cha nods.

"Only snag, what if Mom asks for a phone number where
she can reach me?" I ask.

I'm a prisoner with a false sense of duty, obligation and a
slave to the internalized merit badge system. Bombarded with
rules at home, school, and church. I pray for Grace to set no
bounds for Love, as *She* sets none to hers. I plead with Mother
Mary, the Holy Mystery, and all the guardian angels to protect
Jack and me. *Help us to see.* Bless our union, even though I
can't share our joy with my family for fear of the fallout.

Nature is the one song of praise that never stops singing, it is our religion and *The River* our church. The holiest place is on the rocks, looking out at an *endless River of mercy and infinite abundance.*

Making things better—my task and obligation along with the *disease to please.* I enable the alcoholic father, tirelessly defending him, after every down and dirty, rock'em sock'em blow-out fight with Rae, making excuses for his shortcomings and the long absences. I push to fulfill the needs of the demanding and controlling mother which stem from her mother's loss. *I'm the black belt of codependents.* I juggle to keep everyone happy, but that only makes me miserable. Pleasing everyone was impossible, but pissing them off was a piece of cake!

I'm the lowest Ramirez on the family power totem pole. I go to school, keep the house clean, pick up after a family of six, and make dinner before my mother gets home from teaching. I take care of brother Gus now, nine years old. I've no choice, there's no money allowance, or thank you's, *this is my lot in life.* I'm the familia's *Go-to Girl.*

I have homework, weekly cheerleading practice, and games on weekends. I babysit for the wives of prisoners, Mom's friends, neighbors and family. The extra cash helps, we struggle to survive on her meager Head Start teacher's salary. Our lioness Mother teaches us how to stretch and maneuver with very little.

"Hey, aren't we suppose to have dinner ready before Auntie Alma comes home?" Cha Cha rubber bands me back to reality.

"Let's throw some burgers in a pan, fry up some papas and reheat the frijoles." Tried and true favorites, and the easiest dishes to prepare.

"Dat's cool." She jumps off the kitchen counter where she was sitting and swinging her legs. We're lightning fast at prepping dinner. Cha Cha knew her way around a kitchen. She peels the potatoes. I roll, flatten, and place the hamburgers in the frying pan. The window fogs up from heat and food steam. A homey, rich cloud of aromatic gamy meat fills the kitchen.

Neil Young's *Cinnamon Girl* plays on the radio. Cha Cha moans "Ummm, I Love this song—turn that sucker up!" She agilely bobs and weaves in the small kitchen with the large, round table.

"No torts, eh?" Cha Cha frowns at the lack of her auntie's specialty. *"Ramirez tortillas reign supreme!"* She bellows as her thin hips sway back and forth, dipping on the downbeat.

"No, Mom didn't have time last weekend, she had to study for a test. There's Wonder Bread in there." I point at a beat-up tin breadbox on the counter by the sink.

There's a timid rap on the kitchen door. "Rose, it's me, Jewell." A small voice echoes from the other side of the door.

"Come in. It's open," I shout.

Jewell Johnson lives next door. She's one of Mom's Head Start Mothers. Her son, Jacob, is in her class. Jewell's boyfriend is in prison in Red Cañon. Mom's close to these ladies and helps them, *they're her spiritual ministry.* She teaches the children all day, befriends them in the evenings, and on the lonely, unendurable, manless weekends. *Borracho* Blaze is trapped in the addictive prison inside a Jim Beam bottle.

She helps them fill out food stamp applications, welfare paperwork, and other legal documents. Mom invites them to holiday gatherings, birthdays, graduations, and funerals. They're part of the colorful threads of the family fabric.

"Can you babysit Sunday afternoon?" Jewell asks.

"Oh-lah, *vacina, yessum!*" I give an enthusiastic greasy thumbs up.

"I'm going to a Tupperware party, no kids allowed. I might actually, buy something this time," she said with a weak smile.

"You wanna stay for dinner?" I ask.

"We already ate, but thanks—tell your mom I'll stop by later for a cup of tea, OK?" Jewell waves as she floats like a shadow out the kitchen door. She's a mousy, submissive introvert with brown, short, teased hair. Her boyfriend was doing ten years in prison. Jewell rented the upstairs apartment of the house next door.

Mom, after retiring from Head Start, worked as an advocate for the Prisoner families, a ministry she relished. She learned firsthand, from her mother, in this world we're all connected. *Those with less are our main business—thou art that, compassion, virtue, rests in every good deed.* Even with eleven children, my grandparents managed to take care of those in need. In those days, there was no social safety net of welfare, food stamps, Social Security, old age pension relief, Head Start or W.I.C. for single mothers. *There was only the generosity of good people to help those less fortunate.*

My maternal Grandmother Eugenia was a member of the Secular Carmelite Order, it consisted of lay people, non-clergy, every walk of life, young and old. The call to Carmel is to seek The Almighty's will and presence in the ordinary circumstances of everyday life.

Carmelite spirituality isn't about doing, but rather about being *a certain kind of person.* The vocation is truly Marian. They believe in pure naked faith and devotion to the poor and selfless service to others. Carmelites, like Mary, are *called to a hidden union with God* for the sake of the world. From the heart comes patience, forgiveness, compassion, and through quiet lives of prayer, clean out negativity for Grace to operate.

The ultimate reason for everything is Love. The Supreme Being's Love barrels down into the corridors of the will, *letting us choose the way* of giving Love. The Loving face of Mary is the archetypal image of God. The Blessed Mother Mary is so revered that baby girls are named Mary or Maria, in her honor. Mom's first name was Mary she preferred to go by her middle name.

Mom lived this way of life, until her father's untimely death when all security vanished. She had to grow up fast to help her mother, the worry and fear brought on depression pacified by food addiction.

Catholicism runs deep, in both families. My paternal grand-parents are also, hardy religious stock. I grow up under the tutelage of the church lady of Red Cañon Catholic parish. Grandma Ramirez cleaned, ironed, and prepared the altar for the priests. My grandfather was the caretaker for the church, shoveling snow until his late seventies. They grow an acre of beautiful vegetables and rows of roses every year. A huge, blue and white-robed, Virgin Mary statue, stands on her cement throne in the front yard, protecting the house and family.

I went to Sunday Mass with Mom and Grandmother Grace. She's a tiny, 4 foot 8 inch, 90 pounds, salt and pepper, curly-haired sprite. I grow up watching her fingers dance across the Rosary beads. She prayed fervently for the husband and four sons cursed with the disease of alcoholism. I pray to Mother Mary to forgive me for the web of deceits, and that I'm not disowned for my conniving ways and secret life. Most the time my parents didn't even know where I was, *by the grace of all that is holy,* I'm protected and watched over carefully.

Presence comes alive in the invisible world and *prayer is the secret key* that can heal, bring discernment and wisdom. It sanctifies the world walked upon. *Our lives are held tender in the circle light of prayer,* which holds harmony at the heart of chaos. I tap Mother Mary's calm waters daily—*Queen of the Angels.* At sixteen, I'm totally unaware of the benevolent forces underneath it all working on my behalf.

Blaze Skyward

MY FATHER BLAZE is defined by the precise moment he enters this world—his father's eye catches a skyward beam of light. He tracks a comet-like shooting star streaking across the night sky, as he hears his son's first cry.

Blaze—the meteor *Mestizo* (Spanish and Indian blood) sparks with the sizzle of the stars. A shower of them lights his way. The black, curly-haired, Aztec God-Huitzilopochtli is small and boyish. Up close, he's all macho man in his scoundrel and scapegrace ways. He lives life like he's about to flame out.

Aztecs believed in sacrificing human blood and hearts to the sun god who needed daily nourishment. They were known as *"the people of the sun."* Warriors, who died in battle or as sacrifices, go on to live forever in the bodies of hummingbirds. Blaze is born with the same buzzing energy and restlessness.

He won the featherweight Golden Glove boxing championship in his late twenties. He epitomized Mohammad Ali's famous quote: "Float like a butterfly, sting like a bee." In the ring, what he lacked in technique, he made up for in speed. My small, Huitzil—hummingbird warrior from ancient times reincarnated into a cruel world and swept up by supernatural forces. Hummingbirds bring us the gift of beauty and wonder pulling our attention out of the mundane.

He bought Mom beautiful jewelry with his winnings—her "boxing baubles." While he was working as a lineman for the Rio Grande Railroad, along the Arkansas River in Texas Creek, Colorado, a hobo broke into the small, row shack and stole all of my mother's precious jewelry.

During this happy stretch of their marriage, he'd serenade her while driving the long 30 miles of winding Arkansas River road from Texas Creek to Red Cañon.

"Sing *Red River Valley*," she said, it was her favorite.

"Then come sit by my side, do not hasten to bid me adieu. Just remember the Red River Valley and the cowboy that Loved you so true." He warbles in a velvet baritone.

Blaze, blood brother to the constellations, bursting with charm and effusiveness. Living in Red Cañon proved detrimental with the failure of his barbershop, along with the progressive stages of alcoholism. He walked sideways like a coyote hunting for food, drink, women, and excitement. He staggered from bar to bar on Main Street with a fifth of Jim Beam in his pocket and a cigarette dangling from his mouth. All the wasted days and nights my dad spent in beer joints, pool halls, and seedy jukebox dive bars, I imagine him in heaven watching all the suffering alcoholics warming barstools wishing he could flick a wand and cure them of the dreadful family wrecking disease.

At closing time with nowhere to party and too drunk to drive, he'd pass out in the car. He often had King, my ferocious, overly protective German Shepherd in the backseat barking and snarling not letting anyone near.

As a child, on the rare occasion when he took me bar-hopping, I was treated like a princess, sitting up on the bar, sipping a Shirley Temple or Roy Rogers mocktail. He'd shoot snooker or pool and drop quarters in the jukebox spinning a Freddy Fender or Johnny Cash tune. He puffed on his Swisher Sweets that smelled of cherries.

He stumbles in from a weeklong bender. *"Oh-lah, Papa Bear!"* I'm overjoyed and relieved to see him. I whip up gumbo, a goopy mash of peanut butter and honey. If there's nothing to spread it on, we'd eat it straight out of the bowl, as we catch up with each other's lives. He belts, *"Goodnight Irene, goodnight Irene, I'll see you in my dreams."* Then, tenderly kisses me, his "sweet, baby doll," and staggers off to bed, snoring loud within seconds.

If Mom spots a bottle near him, she empties it out in the sink, so he devises ingenious hiding places. He stashes his bottle of Jim Beam whiskey in the false kick bottom of the refrigerator. Dad barely eats, for an upset stomach he drinks baking soda mixed with water and survives on Alka Seltzer and Pepto Bismol.

Sunday mornings are *quality time* with my father. I'm a Daddy's Girl, his favorite child. He drags himself in from a night of heavy partying and hollers for me: "C'mon *mi'jita*, let's go for Long Johns. *'Put your shoes on Lucy, don't you know you're in the City!"* He drives downtown still drunk from the night before, reeking of alcohol and cigarettes.

Being with my father is like riding shotgun with a mini clone of Poncho Villa—regular rules don't apply. Where Mom was overly responsible, Dad didn't give a damn about the necessities of the family. *Feeling good* ruled his psyche—the *borracho's* lifestyle of booze, drugs, and women went hand in hand. Monogamy is just another rule to break. For some macho

Chicano males, like my father and his brothers, infidelity was part of their social structure and a risky, daring chicken game of the heart.

Daylight Donut shop on Main Street is a heavenly bakery with divine donuts, pastries, cakes, and bread. The German ladies with meat hook hands and portly bodies wrapped in white aprons bake the best donuts in Southern Colorado. It smells of yeast, butter and freshly baked bread. My favorite are Long Johns covered with crusty, maple flavored frosting, filled with fluffy cream, twelve-inch, dough logs of pure delight.

I see through the guilt-ridden bribes of the donuts. Mom lives for sweets, eager to wolf down the sugary peace offerings, happy, until he's missing in action, *again.* The sugar temporarily helps him feel better. He's *a classic addict:* always searching for the next drink, thrill, high, and conquest. He's the favorite Dad among my friends. I didn't know why until a confidant reveals *he got stoned with them,* but never with me.

It didn't take much to make him happy. Dad was different that way. He doesn't confront me about Jack or asks who I'm seeing. He trusts my judgment and believes *emphatically in unconditional Love.*

He was a self-taught, gifted mechanic with innate gearhead skills. He replaced an engine in a car, and it would run perfectly. After a long day of working on hot rods, I'd run across the street to the Kwik Way convenience store to fetch him a treat of Vienna sausages, canned oysters, sardines, Spam, all smothered in Red Devil Hot Sauce.

He has a passion for horses. His father was a ranch foreman for years in the Sangre de Cristo Mountains. He grew up with horses and was the best at breaking spirited ones, a horse

whisperer. My father adored anything with speed and dash—
like the comet he rode in on.

Dad didn't contribute much to the bottom line of the family expenses. He prides himself on bringing home the meat and
comes from people who hunt for their food. Tracking a large
deer or elk is a solitary, religious experience and purposeful
with the ancient wisdom of Mother Earth *that provides for us
every season.* It redeems him for the bad behavior the rest of
the year.

Every fall, the Ramirez brothers, plus Rae, (because she
worked like a man and kept her mouth shut), trekked into
the Sangre de Cristo Mountains for their limit of deer and elk.
Hunting season is that liminal betwixt and between break from
jobs, routine responsibilities, and dealing with women and children. Crazy time to run with the beasts of the wilderness where
drinking, smoking, and brother bonding takes precedence.

Blaze and his two younger brothers, Gil and Bernie, prepared for the weeklong trip. They packed their pickup/campers
with food, camping equipment, supplies, guns, and ammuni-
tion. And *booze—plenty of alcohol.* The annual hunting trip is
twofold: to secure three families a year supply of meat and to
get thoroughly, shit-faced.

They don't drink during the day while hunting for safety rea-
sons and out of respect for the animals, but when they return to
base camp, the *chelas* and whiskey flows effortlessly. Cases of
beer and quarts of whiskey are top priority. The Sacred Troika
of Hunting: *booze, guns, and Swisher Sweet cigars.*

During the summer, they scout locations in the Sangre de
Cristo Range. They inspect deer and elk droppings to check
what the animals are eating. Berries and piñon nuts meant

they're staying low in the foothills. They mark the thin, rib-boned, worn deer trails with tall rock Cairns in case it snowed. They check the *Old Farmer's Almanac* for weather patterns to calculate the perfect dates. A serious commitment required with the cost of hunting licenses, food, gas, ammo, and liquor.

Eyes of Heaven

R AE RETURNS FROM A HUNTING TRIP with a chilling story. The urgency in her voice foretells that if Mom ever got wind of it; she'd put the *kabash* on hunting season.

It's a Sunday evening too early for Jack to call, I'm in a mellow, relaxed mood. Elton John's *Madman Across the Water* album is spinning on the turntable, we sip hot chocolate, and lounge on the bed with the black florescent light on. The bedroom is wallpapered in psychedelic neon posters that glow freakily in the blacklight. There's *Age of Aquarius*, Hendrix, Doors, Janis Joplin, and *The Desiderata: "Go Placidly amid the noise and haste..."*

The trip to Black Table Mountain was difficult. Rae drove the recent purchase of a Bronco-orange 1956, GMC truck. She inched up a steep, snowy grade in granny gear. Gus wedged between her and Blaze. Swisher Sweets cigar smoke filled the cab, choking Gus.

She describes how the truck trudged slowly, moving her-ky-jerky and that Gus yelled: "Let me out; I can walk faster than this!" We laughed. A week's worth of deep snow had ac-cumulated at the Ramirez's campsite. It aided in tracking but made it wet, cold and miserable.

Rae explains that Gus is her responsibility for the entire week. The men didn't want to deal with him. He's chubby, not athletic, the antithesis of Rae. Gus at fourteen is in an awkward pubescent stage—not quite a boy or a man.

Rae instructed him, "Tomorrow, we're up at sunrise, eat a big breakfast and start tracking deer. No whining from you—got that?" They unpack the camping equipment. The men sleep in separate campers with Rae and Gus in a tent. They set up the camping stoves and gathered wood for the week for the large campfires they'll need to keep warm. Gus did his chores in silence to avoid agitating Rae.

The brothers dive into the first case of Budweiser. Rae builds a roaring campfire. They clean and prepare their guns and re-tell the same old hunting stories Rae knows by heart. They laugh and puff on little cigars full of machismo and one-up-manship—especially in drinking. Dad wins that contest hands down, even though he's the smallest and the oldest.

Dinner is tasty lima beans and ham with homemade corn-bread. The prepared in advance scrumptious meals just require reheating on the camp stove. She describes how Gus helps her tidy up, she cleans her .30-30 Winchester rifle and packs the ammo in a backpack. She throws in a first aid kit, binoculars, a compass, candy bars, nuts and a canteen of water.

Rae explains that she lectures Gus about not hearing any excuses from him and that "*I'm shooting a deer.*" They plan to stick close to camp and return for lunch. It saves from having to pack lunches for everyone. Until the animals move up higher into the mountains or go down lower, it's a constant cat and mouse game between hunter and prey.

She stressed how cold it was and the importance of the

campfire. Gus finished roasting and eating his last marshmallow and climbed into the tent. Dad got her a hunting license and she *had to hold her own* and shoot a deer so she can relax. She disliked the ritual of eating the animal's heart and liver that Dad insisted on when taking a life but won't hesitate in the presence of the tough uncles.

Before bedtime Dad underscored her priorities: "Rae, make sure you keep a close eye on Gus your mom will divorce me if anything happens to him," he warns. To them, he was a candy-ass and spoiled mama's boy. It dips below freezing that night. Rae was toasty in a down, army surplus mummy sleeping bag.

"At sunrise sparkling diamonds glinted off the snow piled high. If it weren't so damn cold, I'd enjoyed all that glorious beauty." Rae said as she jumps back onto the bed after flipping over the album.

In the chilly tent, she roused Gus groggy with sleep. He dresses and she shows him how to cook a huge pot of oatmeal. He downs a hearty sized bowl; it's a long time till the next meal. The others were asleep and hungover, judging from the two cases of empty beer cans and two, empty quart, Jim Beam whiskey bottles that littered the campsite.

"I crossed my fingers and hoped they're still alive," she frowned. Dad was passed out in one of the campers. Once awake, he'll start tracking and hunts alone.

They head to a clearing east of the campsite, Gus follows close behind her. "I mentally list what to go over with him to keep him safe. We wear bright orange hunting vests and caps. 'You stay behind me—*ALWAYS*, don't step in front of me, do you understand?' I turn around to make sure he's listening and tell him that I didn't want to accidentally, shoot him. I squinted in *the mean Indian,* take-no-shit scowl to emphasize how important this is."

In the clearing, a few yards on the right, is a wake of turkey buzzards, five perched in the trees, four on the ground. She hadn't seen this many together. They're huge, intimidating birds.

"Oh man, how creepy. I can't stand those scavengers." She grimaced. They're clean animals performing a valuable service of eliminating the remains of decaying carcasses. She recalls from Dad's *Animal Energies* book that *they clean up messes.* We create physical and psychic messes, we don't want to deal with. If a buzzard appears, one has to remedy a messy situation and turn it into something positive.

They hike a few miles from camp without a hint of wildlife, but now, she's tracking a deer each hoof print makes a heart-shaped impression as it lifts away from the ground. *Heaven's in the eyes of these creatures.* She spots a healthy buck 60 yards away, down in a small hollow.

"I scan back to check on Gus, but he's not behind me. He's not anywhere, and I can't yell for him for fear of frightening the buck. I raise the rifle, view the buck in the gunsight. I line up the perfect shot aimed right between the shoulder blades, and was about to pull the trigger...

Suddenly, in a flash, I'm back at home, telling Mom the horrific news that I accidentally, shot my baby brother. Mom falls to the floor in a wave of grief. I blink back to the present moment. Up POPs Gus, ten feet in front of me and in-line of the shot aimed at the buck! I gasp loudly, and lower the rifle to the

ground quick. I look heavenward in to the brilliant, aquama-
rine sky, and let out a huge sigh of *"Thank you."*

"I laid into him so hard," she said. "What did I tell you?
Didn't I say *to not step in front of me?* I almost shot you right
between the eyes! Don't ever do that again, do you understand?'
I yell and ran over to him. He's frozen with fear. I shoved him
hard, almost knocking him down.

"What happened to you? Where'd you go?" I shouted. He
explained he had to pee and stepped off the path, and I kept
going. He got turned around and wandered right into the line
of the shot. He's shaking. I reached and gathered him into my
arms. He sobbed into my jacket.

Rae said, "I remind him that he's okay, and not to tell Mom
and Dad or he won't ever come again." She's relieved and
grateful she didn't take down the stately buck *or kill her little
brother* they made their way back to camp.

Dad was field dressing a huge buck when they arrived. He
got lucky, first thing over a bluff, he stumbled onto this gorgeous creature. He could smell the animals from a great distance. He follows the traditional ways of Apache, Diné, and
Ute. He doesn't plunder or waste Mother Nature which is
of the supernatural and believed in Carlos Castaneda's tenet:
"There is an unmeasurable, indescribable force called intent,
and everything that exists in the entire cosmos is attached to
intent by a connecting link."

Dad knew the animal's patterns and habits and honored their
souls and spirits allowing them to continue, even after their demise. He becomes one with them by eating their heart and liver,

manifesting the creature's spirit into his. My father was grateful for the animal's sacrifice for the nutrients of our family.

She describes how he cut the heart and liver into bite-sized chunks, whispers a prayer of gratitude to the animal while eating the meat. He cut a small piece of the heart and liver and placed it in a plastic bag. Later, he'll share it with me a ritual in our family. He teases his tough older kids who didn't like to eat the organs of the hunt, but the prissy, *la consentida*—Daddy's little-spoiled princess chows it down with no hesitation.

She realized after almost annihilating her little brother that she abhorred killing the beauties of the mountains. It's the best hunt ever all three Ramirez brothers bagged a deer.

Freezers overflowed with deer steaks, venison sausage, and teriyaki jerky. We prepared smothered, chile verde, deer steak burritos, Spanish rice, and venison sausage. Deer meat stew with potato, onion, and pinto beans. Abundance blessed our tables with *manna from heaven.*

Be the Star

And then the day came when
the risk to remain tight in a bud
was greater than the risk
it took to blossom.
—Anaïs Nin

M Y YOUNG MIND WAS LIKE A SMALL FLOWER bud yearning to burst open. I move through a disjointed landscape shifting between poverty, racism and the grandeur of *The River with all its hidden dimensions*: inner and outer world, and Divine Ground.

I'm the Patron Saint of Outsiders, now as a cheerleader, is it possible that I finally snagged a seat at the table? Brown skinned in *Gringolandia*; I'm constantly reminded how different I am. All I want is to fly under the radar, but it has the complete opposite effect. I'm excluded even more, and now, *don't fit in anywhere*. The rich, popular kids didn't want me, and neither do the other cliques who label me as a Judas for fraternizing with the enemy.

Cha Cha's back in school but between the extra make-up homework and taking care of baby Julian, we don't spend as much time together.

Darby Dawn, my only friend from the *noblesse oblige*. Her father owns a chain of hardware stores; she's from a large, Irish Catholic family. Our special ritual is getting high together in the high school parking lot during lunch hour.

Darby, *my angel in a vat of Vultures*. She bounces up to me in the hall with those big glittery, crystal, sapphire eyes, shoulder length, brown hair with fringed bangs, flitting on feathered eyelashes. Her puffy, pink frosted, lips crack a wad of Bubble Yum Gum while yelling over the hallway commotion, "Hey, Ramirez, time to get ripped!" A total day brightener, unless there's cheerleading practice if busted its expulsion from school and the squad.

We recline in Darby's baby-blue Mustang with a joint poised in the ashtray, ready to fire up. The car's bouquet smells of Bonnie Bell, Berry Lip Smackers. *I'm tucked into the most luscious, magical, sweet ride.*

"How's Jack? Gawd, he's a cutie!" She keeps it light and doesn't ask anything too personal. "Did your sister win her softball game last weekend?" Darby's four sisters are excellent athletes and played softball and volleyball with my sister. By the third question, we'd be laughing, too stoned to maintain a decent conversation. Didn't matter, she was an oasis in a desolate, dreary rope-a-dope landscape.

We gleam ecstatic; our bodies' loosey-goosey, the car fills up with thick smoke. Getting stoned with Darby freed me of the usual paranoia; she's exempt from all things negative. A Teflon protected, pot-puffing goddess her every whim and desire granted by the Universe.

Darby and I meet on a Friday night in the dark parking lot next to the football field at Red Cañon High School. We're playing in an all-girl, juniors vs. seniors, Homecoming Powder Puff football game. We mistakenly believed it would be *"fun"* to drop a tab of Mescaline before kickoff. The Lion's Varsity ivory and gold football jerseys that we slip over jeans and T-shirts hang on our petite bodies like flour sacks.

I didn't realize that Mescaline is a psychotropic substance similar to LSD and Psilocybin and I'd be trippin' while playing a violent football game that *I've no clue how to play.* The drug kicks in and my mind shifts into sensory overload with brilliant primary shades of colors flashing.

Darby morphs into a fearless warrior, leading like a general in battle—totally blitzed. *I'm a blubbering mess* who wants to crawl under the bleachers and remain in a fetal position until it wears off.

The bright, football stadium lights overwhelm me. I run up and down the field, my lungs constrict and threaten to explode. Darby charges like a victorious gladiator and executes powerfully. She runs up breathless after a botched play, "Ramirez, are we having fun now?" Crossing those big, crystal blue eyes. "Stay low and out of the way!" she yells over her shoulder. Thankfully, I'm not creamed by the big-boned, Amazonian, senior girls. Juniors win 12-6, even bombed on Mescaline, triumph, and glory are ours: a small victory, *fer sure.*

I doubt Darby got any grief from her inner circle about me, because she probably didn't tell them. Maybe, she's just slumming or pitied me. We don't do anything together outside of getting stoned in her car. I should've pushed her but, *I savor our time.* Selfishly, I'm keen on it being just the two of us—pure unadulterated bliss.

Our secret friendship makes the cruel treatment by the others seem harsher and magnifies my outsider status even more. It's not the constant flow of meanness that cuts the deepest, it's the cold blank stare that looks past, invisibility with diminished irrelevancy, which slams the door of acceptance. I shadowbox all through high school, not sure who the opponent is—the jerky jock slinging derogatory slurs or the constant, *death-by-a-thousand cold-shoulder cuts,* noses up in the air, and the *"you're not one of us"* cold stare of superiority from the popular crowd.

❮———•———❯

I vow to leave Red Cañon and live a large, full exciting life and not look back. I count the days till graduation and freedom from judgmental attitudes, bigotry, and small-mindedness.

Cha Cha and Jack are my safe havens. *The River* my sanctuary. Music is my escape. I'm lucky to be born in the zenith of music's heyday—Jimi Hendrix, Janis Joplin, Joan Baez, Joni Mitchell, Linda Ronstadt, Carole King, Cat Stevens, Led Zeppelin, Neil Young, Traffic, The Who, Van Morrison, The Beatles, The Rolling Stones, James Gang, The Moody Blues, Pink Floyd, Steely Dan, and Ten Years After *just to name a few.* In 1973, Rock and Roll raked in two billion dollars, which was more than what was spent on movies and sports combined.

We basked in the Sixties afterglow an excellent example of a Renaissance type of change. *Power to the People.* The perfect period of life as participation, *it eclipsed everything*: politics, religion, and race. Ideological movements expressed in the music: Monterey Pop Festival, Woodstock and in protest songs still sung today.

There was a *connection between people*. An amalgam of political and cultural changes. This generation raised the bar on how men should treat women and how women should treat themselves. That unity was key. The youth-led counterculture was on the brink of a non-violent revolution of a liberated lifestyle. We blasted out of the confines of society until the hippies turn into parents, secured square day jobs and were forced to face the responsibilities of adulthood which heated up ravenous consumerism and a culture of greed and corruption.

Music, a psychic salve on my soul, a constant companion, and a temple of shelter in my Tilt-a-Whirl cosmos. In the lyrics, I heard cryptic messages of hope and Love that inspired me *to be the star in my life*, to weave the pattern of my destiny, no matter how difficult or impossible.

I'm all in, *I Love Jack, more than I fear my family*. Music, Jack, and The River are my lifelines, lifting and fulfilling me so completely that I could suffer through anything. The only limit was the capacity to receive. The Infinite Spirit flows in both directions, or there's no flow at all. Jack's presence confirms an omnipotence of a higher power.

Growing up in the thick of the sexual revolution became a generational marker for me as a Catholic. It opened the floodgates to Feminism, abortion rights, gay rights, and Civil Rights. Conservative members flung derogatory names like "Cafeteria Catholics" at liberal progressives attempting to reform the old doctrines and moral teachings of the church.

The emerging church is nurtured by realistic Catholics that don't accept the intolerant and shaming ways of a religion that refuses to keep up with its followers of Jesus Christ. The focus should be on true conversions of heart and less on doctrine purity. Jesus teaching was simple: God Loves you. What does God expect in return? *Love God and Love others. It's that simple.*

Lotta Love

If I got rid of all my demons,
I'd lose my angels.
−Tennessee Williams

JACK STAYS AT THE BOARDING SCHOOL during Thanksgiving break. He'd have plenty of time with the family in New Zealand during the month-long Christmas vacation. He invites me to spend a quiet evening with him in his dorm room. The campus cleared out, and even the prefects went home for Thanksgiving. Everyone left except the ubiquitous monks and priests who live at the monastery.

Kids at an empty school during a holiday break—ideal conditions *to just be together.* I bike to the school around dusk and stash it in the bushes that grow along the ditch, directly across the field from Hedley Hall, the junior/senior dormitory.

I trudge through the long, grassy field to his ground floor dorm room and tap on the window, he slides it open and helps me climb down into the room. It's a small, white cinderblock cube, so clean and orderly. *I'm shocked by how small it is.*

"Wanna drink? I've got beer, do you want a glass?" He pops open a Michelob. I get a whiff of the hoppy, beer mixed with the cool, night-wind of mountain air that blew into the room. The brightly lit space has a harsh, cold bluish tint. I'm keyed up from the strenuous bike ride.

"No thanks, bottle's fine." Giddy, he picks me up and playfully, flings me on the small, twin-size bed.

"This is it, are you disappointed?" He reads my tentativeness.

"Gawd, no, so cool to see where you sleep and *dream,* it's so tidy. I'm impressed, you'd hate my messy room, *it's pandemonium.* Sharing a room with a slob sister is the worst." I don't admit that I'm the messy one.

"We need music," he flips off the obnoxious, buzzing, fluorescent ceiling light, and clicks on a desk lamp. I'm on the bed watching him and read Goethe's quote tacked to the bulletin board. "*We are shaped and fashioned by what we Love.*"

My heart is thumping so fast, even though I'm not going to sleep with him. I'll stay a virgin until the time is right. He puts on Neil Young's song, *Lotta Love.* My heart melts, my whole body relaxes from the first bars of the familiar song. *He plays dirty.*

"Not fair, I'm a sucker for Neil!" I cry.

"I'm a rat bastard, let's get high." He limps over to the desk and lights a joint. We kiss... I'm excited but scared, my mind races, I stop myself, *savor this moment.* His tender soft kisses aren't rushed, he doesn't push, or try to control me, hmmm... *how in sync we are.* I'm too high—why did I get stoned? His hand is on my breast I jolt from the reverie.

"It's OK if we take it slow, right?" I look up at him.

"No worries, I wouldn't ask you to do anything you're not comfortable with." He moves his hand away. We kiss deeply; he's halfway laying on top of me but I don't freak out, I relax knowing I can trust him; *it's pure bliss.*

I imagine we're at *The River* making Love in one of the willow-stick huts in Munchkin Land. Our Love fills the whole town with positive ions. The divisions between townies and private school preppies evaporate, racial hatred wiped out, divisions of rich and poor zapped, *GONE!* My eyes are closed with a slight, smile on my face.

"Hey, you're not falling asleep, are you?" He playfully nudges me.

"Nope, just transforming the world. Don't you wish pot was legal? It'd solve so many problems." I reason.

"Hell, yeah! In some countries, the laws aren't as strict as the States."

We drink a couple more beers. There's a firm knock on the door. I'm startled. I thought we had the campus all to ourselves. Jack's face darts up; a pair of beady eyes, framed in black, horn-rimmed, Buddy Holly glasses peer at us through the long, thin window in the door.

"Oh shit, quick, hide in the closet! It's a monk checking on me," Jack whispers.

I jump off the bed, dash across the room, slide open the pocket door to the closet and duck in, sliding it closed. Jack ditches the beers under the bed, smoothed the blankets and walks calmly, the few steps to the door. "Hey, how are you, Brother Daniel?"

The monk blasts past him and slides open the closet door. Squats down, eye-to-eye with me: "You need to leave young lady, right now." He stands in front of the door blocking my exit. I blink like a rabbit cornered by hounds and calmly proceed over to the dorm window. Jack slides it open and hoists me up and out into the heavy, tingling, piney frigid night air.

I bolt through the barren, frozen field in front to the ditch, and jump on my bike. I'm tipsy and high and numbed by the bone-chilling cold, but my biggest concern is for Jack. He calls me later, and we giggle about being busted. Brother Daniel lets him off with a warning but advises against visitors in his room. We wouldn't be brazen enough to try that again.

The vortex of Eros; an invisible *Divine Reality* that at our age is incomprehensible. It swoops in, sparks fly and ignites change. An eternal treasure that is unexpected and undeserved precious beyond measure transforming experience.

I gleam *inexplicable Love* unable to grasp its profound sacredness. It brightens every aspect of my life, *and through it, I see the Great Spirits tender smile.* Our worlds are so completely different, but when united there is a newness and a flowering of souls. *Nothing lasts forever, but something special can last a lifetime.*

Pocha Princess

A Mexicana is a very strong woman—
mujeres muy mujeres.
–Chavela Vargas

Y SISTER RAE AND I drill each other on the new tennis hard courts at Rio Vista Park located across the street from Red Cañon High School. The city pool is kitty-corner and has racquetball and handball courts. In the summer, we spent all our free time at this *happening hot spot*, a strong second to "dragging the gut" on Main Street.

The beautiful, tree-lined grassy park has new tennis hard courts, picnic tables, barbecue pits, playground with a teeter-totter, merry-go-round, and a scary, twisty slide. All summer, we'd hit the tennis and racquetball courts at least once a week and during mild weathered holidays, a welcome retreat and escape from the crowded house.

Rae prefers racquetball over tennis. My infatuation with bad boy Johnny "Mac" McEnroe and the perfection of Chrissie Evert fueled my interest in tennis. Our practice sessions bordered on the ridiculous and we didn't even know how to keep score. Once I was clobbered with such force with a tennis ball right between the eyes that it made them water. We laughed so hard, that I forgot about the pain, until later when an egg-shaped knot formed on my forehead surrounded by a purple-bluish bruise.

I cruise on my bike to Sacred Heart School to play a couple of sets with Jack on a mild, winter Saturday. I bring along my sleek, Chris Evert wood racquet and extra tennis balls.

Jack introduces me to Fernando Fernandez; I'm upset it's not the usual mix of man-children. He's handsome and brash, full of cocksure machismo. I've grown up with this breed of male. Back home in *Nuevo Méjico,* Fernando's a tyrant to his family: life revolves around his needs and wants. He lives for the next narcissistic fix. Fernando's angry that I'm dating a *gabacho*—white guy but the bigger blow, I annihilate him on the tennis court.

The deteriorating cement tennis court at Sacred Heart School is the *worst surface* to play on. When a ball hits the large cracks, it's a lucky guess which direction it will bounce. I smack a perfectly timed tennis ball on the sweet spot of the racquet rocketing it through the air and painting the line. It's turning dark; the courts didn't have lights, so we wrap it up.

"You don't think anything will come of this, do you?" Fernando baits me when Jack runs to retrieve balls hit over the fence. I glare at him.

"Excuse me; I don't give a shit what you think." I snap. It took major restraint to not smash my prized racquet over his head. I'm as angry with Jack for bringing this buffoon to play. I gather my things and stuff them in the backpack.

"You're out of your league, *honey.*" He smiles through coyote-like teeth.

"It pisses you off that Jack is white, but *Love has no boundaries.*" I tamp down the wild Apache temper.

"You're delusional, keep lying to yourself." He hisses at me. Fernando puffs up like a peacock to appear powerful. He oozes poisonous, judgmental thinking.

"*Stay away from us and stop pretending to be Jack's friend.*" I throw the backpack over my shoulder and run over to Jack.

"He's one big asshole I don't want to see again!" I shout.

In Fernando's mind, he's superior to the boy I'm in Love with. He's obsessed with measuring, counting, keeping track, weighing up or down, mostly down, the typical dualistic mindset. Fernando watches me run to the ditch to my bike. He vows to wreak havoc and destruction in our lives. If he can't have me, he'll make it impossible for Jack.

Fernando Fernandez or now, as I refer to him as Fernando Fernan'*dick*'ez, after he spreads rumors that Jack's nailing some local tail: *Rose Ramirez—the town puta,* whore.

"She puts out to anyone, for a good time, call Rose Ramirez." He scrawls my telephone number on the walls of the pay phone booth and in the dorm bathroom stalls. Jack removes it and asks friends to do the same whenever they see the hideous filth.

The guys know what a windbag Fernandez is and don't believe him. Oliver keeps me up to date. I worry Jack will stop seeing me, but *it makes our Love stronger.* He learns a valuable lesson: to bring only his most trusted friends around me. We refuse to allow negative drama and toxic people to poison our relationship. Fernan'*dick*'ez was an emotional pox; we'd stay clear of.

❖————◆————❖

I don't perceive myself as different and agree with Eleanor Roosevelt that no one can make you feel inferior without your consent. I loathe the snide judgmental remarks and the awful insufferable question: "What nationality are you?" Shorthand for *you're not one of us*. Insidious racism where differences are pointed out in a derogatory way. I'm remarkable inside until manipulated *into feeling less than* by the racist gaze of contempt and pity and told that I don't belong.

Ironic since my ancestors were the first people to walk *la tierra encantada*—the enchanted land. I'm a proud, Pocha Princess a fifth-generation, Southern Colorado native with limited Spanish vocabulary. A Spanglish speaking born and bred *Méjicana/Chicana*. We aren't taught Spanish to spare us the terrible discrimination our parents suffered growing up. Our parents wanted to protect us from the beatings and ridicule and know English is *the most powerful weapon for success*.

Mestizaje is another definition for us, a person of mixed race; of European (Spanish) and indigenous descent of mixed blood. I was not born in Mexico; neither were any of my family members. We are Mexican Americans. I'm an Indigenous Chicana whose incensed when told to "go back to Mexico." *When Mexico ceded the territory to America, we did not cross the border; the border crossed us.*

Mexican Americans transform the definition of what it means to be mainstream American, *by the enormity of our numbers*—the new American majority of non-whites. Slowly, the face of America is changing—*she's turning brown*. Every year, 1 million Chicanos born in America reach voting age. We spend over 1.1 trillion dollars a year. If we were a country, we'd rank 16th in the world. We're too large of a demographic to ignore or marginalize.

What innovative ideas could immigrants come up with if allowed out of the shadows? We can't risk living in a society where Chicanos become a permanent underclass. Voter's rights, Women's rights, racism, classism, homophobia, environmental awareness, and care for those living in the margins of society. All problems that need dealing with in compassionate ways and with Loving solutions.

Those excluded on the edges of society, hold the answers to the wholeness of us all. They represent the feared, rejected and denied parts of our souls. The acceptance of the outcasts— immigrants is actually how we all are converted and renewed.

Religion in the past greased the wheels of human consciousness towards Love, non-violence, justice, and inclusivity. The immature religion that prevails keeps us stalled and is a big part of the problem. *Mystical experience is our one, big hope,* connecting us at new levels. Universal belonging and connecting *is the definition of Heaven on Earth.*

Emmet Fox's beautiful explanation of how it's not "My Father," but *"Our Father,"* is the clear truth of the brotherhood of man. It cuts away the illusion that members of any nation, race, territory, group, class, or color, are in the sight of God, superior to any other group. *We are the limbs of one body.*

I linked the sacredness we experienced at *The River* with how we honored it in each other, regardless of the color and class distinctions. As Jimi Hendrix said: "When the power of Love overcomes the Love of power, the world will know peace." Loved people have the courage and energy to imagine new things. Richard Rohr, a Franciscan priest, described it best: *"It's Uni-verse, means to turn around one thing."*

A Seat at the Table

Diversity is being invited to the party.
Inclusion is being asked to dance.
–Vernā Myers

THREE YEARS ON THE CHEERLEADING SQUAD and *I lived in the belly of prejudice and paradox.* Every year the new captain of the squad devised "team building" activities. Most were lame and superficial; nonetheless, I had to participate.

The "Wake-Up" sleepover is the epitome of cruelty. A carload of boisterous cheerleaders at sunrise go to each squad members house wake them up out of bed in their pajamas and whisk them off to the captain's house for breakfast. They spend the day together and extend it to a sleepover.

Katie Kapperling is Captain my sophomore year. She shines like a copper penny with satiny brown, page boy hair, and at six feet tall is all legs and giraffe-like. A harsh and dismissive giantess with a permanent smirk that doesn't acknowledge me the entire year. Her eyes slide past me like I'm a piece of furniture.

At Katie's house, we rolled out our sleeping bags in the great room by the fireplace. We're up all night gossiping about the in-crowds' sex lives. There're tons of junk food, movies, games;

Twister, Truth or Dare, chats about makeup, clothes, and expensive vacations.

We prank-call the Varsity football and basketball teams. They date them and have their telephone numbers and schedules. Her mother feeds us waffles, pancakes, and eggs for breakfast and mountains of pizza and snacks for the rest of our stay.

The hypocrisy of these outings is *pretending we're friends.* It's even harder for them. They can't be too cruel to me— we're supposed to be a team, but they didn't have to like me. There's a *"Fernando Light"* female version on the cheerleading squad. She's not quite as diabolical, but by being Italian, it still smacked of ethnic betrayal.

We're both short with brown skin, long black hair and brown eyes. We could've passed for sisters, if not for the glare of disgust down her witchy nose at me. She is Fernando's evil twin: it's not the wealthy, white boys at Sacred Heart School that made me feel less than, *it's one of my own kind.*

Coco (Chandler) Cabrini, *is a bad apple,* which is all she ate to maintain her scrawny, 90-pound body. She has a mouthful of steel braces, long, frizzy, black hair and a small, dark mole on the side of her mouth. She chomps on gum snapping it without mercy.

I endure whispers and giggles with rolled eyes behind hand-covered mouths. I want to fit in and stand out at the same time. Coco is accepted because her daddy owns a large, construction company in town. Money, it always came down to that, it wasn't just about race. *It's what people of privilege do to close the doors to the outsiders*—the haves versus the have-nots.

I didn't expect to be close friends, *all I want is a seat at the table*. I worked just as hard, show up and care passionately about the success of the team. Look past my brown skin and *see me and my abilities* of strong will and determination.

I recall the lonely, long road trips to out of towns games on the school bus. No one would sit next to me. I'd sit stone-faced and glare out the window, holding back tears, *because I didn't want those bitches to see me cry.*

Cha Cha and I plot revenge on Coco Moco "Fernando Light." We drive to her fancy neighborhood to TPee her house.

Cha Cha: Are you sure this is *ese pendeja's* house? I don't want to waste all this toilet paper/trees on the wrong, damn house. This mother's a monster.

Me: Positive—I spent one of those insufferable, sleep-overs here. I gagged the whole night, almost asphyxiated myself.

Cha Cha: You sure you want to do this, crazy *vata*? She asks with a nervous twitch.

Me: Hell, Yeah! I shout, determined.

As we debated, a large dog trots toward us. He's dark brown, a Sheepdog/Husky mix, he looks harmless, until he's closer and barks viscously and bares his teeth. We look at each other and consider it an omen, "Let's boogie!" Cha Cha cries.

I was taught to *eat at a bigger table* with new people-the oppressed and excluded. Set a bigger table overflowing with compassion and mercy.

Stick to Your Guns

You can't test courage cautiously.
–Annie Dillard

JACK CALLS ME THE EVENING before his departure for the month-long Christmas break.

"I need to see you before I leave for New Zealand." I hear urgency in his voice.

"When? You're leaving first thing tomorrow," I ask, puzzled.

"Tonight. Can you sneak out at 2:00 a.m.? Your parents will be sleeping."

"Oh no, Jack, that's too dicey. What if we're picked up for curfew? It's at 11:00 p.m. for anyone under eighteen," I warn him.

"We'll stay close to your house, *please*. I promise we won't get caught."

I agree to meet him. I hang up the phone. Why didn't I *stick to my guns* and say no? Am I so willing to please him, even if it means risking trouble with the law and my parents? I'm angry at myself and have an uneasy feeling about this.

I peek out my bedroom window, "Hopefully, he won't show," I whisper. Exactly at 2:00 a.m. he's standing in the shadow of a big elm tree in the front yard. I throw on a jacket and tiptoe to the front door. I place an inflated inner tube between the squeaky, screen door and frame. I run down the porch steps, push through my fear, and the thick weight of the arctic air into his warm arms. The bolt of cold air hits me, bristles my nostril hair and stings my cheeks. I want to see him but not like this. *It's way too risky.*

"We're sooo outta here!" He's happy to see me one last time before he makes the long journey to New Zealand. We're at the corner in front of the Mobile Gas Station, *next door to my house* when we're blasted by a jarring, blare of a siren and flashing red lights. My dad's startled awake by the loud noise and red flashing lights blinking in his bedroom window. He listens for a moment for any familiar voices or sounds and then, rolls over and goes back to sleep.

A police cruiser pulls up. "Damn, we didn't even talk! *I'm so sorry.*" He's crestfallen. Jack walks over to the police officer and tries to reason with him.

"Please, sir, this was my idea. I talked her into it, she didn't want to meet me. Take me in, she lives in that house right there." He points to my house, less than 50 yards away. He desperately pleads with the cop.

"Sorry, son, you're both going in and will have to be picked up by your parents," he tells Jack. I begin to sob, I'm so scared. We climb into the backseat of the police cruiser. I'm trembling so hard, I ball up my shaking fists and stuff them under my thighs.

"If your parents didn't like me before, this will make it difficult for us. Such a knucklehead idea, I just wanted to see you one last time." He holds my hand. A priest picks him up from the police station around 4:00 a.m.

My father comes for me. He doesn't lay a finger or say a cross word because he Loves me more than life, but I don't ever, *again, want to experience*, his closed face and those hard, disappointed eyes. I learn an invaluable lesson: to listen to and trust my instincts.

Blaze and Alma sit next to each other on the couch in the small, alcove television room with the garish lavender floral wallpaper. A peeping Tom might think he stumbled onto a happy couple. There's a loud knock on the door. "Ah, come in." Mom greets her favorite nephew, Don, Aunt Lucy's adopted son. Blaze called him after my arrest.

"*Mi'jito,* so glad you came, we've serious business to discuss." He offers him a seat.

"Tío, what's this about?" Don's a handsome, Anthony Quinn looking, nephew. There's no Mexican Mafia in town, but if Blaze ever needed anything—*he's the guy.* Don idolizes his Uncle Blaze. Auntie Alma's his mother's younger, sister; *he would go to the ends of the earth for these people.*

"Rosie got arrested last night, I shit you not." He shudders. "My angel has met a boy at that damn, private school on the edge of town. He talked her into sneaking out at 2:00 in the morning—*what asshole does that?* I want you to keep an eye on my girl. Put the word out: if anyone sees her with this Jack Dillon person or any of those prep school punks, let me know. I'll replace the engine in your car, cut your hair, buy you drinks at the bar. I don't want my girl hurt by bastards who will use her. So, you in?" Blaze asks.

"Tío, I don't run in her crowd, I'm six years older and don't hang out at the same keggers—um, parties. How can I watch her if I can't get close?" he asks.

"Yeah, we got okey doked big time. This girl's crafty and cunning and lies with a straight face. Use your street smarts, tail her moves and report back to me. Right now, I'm in the damn DARK! I just want to keep her out of harm's way. *Rosie's our most precious gift."* He lowers his eyes.

Don's the adopted son of Aunt Lucy. She's loathed and resented by her oldest sister Manuelita's seven children, all legally adopted by her and Uncle Carlos. Mom helped Manuelita care for them until Aunt Lucy alerted the County Child Services about their living conditions.

A case of the strong-willed taking advantage of the weak. The iniquitous narrative is Aunt Lucy stripped the children from her for the welfare money. The adopted children are bullied, treated as outsiders and *less than* Lucy's children. Half of them continue the cycle of alcoholism and poverty.

Don's all Navajo with root beer tinted, wolf eyes, a long face, high cheekbones, and a wide forehead. He's shy and avoids eye contact. The adopted children have poor social skills. Don clears his throat. "This is narc work, I don't want to betray Rosie's trust. She'll be pissed that I'm snitching on her."

Mom's been sitting quietly on the couch: "Imagine having a daughter pure and untouched until she meets a boy who talks her into who-knows-what. Would you *stand by and do nothing?"* she asks with outstretched hands.

"Oh, no Tía, I'll help you, Rosie's a smart girl, she wouldn't do anything to damage the family," he said.

"Don, that's damn straight, but *pobrecita,* Cha Cha at such a young age her life ruined by a man who didn't give a rat's ass. Keep an eagle eye on your cousin and alert us. Enough of this bullshit, let's have a beer." Dad stands up. After a couple of drinks, they shake on it. Don agrees to help his auntie and uncle.

Later that evening, I receive a stern lecture from Cha Cha, "Damn, you little *Vagamunda!* Even I wouldn't have taken such a huge risk. You live just two blocks from the cop station. That *cabrón* was ending his shift and returning the cruiser when he saw you. You're lucky Tío didn't kick your rosca up one side the street and down the other. Next time, *listen to your gut,* she's always right. The biggest whoppers I've made were against my better judgment. Learn to say no, it'll save you so much pain and suffering."

Experience—the tuition is high, but there's no better teacher.

After the holiday vacation break I receive a call from Oliver. He said the night we got arrested he watched Fernando Fernan*'dick'*ez from the lobby of the dorm. Fernando saw Jack leave through the field toward town. Oliver tailed Fernando as he strutted down the hallway to the phone booth, and dialed the number to the Red Cañon Police Department. Fernando waited to call giving Jack ample time to reach my front door.

Oliver overheard Fernando's telephone call: "Red Cañon Police Department, "Hello, I'm Father Michael from Sacred Heart School, I want to report a missing student, Jack Dillon. He might be on U.S. Highway 50, near the Mobile Gas Station. He's violated school rules and curfew. Can you send a car to pick him up?" Fernando asked. Oliver was incensed to hear Fernando whistling *Felize Navidad* on his way back to his room and muttering "Merry fucking Christmas, kids," chuckling as he unlocked the door. Ollie fell asleep waiting for Jack in his room and relayed what happened when he returned.

Chicano Power

what didn't you do to bury me
but you forgot I was a seed
–Konstantinos Dimtriadis

THE BOYS PATIENTLY WAIT for the townie girls at *The River* on a late, Saturday afternoon in January with swirling, cirrus clouds overhead. I just got my driver's license and a bomb of a car with the help of my sister's $100 loan: *it gives me complete freedom*. It's impossible that such a free, and happy life could exist.

The white and tan, 1957, Star Chief, Oldsmobile is jam-packed to the headliner with girlfriends; the Morgan sisters, Cha Cha, Meg, and Jenny, along with guitars and camping gear. The cavernous car buzzes with rowdy chatter, laughter, and nervous excitement. The radio blasts: Zeppelin, Hendrix, Santana, and Neil Young... *the Beat Goes on.*

We're bundled up in down vests, coats, hats, scarves, and gloves. Cha Cha's decked out in her favorite oversized army jacket. We discover at the Army Surplus Store, army jackets, fatigues, and cargo pants years before they go mainstream, selling $700 million a year. My warmest piece of outer clothing, was a slate gray, down vest: the *hip-de rigueur* of Colorado winter gear which I found *at the Segunda,* the Salvation Army Store.

We pile out, onto the ribboned path that leads to *The River.*

"Oh-lah, *guapa chicas,* hope you dressed warm, it's cold as soon as the sun goes down." Sadie sidles up to me, hangs an arm over my shoulder, nestled together; we scurry down the path. She exudes a warm, Loving, effervescent radiance. She's a trustworthy confidant. We write poetry together and share a simpatico Love of music.

At the campfire clearing, we're greeted with a song: "*Wooo Hooo! Ho He He, Hi Hi Ho, I Love homosexuals!* Y'all made it." Oliver gallops up with a Frisbee. Eager as a frisky puppy, full of reckless, silly enthusiasm. He's wrapped in an old Mexican blanket with a ragged, brown, cowboy hat, too big for his puny pinhead.

"Who wants to play Frisbee with me? I've cleared a flat spot *over there.*" He said.

This is our first meeting since the arrest before Christmas break. I wrap my arms around Jack; he picks me up by the waist and swings me like a rag doll. I'm overjoyed to see him.

"What took you sooo long?" He asks with forced politeness.

Caleb is sporting a jean-jacket, tight Levis, a black, cowboy hat and boots—a Jon Voight dead ringer from *Midnight Cowboy,* he saunters up. "Who are all the new faces?" His wry smile and coolness factor puts the girls at ease.

Oliver's ear-shattering yell, "*¡Ay, Chavela! The hell on wheels Chicanita who needs no introduction!*" He jiggles an excited, happy dance. Cha Cha pulls his goofy hat down over his eyes, "This is Meg and Jenny, now fire up the wacky tobacky."

She chases after Oliver and his Frisbee. Caleb turns and smiles at Jenny, a freckle-faced, brunette, a baby beatnik wearing a similar jean outfit with a red handkerchief tied around her neck.

Other boys stop skipping rocks and move in, eager to meet the girls from town. The crackling blazing fire, shoots explosive sparks. A Jethro Tull tune booms through the campsite. I inhale deeply and gather it all in—the coil of smoke, *the roaring river,* and musky, teenage hormones raging.

Jack and Caleb gesture to assemble around the campfire. Jack announces: "Everyone's free to visit and explore Munchkin Land. Don't wander too far, at dusk we'll make s'mores, play music, and get stoned."

Oliver's bobbing up and down waving a small rainbow flag: *"Let your freak flag fly!"* Martin with his Armenian mane of wild black curls, guitar in hand, runs up to Scarlett as she pulls out her guitar. They tune their instruments, smiling and nodding at the right chords. Music, a mutual friend that instantly bonds them.

Jack and I wander off in search of firewood and privacy.

"Everyone seems to like each other." He stoops to pick up a large broken branch.

"Did you think they wouldn't?" I glance at him.

"I want everyone to have fun. *I know I'm going to.*" A pleasant smile broke over his lips. I half closed my eyes and inhale his Old Spice and woodsy smoke scent.

"Hey, Earth to Rose... I lost you for a second." He jostles me.

"Come here and gimme some sugar." I hug him roughly, he tightens his squeeze and tucks me under his shoulder. We stumble and roll onto the mellow needle duff. I slip my cold hands

under his wool jacket and run them over his warm, smooth back. He puts his face in the nape of my neck. We lay still, and I wish . . . time . . . would . . . stop.

As dusk descends, we gather logs for chairs and large rocks to sit on. One of the boys shouts, "There's the Great Blue Heron!" We all stand up and strain to see the pristine beauty. The enormous bird perches nearby on a rock; posing regally for his audience.

Martin kicks off the evening with an original song, *9th and Main*. It captures the buoyant, carefree nature of *"dragging the gut."* The last, rich note riffles through the air and rides a wave down the rustling water. A quick glance around the campfire, I'm warmed by the firelight gleam on the ruddy belly of the guitar with our feet spread toward the blaze, beers in hand and excitement beaming from our eyes.

Someone hollers from the shadow, "Let's play Truth or Dare."

Cha Cha stands up, "Ask me anything. I won't hold back," she said.

"What's the scariest experience you've ever had?" a faceless voice inquires. She puts a hand on her side and a finger under her chin and sits down.

"In 1970, at the tender age of thirteen, with a brave skinny, white chick, my girlfriend, Donna, we hitchhiked from Red Cañon to the west side of Denver. I'd been writing letters to a boyfriend who lived there. I'm crazy in Love and dying to see him. Upon arrival, I find him with another girl and we had no place to stay. He suggested we check out the Brown Berets at La Raza Park.

Two of Rose's uncles are delegates in La Raza Unida Party, so I'm familiar with the organization. We made friends with the foxy, young, Brown Beret college students and they invited us to a meeting in a church basement in northeast Denver. The packed room was full of eager Chicanos. The electricity in the air foretold *something powerful was about to happen.*

A handsome man in a blue suit with dark wavy hair, a thick mustache, and intense brown eyes, appeared at the podium. It was Rodolfo "Corky" Gonzales, the honorable leader of the Crusade for Justice, a national activist organization based in Denver.

Corky said: "Understand to make progress and to gain justice in a greedy, capitalistic, corporation loving society—*you have to take a stand.* Let's connect and work together with the American Indian Movement and the Black Liberation Movement." He paused and scanned the room of the large, enthusiastic group of young people gathered.

Cha Cha's excitement bubbles over, she jumps up and roars *"Chicano Power!"* Her right fist pumps in the air. *"¡Que Viva La Raza Indígenas!"* Startled, but captivated, the campers jump at the outburst.

She continues with more of Mr. Gonzales's speech; "There can be no justice when the prison population is forty percent of our people. We're not liberated, as long as the corporate structure controls the country. We can't land jobs that we deserve. The progress of people is judged by how many are in prisons versus how many are in universities. *We are a new Chicano.* Recognize if our young belong to the people or to the establishment. They not only need to make money but also, need to *give back to their communities.*

We are the fastest-growing minority, we have grown because our parents were strong enough to face racism, repression, oppression, and brutality. They've worked ten times harder than us. It's up to you now, our youth, to carry on and take us in a new political direction.

People are loyal to corporations for the check. But our people liberate themselves for the *Love of each other,* and that is the most important thing we have. Nobody can destroy that or an ideal or philosophy. *They can't destroy Love.* We are going to win, whether it takes this generation, the next generation, or the next. We are going to win! Viva La Raza! Viva La Raza Libre! Viva! Viva, Aztlán Libre! *Education is the answer; it's how we make a difference.*" He said.

"He ended by emphasizing that we win by going to college. He was passionate and vibrant. I saw a strong leader that night that continues to be a major influence in my life. After his speech, the Brown Berets took us to their house and under their protection. They were to treat us as little sisters, *la Adelita's*— these are the women soldiers that traveled with the comrades to help with chores and heal the wounded. Corky explained to the young men that we are someone's daughter or sister and to respect us as you would your family.

Later, they shared that he was a feminist, a writer, and a poet. They let us sleep on their pool table for a month, till we returned home to Red Cañon. It was during summer vacation, so we didn't miss any school," Cha Cha added.

As Chavela wraps up her story, almost on cue, Rodolfo's spirit materialized—smoke from the campfire spirals and permeates the group. The thin ribbon of smoke circles Cha Cha and me, then heads toward Scarlett who waves her hand back

and forth violently. Cha Cha still excited by the connection
with the old leader chases after the smoke. Yelling "Corky,
please come back!" She sits down next to Sadie.

"*I hate rabbits,* she murmurs mantra-like, *I hate rabbits!*"
Sadie says and repeats it over and over.

"What are you saying?" Oliver squeaks.

"Our family ritual, on camping trips we'd chant: *I hate rab-
bits,* and the smoke would change direction," Sadie explains.
Obediently, the smoke snakes the opposite direction toward
The River. Prest-O Change-O.

Caleb passes a joint around the boisterous group gathered
at the glowing campfire. Sleeping bags are propped up against
makeshift logs. A mellow, hang-loose vibe blankets the party.

Hot chocolate rolls to a frantic boil in a saucepan set in the
fire ring. Whiffs of sweet chocolate mingle with smoke. I bust
out the grocery bags with the s'more making supplies. We scat-
ter to find marshmallow roasting sticks and the s'more making
commences.

Sacred Spaces

Do not plunder the Mystery with concepts.
–Zen Masters

TWO NIGHTS LATER, I'm sprawled out on my bed in my room tackling difficult algebra homework when the phone rings it's too early to be Jack, but I run to answer it.

"*Qué onda, muchita?*" Oliver chirps.

"*Hola*, Ollie!" I'm thrilled to hear the airy, high-pitched voice.

"We need to move forward with building the Labyrinth at The River. A fantastic idea sounds like y'all were inspired by that first visit to *The River*. Lots of details to tend to, little, sassy, amiga. Gotta hit the ground running; this is where the rubber hits the road," he said.

"Are you done with the tired clichés?" I giggle.

"Rosie, do you realize how vital this Labyrinth is to us boys? Rational thought is shoved down our throats. *We need this sacred space* which is a magical, right brain spiritual enhancer. Sacred spaces as our playground, *if you're doing what seems like play—you are IN IT!* I learned about sacred spaces in Marie Noonan's class, that's one cool, she-Shaman teacher. Wonder what it would be like to drop acid with her. Hmmm...

The Labyrinth will symbolize our time together like a memorial, a win-win for all." He cheers.

"Let's set the date to clear the space at *The River*, build the foundation before winter sets in and the ground freezes," I suggest.

"Perfect, the area has to be dowsed with a divining rod to find the energy leys to figure where to place the rocks. Each riverbed rock is dowsed. The more we use this sacred space to develop our intuition and enhance the spiritual realms, *the more Mother Earth will speak to us*. She's alive and wants to connect. The Labyrinth is a conduit for Mother Nature to heal us, allowing *our souls and hearts to reset* to our deepest truth and rhythms. Oliver Cromwell and Theseus delivered the death blow to sacred spaces, logic over intuition, might makes right, male dominance and all that rot. We're too analytical and scientifically fact-oriented, we've lost contact with nature. *There needs to be a balance between the rational and intuitive*." He said.

"Whoa Ollie, you're a wisdom-filled fortune cookie." I chuckle into the phone.

"I wish, it's years of Catholic indoctrination—a blessing and a curse."

"Oliver, The River is a sacred place, I knew it immediately. I experienced *pure and innocent Love* let's share it with everyone."

"Oh Rosie, when I came upon this place—the swift, flowing river, a safe, neutral spot removed from judgments, and feeling out of place. At The River, there is room for every part of me, to be myself, and not have to look over my shoulder. Every hurtful glance, word, and mean act, is discarded in *The River* to wash away and remove it. I have feelings, but feelings don't have me, don't over-identify with negative feelings. I haven't shared this with anyone, but you're my best friend, so I'll trust you to keep a secret. I'm a female trapped in a male body. Someday I hope to receive a sex change, but until then I have to live this lie." He sniffles.

"Ollie, it'll work out, just look at the miracles The River has manifested, it brought you, Mary Noonan, and Jack into my life; a poor Chicana townie. Years from now when you're living your dreams with a gorgeous husband you'll forget all this sadness." I hold my breath, close my eyes, my vision left me for a second.

"I hope She's listening up there and grants all my wishes. For now, we've got to focus on the Labyrinth; those old farts killed off a female-centered, Goddess celebrated world. Back in the day, sacred spaces were commonplace, found in villages, and in homes. *Goddesses were everywhere.*" He's Waldorf educated and revels in Greek Mythology.

"Funny, you mentioned Goddesses, Chavela's crazed with them lately. Ollie, I'd love to visit more, but this Goddess has a shitload of homework." I beg off.

"I gotta boogie too—thanks for the heart-to-heart, spot cha' later Rosie!" He hangs up.

That evening, Don's staked out across the street in his car. He spots a weirdo lurking at the end of the block, eyeing the Ramirez house. He pulls up to the curb, bolts out of his car. "Hey, what the hell are you looking at? Who are you?" He growls. Don grabs the culprit by the scruff of his jacket, lifting him up, off the sidewalk, feet dangling.

It's Fernando Fernandez, shaking and scared. "I'm just walking to town. I go to Sacred Heart School." He squeaks.

"If I *ever see you near* this neighborhood again, I'll beat the living crap out of you. Any of the dip shits from that peckerhead, country club pretending to be a school!" Don bellows setting him down on the sidewalk then shoves him hard.

"No Sir, you won't see me again." Fernando runs in the direction of Sacred Heart School not daring to look back. The brawny cousin watches him and stands with arms crossed, legs spread wide apart on the sidewalk.

"*Chinga tu madre, Piojo,*" Don yells and spits on the ground.

Murder in the Cathedral

Some find their paradise
others come to harm.
–Amelia by Joni Mitchell

THE TOWNIES TAKE PART in the Sacred Heart School spring play, T. S. Eliot's *Murder in the Cathedral*. The theater director was Brother Owen, a.k.a. *Mad Monk*. He's in his thirties with light, brown hair and lively, blue eyes. He taught music, theater, and was the Director of the Glee Club Choir. He built the special stones for the Labyrinth at *The River*. Oliver was close to Brother Owen; he was like a big brother to him.

Oliver and Gonzo land leading parts. We go twice a week to rehearsal for two months. It allows me to be on campus without risking anyone's explosion. Jack and friends don't audition so we meet a new group of boys. I knew one "day-hopper" (a local student) since elementary school. Mention his name, Miles Layton, to any girl, and you'd get a sigh of exhilaration. "I've got the biggest crush on him," or "hubba hubba, he's sizzling hot!" He's not only handsome but intelligent with a musician's confidence. I had Miles Layton Fever since fourth grade when it was electrifying but daunting to be seated next to the cutest boy in music class. *He had the most beautiful hands.*

He's obsessed with the Beatles and the British Invasion and wears long hair since third grade and even is suspended for it. In junior high as a new, seventh grader, the ninth grade stomps—cowboys, jumped him after school and punched him and cut off a chunk of his hair. After that, he wore a short-haired wig all through junior high.

In grade school, my friend Sally and I sang songs in my backyard, pretending to be famous singers. We'd act out TV variety shows. "This one is for my boyfriend, Miles Layton." I'd belt out John Denver's *Leaving on a Jet Plane*. Performed under the apple tree with my dog King, as our audience.

Red Cañon High School had mandatory ROTC (Reserve Officer Training Corps). Long hair wasn't allowed in the dress code. Miles's Father arranged an interview with Headmaster Rawleigh Rio who accepted Miles after a quick meeting. The headmaster *even grew his hair long* in solidarity with Miles. He took a keen interest in him. They jogged during the summer when he tutored Miles in Liberal Arts classes to help him through high school a year early. Rawleigh saved his life by getting him into college at sixteen. He is a successful doctor.

The female cast performs as a chorus of village women who chant lamentations over and over. A dreary, dirge of a play, as adults we laughed at such a downer show for high school kids. The one phrase chanted throughout was, *"Bar the door."* It becomes a catchphrase at parties at *The River*.

It exposes us to theater that influences our paths as adults. Cha Cha on tech rehearsal night: "Check out the old lady costumes. I wish Brother Owen had picked an upbeat musical, like *West Side Story*." The Morgan sisters are cast, also, Meg and Raven, my friends from high school. Girls from Scholastico

Academy round out the village women. Opening night, I'm thrown off by a harsh remark by Scarlett.

"Why did you help yourself to the best costumes?" Scarlett yells at me.

"What are you talking about, I just picked what fit." I'm shocked at her attitude and upset this happens during the chaotic rush of opening night. I hang my head into my shawl and cry throughout the play. Later, I left without saying a word the cast headed to *The River* to celebrate.

I run toward Hedley Hall, to Jack's dorm. I knock on the dark window of his first-floor room, there's no answer. I look across the field and see Miles strolling by in his massive gorgeousness: the long, dark brown hair, sweet brown eyes one could drown in... He couldn't see me crouched in the dark. He's the poster boy of unattainable and unrequited Love.

Sobbing harder, I stumble to my car parked in front of the theater. Angry, loud shouts echo from the crowd gathered by the Scholastico Academy's bus. "What's happening?" I ask a bespectacled, pimply, freshman.

"Brother Owen punched a student by the bus," he said. A red-faced, angry, Brother Owen emerges from the center. He's dragging by the arm a roughed up, disheveled friend of Martin's, a "day-hopper."

The student, Rich Rodriquez, exchanged punches with Brother Owen after he pulled his hair and accused him of smoking. Rich escapes Brother Owen's grip, jumps in his white, Volkswagen Beetle, and peels out, burning rubber on the asphalt.

He returns with his father who explains to Headmaster Rio that Brother Owen attacked his son. Rich was innocently walking his girlfriend to the bus. Mr. Rodriquez demands punishment for the abusive teacher; "This kind of behavior is unacceptable and not tolerated." Rich is cleared of all wrongdoing.

The older students know to stay clear of Brother Owen. Upon seeing him, they'd sing the Three Dog Night's song: *"Momma told me not to come! That ain't the way to have fun, Son."*

He lives in an apartment above the theater. One party room was completely lined with Schlitz beer cans. On weekends, he'd invite the younger, clueless boys up to drink, get stoned, and party. His favorite attire is a see-through silk robe and gave these to his devotee's to ogle them as they paraded around his apartment.

The naïve younger students were easy pickings. Informality and a no boundaries setting is the perfect breeding ground for the crimes committed. He banked on the tyranny of secrets that allow him to violate the innocent. The victims too ashamed remain silent. Always tell someone, *never be silent, it encourages the tormentor, never be neutral, it helps the oppressor, never the victim.*

Why is it some of us skate right past these dangerous hot zones? I'm raised side by side with Cha Cha and was not inappropriately touched. An older, cousin molested her at five years of age which deeply affected and warped her self-image.

Predators plow roughshod through their victim's tender psyches, not caring about the wreckage and carnage. Child molestation leads to low self-esteem, severe depression, and suicidal ideation. Also, promiscuity, unprotected sex, alcoholism, drug abuse, and sexual dysfunction. The absolute worst result: *death from suicide.*

Shameful that the Abbot and administrators knew of his activities and other's pederast misdeeds and did nothing choosing to protect the institution over truth and mercy. The boys, I befriended at Sacred Heart School told me the school had saved them or drastically changed their lives for the better. There might be the same amount that could declare the opposite effect on their young lives.

Into the New Future

ON A FRIGID, JANUARY EVENING, Chavela arrives with the first edition of *Ms. Magazine*. She blasts into my room singing, *"Didn't I blow your mind this time?"* She's wearing a fringed, buckskin leather jacket, blue jeans and a black beaded, Indian Thunderbird headband—a perfect, Mini-Buffy Sainte-Marie double. She tosses the magazine to me, an image of a Goddess with Hydra multi-arms is on the cover, *"This is super fly!"* she cries. I quickly leaf through it.

We do a word-for-the-day practice in our note passing she gravitates to Spanglish cuss words. "What's this? Define it in ten words or less, with no adjectives." I challenge her.

"Híjole, not possible, it's mind-blowing, guano, baby. *The Revolution has begun!"* She thrust her fist militant style in the air and marches around the bedroom.

"Chica power! 1972 is The Year of the Woman!" she shouts, stopping to adjust the headband that slips down across her deep-set eyes. She quotes Jane O'Reilly: *"Step out into the new tomorrow."* And Joseph Campbell: *"Free fall into the new future where the old models are not working, and the new ones are yet to appear.*"

She points to a photo of the founder of Ms. Magazine, a hip, foxy, Gloria Steinem with flowing hair and aviator glasses. Gloria defined the beginning of every movement when people are being treated like they are invisible. "You are not alone; we can change unfair and unjust treatment. *We can choose to live differently.* Equality can transform everything. We are all linked, not ranked. Why do we focus on adjectives that divide us? He—she, the Cherokee don't have separate words for gender. Women tell the truth and live authentic lives." *She uncorked the bottle and let the Genie out.*

Betty Friedan, the Mother Superior of the Modern Liberation movement: "The only way for a woman as for a man, to find herself is by creative work of her own." These bold women, along with Billie Jean King, Bella Abzug, and many others through courage and hard work, fostered equal pay for women in the workforce. They also administered the Equal Rights Amendment, Roe V. Wade, Title IX Sports Programs, and the National Women's Political Caucus—To Make Policy Not Coffee. You either have a seat at the table, or you're on the agenda. Women *need to set* our agenda.

They changed the 1950s mindset of housework and child-rearing as "*Women's work.*" The point of feminism is *humanity.* What it means is men can, should, and must, become parents who spend as much time with their kids as women do. It takes many hands that include both sexes. *We are not defined by our children, or our husbands, but by ourselves.* The challenge is to flower as individuals.

Cha Cha's marching morphs into a dance, and a singsong Goddess rap: "Butterfly Maiden Goddess of *Transformation.*" Thrusts her hips back and forth. "Maat Goddess of *Fairness,* Brigit Goddess of *Don't Back Down—Stand up for what you believe is right,*" A full freak-out shimmy. "Bast Goddess of *Independence,* Green Tara Goddess of *Delegating—Never Give in, Don't feel guilty,* Ishstar Goddess of *Boundaries— Love yourself enough to say no to demands on time and energy,* wraps arms around her body. "And Kali Goddess of *Ending and Beginnings—the old must be released so the new can enter, next stop... Human Liberation!*"

She whirls into a Go-Go dancing frenzy doing the Jerk, the Mash Potato, and Twisting, shaking the fringed leather frantically on her jacket.

"*Oh-lah, mujer!*" I jump up on my knees, on the bed, clapping with enthusiasm.

My mother and her two sisters Lucy and Lana were pioneers who unknowingly participated in the Women's Liberation Movement. Before this time, unmarried women couldn't receive birth control, serve on a jury, get a credit card in their name, have an abortion, or sue for sexual harassment. *We're only as* great *as the double doors we blast open.*

Lucy's confident, cold focus, and fierceness, made her the strongest willed of the sisters. Always in charge with a powerful, *senior-self* air of authority. Every bit Indian with a short, thick, compact body, a long nose, high cheekbones, the Navajo flat forehead, and the firm "*take-no-shit*" scowl. A face untouched by makeup and wore only pants before it was fashionable. The severe, short hair, made her look manly. A hard-working staunch Baptist among a sea of Catholics and the polar opposite of Lana and Alma.

Lana's the beauty of the Chávez clan a Rita Hayworth look-alike with auburn hair and porcelain skin. She glistened with stardust like Glinda the Good Witch. Her goodness glows with a personality similar to Mom's, they liked the same food, entertainment, music, and dancing. Extroverts to their core: *both Loved being the center of attention.* Lucy and Lana were perfect examples of how the single, most important decision one makes in life *is whom you marry.*

They battled, about the silliest misunderstanding, not lasting long. No matter the severity of the dust-up, not one negative word was said about each other. Loyalty and *a united front always.* Lucy—the rock, Lana—the pearl, (my mother's delight) and Alma—the heart. Love is inexhaustible, divides endlessly and doesn't extinguish. A *circular bond of Love, safety, and belonging.*

I overheard my mother's heartbreaking phone conversations with Lucy: "He didn't come home again last night." She confided.

"Throw the *pendejo's* things out into the street, that'll teach him," Lucy said coldly.

"He'll just take it out on one of the kids." Mom knew not to agitate him.

"You train people how to treat you, Alma," Lucy said.

Lana always on the verge of giving a party inviting Mom to the next wedding, baby shower, or family reunion. The sisters provided a life preserver role in her overwhelming fight for survival. My mother who tapped into her *Wonder Woman* power, despite being born into a frustrating and challenging world. I absorbed at a young age, her strength and quiet rage. I'm not slapped, spanked or physically punished. *Mom's switch or belt was words* and there wicked power over me. She exerted menacing mind control, even as an adult, it affected me.

I'd bristle when in a catty tone, she asks, "Why are you always running? What's the point?" Her eyes slant and calculating. A jarring way of questioning my effort to stay in shape. She was obese most of her adult life. My coping mechanism was to ignore her; as a teenager, I'd roll my eyes at her negative outbursts. She retaliates with; *"Don't you dare* roll those eyes at me!"

Mom instilled in her daughters and Chavela, fierce independence and to stand up for what is right. Children of the sixties grow up with the spirit of unfettered individualism. The Women's Movement caught on like wildfire. The invisible revolution changed the world in unfathomable ways. The twentieth century will be known for the emergence of the feminine mind into mainstream consciousness.

Fortunate Son

Who won your war?!!!
—Wooden Ships
by Crosby, Stills, Nash & Young

MY MOTHER STUMBLED UPON HER TRUE purpose in life: *to teach*. A poor Chicana growing up without a father and no high school diploma. Paid for by her employer—Head Start (U.S. Government) she goes to college and supports a family on a meager income. She attends night school at a Junior College in Pueblo, 40 miles from Red Cañon. *My family is living proof that government programs can break the poverty cycle. Doors open, but not easily.* She didn't drive and depended on co-workers, Grandma Grace, and eventually, her grown children to drive her.

Essé, my older brother, is not as lucky as our mother. He struggles in this oppressive town. He's failing high school. He falls in Love with a white girl who sees him as a way out.

I come home from school on a mild, Indian summer, October afternoon my sophomore year, Essé's senior year. My mother is home early from work—*that never happens*, I'm instantly, alarmed. She chokes back tears, seated at the kitchen table with a pile of Kleenex in front of her. Her eyes are bloodshot and her nose is crimson red.

"¡Aye, Dios mío! Mom, what's wrong? Did someone die?" I throw my backpack in the corner and plop down at the table, bracing for the worst.

"No, but your brother's high school career is definitely dead. He quit school, joined the Air Force and *he's getting married, today."* She blows her nose; tears stream down her cheeks.

"Are you serious? What a bummer, they're too young! Can't you talk sense into them?" My heart aches for her, knowing how she values education. She didn't care about the marriage as much as him quitting school.

"He's eighteen, he informed me and can do whatever the hell he wants. *Throw his life away. ¡Sonso!* He's going to Vietnam. We'll need to pray for his safe return." She does a big, double inhaling sob. I wince.

I'd never seen her this upset before, I jump up and wrap my arms around her. "Mom, it'll be OK, we'll ask Grandma Grace to work her Rosary bead magic. He's a stubborn *burro."*

"Yeah, *MR. BIG man,* who doesn't know shit from Shinola." Her sorrow turns to anger.

He eloped to Denver with his teenage girlfriend, Renee and is sent to Spokane Washington for basic training. *He lands in the middle of the Vietnam War.* Summer of my junior year, before he shipped out, I go to visit him and his new wife. We play cards and bake Toll House chocolate chip cookies. *We're so innocent and naïve.*

One evening, Essé and I have a heartfelt talk in the driveway of the storybook farmhouse, perched on a rolling green hill. They rent the apartment above the garage. He's installing new, Bose speakers in his yellow, Opel Kadett. I ask why he enlisted. Essé's never lived outside of Red Cañon. He's good-looking with ebony, deep-set eyes, coal black, curly hair, and a cherub face. Short but stocky, he is smart, resourceful, a hard worker who always had money.

He explains why he abruptly quit school, elopes and joins the Air Force.

"It's my ticket to take Renee away from that skuzzy stepfather. After four years, I'll have the GI Bill and job training to support our family." I choke back a laugh; when did my brother become an adult? "Why sign over your life to the Air Force during an unpopular war? Why not graduate, move away and find a job?" I ask.

"Things got too crazy at Renee's, that bastard smacked her around. I wanted to kill him. It was either the Air Force or prison. No one knows what goes on behind closed doors. *Don't EVER* let a man knock you around, any problems you let me know." He raised a clenched fist.

The Vietnam War raged on. Two years earlier, the Ohio National Guard killed four college students in Ohio, at Kent State during a war protest. Time magazine had a photo of Allison Krause, one of the students killed, Neil Young saw the carnage was moved with sadness and disbelief, and wrote the song "Ohio" in fifteen minutes.

I monitored the war protests organized by Joan Baez and her husband, David Harris, a journalist and anti-Vietnam war protestor whose imprisoned for draft resistance. The Peace Freaks constantly protested some burned their draft cards, demanding Nixon end the war. The hard-core war resisters hightail it to Canada avoiding the draft altogether. Jane Fonda was labeled Hanoi Jane, spat on and ridiculed for her anti-war stance. The peace movement was an integral part of the *counterculture* since the 1960s.

Nixon's impeached for Watergate during the 1972 election. Hunter S. Thompson was fear and loathing on the campaign trail and drugs, especially, marry wanna (Marijuana) flowed in the streets.

There's an engraving on a Zippo cigarette lighter Essé brings back from Vietnam. He didn't smoke; it was a rite of passage. *"We the unwilling, led by the unqualified to kill the unfortunate, die for the ungrateful."* An apt, soul-sucking summary of the Vietnam war.

The full-out draft is more diplomatic than the volunteer system in place today, which sweeps up the poor, letting the rich skate. *"When Senators' sons go to the front lines, wars will lose their false luster."* John Fogerty's song, *Fortunate Son,* summed it up concisely.

Freethinking American citizens after Sixties radicalism question the government and demanded their voices be heard. There was no strategy but attrition in Vietnam. Marine hero, Ron Kovic of *Born on the Fourth of July* fame, a Vietnam veteran paralyzed in the war who returned to fight against it: *"The war is between those who catch hell and those who give it out."*

Essé spends four, hellish years as a gunrunner, guarding the medic helicopters in Vietnam, rescuing the wounded in battle. It scars him for life, but now, *he's one of the lucky ones.* The elites didn't fight; the poor, minorities, and white middle class fought the war.

During his absence, I replayed in my mind the top hits of our childhood memories. The most traumatic one: returning home from the movie after watching the Beatles in, *A Hard Days Night.* I was riding in the long, over-sized monkey handlebars of the home built yellow Sting-Ray bike. We hit a nasty pothole, I bounced off and flew, like Superman. I got skinned knees and road rash on the palms of my hands. At home, he cleaned and bandaged my wounds.

Essé and Rae came to my rescue when I was a ten-year-old trick-or-treating with neighbor kids, and a gang of high school punks stole our bags of candy. Rae and Essé hunted them down, even got shot at, but they returned the candy.

I missed the late night pig-outs of crispy brown fried potatoes smothered with extra cheese and salsa and his anchoring presence in our family. He watched over and protected us his entire life. He got a kick from taunting my sassy soul cousin: "Hey, Cha Cha, you're here *again*—don't you have a home? We're gonna start charging you rent," he said with squinty, badass eyes, then, melting into a wide, *Felix the Cat,* mischievous grin.

We listened to the progressive, FM radio stations. Rae and Essé got their hands on transistor radios, (the rage) stereo systems, and the latest albums. In a letter from Essé in Vietnam, he wrote that they listened to Santana, Hendrix, and Fogerty. After Woodstock in 1969, music turned into a fundamental matrix of people's lives. It soothed and helped to deal with the hard rigors of reality.

Music was at the apex of everything. American Bandstand was on every Saturday morning. Music variety shows such as Carol Burnett, Ed Sullivan, Johnny Cash, and the Sonny & Cher show, were on the four television networks; ABC, NBC, CBS, and PBS.

Baby boomers adore their music—the soundtrack of our lives, it lives on today. Steve Jobs made music accessible by the touch of a finger: *music in our pockets.* His spirit was an eternal force at the crossroads of art and technology.

Essé returned home and landed a union job at the Steel Mill in Pueblo. He buys a bright, banana yellow, Harley Davidson. He suffered from PTSD, sleep apnea, flashbacks, depression, and drank heavy for ten years, then quit. The teenage marriage doesn't last. Many years later, his daughter would work counseling Veterans returning from Afghanistan and Iraq with shell shock, and battle fatigue. *War is never over.*

Easter Sunday of his forty-ninth year, returning home from an egg hunt on his Harley Davidson with his nine-year-old son. A speeding car, in a busy intersection, hits them. Macho to the bone—he didn't wear a helmet; he died at the hospital. His son survived with a broken ankle.

The day of his funeral, a thousand people overspill the church; the loyal bikers came from far and wide. I peer out the window during the funeral procession and see bikes that ribbon for miles, winding up a large hill and over the horizon. He receives a full Military Funeral with a 21-gun salute and is buried in a cemetery with his Air Force brothers and Vietnam Veterans.

Earth has no sorrows heaven cannot heal.

Draggin' The Gut

CHA CHA AND I GET OUR JOLLIES from dragging Main Street (*Draggin' the Gut*). We cruise up and down a four-block radius of downtown, with Allman Brothers' *Ramblin' Man* booming out of tinny, car speakers. Far out fun times, floating at lowrider speed in my white and tan, 1957 Star Chief, Oldsmobile with its exquisite amber Indian Chief hood ornament magically glowing in the night sky.

A dreary night explodes into action when Ky pulls up in his blue, pickup at a red light. *"KEGGER, follow me!"* Adrenaline pumping the night blossoms with promise.

If the usual suspects aren't around, we'd wander into three different pool halls. Two serve beer, the other is a youth recreational center—the *Rec* with pool, snooker, pinball machines, foosball tables, and video games. Its purpose is to keep bored kids out of trouble.

My sister Rae, an excellent pool and snooker player, made serious cash running the tables. She lived for the crack of the ball break. The pool halls are her domain. I prefer *The River* to Main Street. The constant police presence scares me. "Cha Cha wants to *get down!* Man, oh Man, where's the party tonight? Let's paint this sorry ass, hick town RED!" She howls. We're eager for excitement. It's a rare Friday night when I didn't have a game, cheerleading tied up my weekend nights.

"Let's go check out Chautauqua Park, and maybe we can find a kegger," she suggests.

I slip a homemade cassette of Martin Piruzian's music in the dash. The song *9ᵗʰ & Main Street* fills the cab. I hear Leo Kottke's influence in this song. Main Street was our entire social outlet where eye contact is a mating ritual. Cars parked in front of the pool hall on a weekend night is ground zero for parties, keggers, and meetups.

Chautauqua Park is a block from Cha Cha's parent's house. We used to cut across the railroad tracks and through the park to walk back and forth to our houses. During the summer on weekends, bands played *"Chautauqua"* performances. The park had a vast area of thick grass and a playground for the kiddies. Located on U.S. Highway 50, exactly one mile from my house. Railroad tracks and the Arkansas River ran parallel to the park on the south side.

Driving down Main Street, I see in the rearview mirror, my cousin Don is following us. *Such an amateur, he doesn't even know to keep his distance, my parents must be behind this,* I thought. I turn into the park off the west end of Main Street, it's empty *no one's around.* He follows and parks under a low-hanging branch next to the tree-lined, railroad tracks.

I turn to Cha Cha, "Wanna roll around and make grass angels, like we used to when we were kids?"

"Chore, maybe, someone will feel sorry for us and give us beer." She chuckles.

I park the car as I'm sliding out, I'm hit with a sudden memory of a sun-kissed, summer, Saturday afternoon. I'm with Cha Cha at a *Chautauqua* Battle of the Bands event. The park is packed with families and kids from school.

We sit cross-legged on the grass with our drugs of choice: Dr. Pepper and M&M's. Exuberant ingénues anxiously waiting for Miles Layton's band—*The Galactic Sound Factory*. We breathe the same rarefied electric air as Miles, who is always at the white-hot center of things. I've Loved Miles since fourth grade when Love was simple.

A small, portable white stage is set up. The band runs onto the stage to their instruments: a bass, rhythm guitars, and drums. Miles picks up the bass guitar. A vibrating starts at the crown of my head and ripples down through my body lingering in my solar plexus, then down my legs and out my feet. *What a rush!* Flustered, I take a couple of deep, calming breaths. The enchantment is complete. Wow, I can relate to the silly girls that faint at Beatles concerts.

Miles is resplendent with long, satiny, brown, hair that falls over russet, deer eyes with black, downy eyelashes. His jarring handsomeness secured by a square jaw. His direct, self-assured way projects out to the audience. He's wearing jeans and a button-down powder blue shirt.

The band launches into a garage version of *For Your Love*, by the Yardbirds. We shimmy and sing along at the top of our lungs; *"Fo yo laa, I would give the stars above, I would give you all I could. I'd give the moon if it were mine to give. I'd give the stars and the sun for I live."*

I'm ruined before I even begin. *No man will ever compare to Miles—EVER!* A naïve concept at the tender age of fourteen; no matter that I'm invisible to him. My pure heart untouched by abuse and hardness. Life hasn't sunk its teeth into me—*yet*. I'm a fresh soul, free of mistakes, an unwounded, bright-eyed innocent, unaware of deception, and false promises. I haven't experienced the *horrible and wondrous* things men will do to me.

He'll forever be my *La Douleur Exquise*: the exquisite pain of wanting someone you can't have. I ricochet back to the present.

I walk over to Don, slouched down low in the car seat. "*Oh-lah, primo*, got any beer?"

"Hi Rosie, even if I did I wouldn't give you any." He smiles with big pearly teeth, a Mexican Elvis with slicked-back hair, a shiny black, curlicue curl dangles from his forehead.

"We're off to find a kegger, want to ride with us and save gas?" I offer.

Don let loose a deep, hardy guffaw. "When did you get so cocky? I remember you running under Aunt Lucy's kitchen table and kicking Uncle Carlos in the shins. I'll leave you alone but stay away from those Sacred Heart Schoolboys." He narrows his eyes.

"Don, you're my cousin, *not my father*. Take care of your business, and don't stick your nose in mine." I flash him a stern look.

"Fair enough, I'm in the shadows if you ever need me."

"My parents need *to back the hell off*. I can take care of myself." I step away from the car, and he pulls out.

I return to Cha Cha, sitting on a green picnic table deep in thought.

"That goofball is spying on me. *The nerve*." Cha Cha's been hanging out with a drug dealer. There's something dark about a grown man befriending a high school girl.

"What's going on with Nick?" I ask.

"Not much, he picks me up from school, we go over to his place, get high, and frisky, and that's about it." She shrugs her shoulders.

"Are you in Love with him?"

"Hell, I don't know, he's not the type to take home to my parents," she said with a nervous laugh. She worries about the kind of father he'll make for Julian. My instincts are to steer her away from this guy, but I don't push it. *He's bad news* by ditching school to be with him, she falls behind and drops out of high school, a disastrous decision with a downward spiral effect on her life. Our precious dragging Main Street halcyon days are numbered and about to come to an end.

Rae and Jen

Love is friendship with erotic moments.
–Antonio Gala

GROWING UP, I QUESTIONED IF RAE was a real lesbian or turned into one after watching Mom suffer in the web of Dad's destruction. She was born a lesbian. Being Queer is to live as a man in a woman's body. The sorry state of our parent's marriage just reinforced her orientation.

She was always chasing some girl before meeting Jen. She'd develop a crush on an attractive cousin or friend at school and bring me as the cute distraction, like a puppy, to lure the intended conquest. She peppered me with questions to ask the girl, the most important one—*did she have a boyfriend?*

Rae wins the Lesbian Lottery with a partner she met at work, the winter after graduating from high school. Rae and Jen meet at a kite factory, located on the outskirts of Red Cañon. They worked on the swing shift and become friends. The chances of Rae finding a mate in this narrow-minded, redneck town were slim to none. End of my junior year in high school, they move into a small apartment on Main Street, half a block from the Ramirez house. *Perfect for me,* a be-bop down the alley to hang with the Lovebirds at my new second home.

In this conservative, small town, their relationship couldn't emerge from the double door closet of secrecy. To the outside world, they were friends and roommates. For me, it was a sanctuary from the chaos at home. A quiet place to do my homework and watch television together. They had a fluffy, white cat that I smothered with affection. Mom didn't like cats, so I wasn't allowed to have one.

Jen is Italian and an excellent cook, she cooked delicious dinners and baked on weekends. Italians like Mexicans *spoil those they Love with food.* By her example, I learn a homemade cake was far superior to a store-bought one and *meant so much more.* She reveals by the simplicity of the ingredients used—*the sacredness of spaghetti sauce.* How at Christmas no one should ever go without homemade fudge and cookies. Especially, pizzelles, which require a special waffle maker to press them.

Jen and Rae subscribed to *Ms. Magazine.* I scoured every glorious issue thoroughly. It's my *Life Survival & Handbook Guide.* We're participating in *The Second Wave of Feminism* and a youth-led revolution. Radical social and cultural tectonic plates shift and spread waves of new consciousness.

Her lesbianism is not an issue with us siblings. Essé prefers it, at eighteen months apart, it's like having a brother. *They always had each other's backs.* A big eye-opener for him when she's beaten bloody by the police. Rae harassed two ditzy teenage cousins who were dating married men. They retaliate by tipping off the police that she didn't have a drivers license because of speeding tickets. She kept driving, unaware that if caught you went directly to jail.

On the Friday night of her arrest, Rae is driving a drunk

friend home, in her souped-up metallic, dark blue-green, 1967, Chevelle, Super Sport hot rod. They're pulled over on Main Street by two of Red Cañon's finest.

Rae's recalcitrant and combative posture got her hit in the face and body and wrestled to the ground and cuffed. She was black and blue for weeks after the arrest. We took pictures of her battered body, but we had no money for a lawyer.

Our parents acted oblivious to her sexual orientation. As she got older, *they know.* A grown woman who doesn't wear makeup or dresses, or ever had a boyfriend. The slicked-back, short hair worn in a ducktail drives Mom crazy.

"Do you have to wear your hair like that? It makes you look so manly," Mom said in disapproval.

All through high school, she wore men's cowboy shirts; button fly Levi's and cowboy boots. Essé called them shit kickers. She was strong as man, walked like one, and had an explosive temper when mistreated or abused.

Rae hasn't had sex with a man. She's a Gold Star Lesbian, a combination of soft butch and a sports dyke. She researched a sex change until the cost nixed that lofty idea. Living the life of a lesbian is her destiny. *Fait accompli.*

At sixteen, she converts our dank dungeon of a basement into a workout room. I drop in to listen to the cranking music and gape at her voluptuous, perfect, 36 C *chichis*. She works out in a sports bra and gym shorts.

Rae despised them and complained how in sports they got in the way and hurt her back. It's difficult to act like *"one of the guys"* with the perfect protruding mounds.

The workout room had weights and an old mattress on the

cement floor for tumbling exercises. Rae is an excellent gymnast practicing backflips and round-offs the length of the small basement floor. Her senior year she was the Lion mascot that *backflipped the entire length of the basketball court* that got everyone on their feet to cheer.

Feeling mischievous Rae would flip up her eyelids, turn them inside out, exposing the red fleshy tips scaring the bejeezus out of Cha Cha and me. The flipped eyelid trick began as payback for sleeping with my eyes open as a child that creeped out my siblings.

Why is it that the lesbian got the perfect breasts and the long, thick eyelashes? Natures genetic discrimination of parceling out the goods. To get even, Cha Cha and I pin her down and apply mascara to the lush eyelashes that point slightly downward. She abhorred makeup, so this was *the ultimate torture.*

After she moved in with Jen, she joined a semi-professional women's softball team. They win the state championship. She trains to be a softball umpire for the city recreation department.

Jen and I get along famously. She doesn't give off a lesbian vibe. I sense she isn't one. She's attracted to Rae and falls in Love with her regardless of the gender. Rae falls in Love *with the one person* who proves to be a faithful, loyal, and loving partner. In this small-minded, conservative town it's like finding a needle in a *cosmic sexuality haystack.*

I spent quiet afternoons at the apartment filling out college applications to begin my exit plan out of Red Cañon. An auspicious time between Rae and I, we're not close, but now, we're having fun together. I'm finally, *experiencing true sisterhood with her, Jen and Cha Cha.* A circle of wild *chingonastres* and a sweet, loving *Italiana.*

On warm spring nights we'd all pile into Jen's sleek black Buick Skylark with the white leather seats. Rae buys a pint of blackberry brandy and we'd sneak sips on Main Street while *dragging the gut.*

This period with Rae and Jen, filled me with hope and security I never had. I'm inspired by their coupling and *the longevity of it, going on forty-six years.*

Raining Rocks

Come to me Take my hand
Look into your heart There I'll be

Roses shall divine Holy mother
Mother of gold Mother with stories

Told and retold She felt our tears
Heard our sighs And turned to gold
Before our eyes She rose into the light
—Mother Rose by Patti Smith

LOOKING BACK, THE ORDINARY MOMENTS, *become the Big Ones.* Mom and I fall into a pattern on the weekends when I'd return home from cheerleading. Mom's propped up comfy cozy on the sofa in front of the TV engrossed in a favorite late-night horror movie. Vampire and werewolf genres are favorites. But, if King Kong and Godzilla battled, she'd pull an all-nighter.

As soon as I walk through the front door, she perks up, "Let's go have breakfast at Sambos, *my treat!*" She slips into her shoes, grabs her jacket, purse, and within 15 minutes we're sitting at the restaurant with pancakes, eggs, hash browns, and a pot of boiling, Lipton tea, spread out in front of us.

She Loves to share stories about her childhood. I learn about Grandmother Eugenia, who died when Mom was just seventeen. "My mother had eleven children, and when asked who her favorite was, she said, 'Children are like fingers. Do you have a favorite finger?'"

Growing up in a large family in Red Cañon, there was always a softball game going on in an empty lot, next to the Chávez house. One hot summer afternoon when Mom was eleven, during a dusty, boisterous softball game with the neighborhood kids, "So eerie, it's a clear, sunny day and within minutes the sky darkens, and *it's raining rocks!* Rocks of different sizes fall from the sky. Kids scattered like rats running for cover." She pauses to squeeze lemon in her tea and takes a sip.

They made it home safe, and her mother explains that a sinister and evil force has invaded Red Cañon. Another incident happens at a beer joint. A handsome, well-dressed man dances in a crowded bar. The woman he's dancing with is missing an earring and while down on the floor searching for it, sees the man has hooves! She screams and the dance floor clears—they run for the door. People are afraid to go out.

Mom's scars lie deep because of Grandpa Juan's death. A tragic event that reverberated through the years for the entire family. The Friday night before her First Holy Communion, miscreants savagely poison her father. He returns home after he drinks wine with a group of Mexican vagrants. He dies the next morning around dawn, the day before her big, religious rite of passage. *She never feels safe and secure again.*

This period of her life is *the Black Sorrow,* such devastation, and abandonment for the three youngest children. It takes four generations for a family to heal from a violent death.

The Chávez clan consisted of eleven children with the three youngest at home. The four eldest boys were in the armed services, fighting World War II. The four older married sisters lived in the area but had large families to take care of. Grandmother Eugenia lived ten years after her husband died with the generous support of her children. They pooled resources for the survival of their mother and the three youngest siblings.

The murderers aren't prosecuted. The close-knit Chicano community kept track of them; all died untimely violent deaths, one struck by lightning. Mom tried to recover from his death but feared he'd be forgotten. A cycle of sadness that haunted her throughout her life.

Evil continued after Grandpa Juan's passing. The youngest daughter, five-year-old Adele is stricken with a mysterious illness. Her hair falls out, and she's bedridden for weeks. Her condition baffles doctors. During her sickness an owl perched on her bedroom window. The Night Eagle's a mysterious messenger from the darkness who comes to those about to die.

Grandmother Eugenia cured Adele with the aid of a *Curandera*—healer, who performs the Basic Egg Limpia spiritual cleansing ritual that required a raw egg, Holy water and praying the Apostles' Creed over energy centers of Adele's body. It drove out the sickness. Grandmother Eugenia questioned Adele, and she confessed that she ate candy from a stranger at Grandpa Juan's funeral.

My mother shared a close bond with her two older sisters, Lana and Lucy, who lived in Red Cañon. They were always nearby with support and a helping hand. Mom received orders to become a Franciscan nun but had to decline because of her mother's diagnoses of ovarian cancer. Grandmother Eugenia, the matriarch of the Chávez family, succumbed to ovarian cancer at fifty-two.

It devastated her, but she quit high school to work cleaning doctor's offices. She had to earn money to support the siblings. My mother at the tender age of seventeen has to raise the two younger children Adele, fifteen and John, thirteen. During this difficult time, girlfriends introduce her to Blaze, who helped shoulder the huge responsibility. They marry and start a family.

The conversation always turned nostalgic. "With the other children I craved different foods, with you, I craved books and read everything I could get my hands on." She said. I want to tell her about Jack but can't risk it, fearing she might overreact and demand I stop seeing him.

My mother cultivates in her children reverence and obedience toward her. A way of controlling the unruly, *animals* as she calls us, half-jokingly. Rae and Essé tape her with a small, portable cassette player, in the midst of a yelling frenzy. She screams *"animals!"* They play it back to her as a joke. They use it against her when she can't coerce them into giving in to her. She even laughs at it.

Our lives are usable by God. We don't need to beat rules into our children to teach them. *We don't even need to be effective, just transparent and vulnerable.* Mom recites the Fifth Commandment after one of us misbehaved—the motive so obvious: "Honor thy father and thy mother: that thy days may be long upon the land which the Lord thy God giveth thee (Exodus 20:12). Underneath the lesson of the Fifth Commandment is divine metaphysics because our *real father and mother is God.* It brings in two opposites, the male, and the female.

In the Bible, mother means the feeling nature and the father is the knowledge nature. Most people have one side or the other more developed. We fail when we don't honor and balance both sides.

The five Indians that we saw at *The River* were symbols of continuity. Their wisdom acquired through the generations, we build on their shoulders and raise up by their noble stature. They're a vital part of the *Eternal Mystery* unfolding through time.

We learned from the missteps of other cultures, which in the past, mistakenly killed off their heritage. The beautiful Cathedrals in both England and France during the Reformation and Revolution, let hatred destroy their art. We're transformed by everything that comes before us. We learn from our past mistakes, our pain, it's how we grow. Grace comes in through our wounds. Transformation is different than education. *Love is at the core of evolution.*

The egoic mind doesn't allow to see things whole, only in fragmented parts. It divides our country between Liberals and Conservatives which are simply two different methods to be in control. We live in despair, in impossible situations, full of illusions, leading us to be an addictive society. Only Larger than Life people can be patient, forgive, and hope. It's not about being correct; *it's about being connected.* At all costs stay connected. We cannot accept that God objectively, dwells in us. Our holiness is by participation and surrendering to the *Body of Love.*

To Mom, family was the end all, as absent as Dad was— she more than over-compensated. *She was the nurturing Mothership, our anchor, security, and Bodhisattva.* The hub in the wheel of our lives, our center of gravity. Her Love and attention equivalent of the Goddess Artemis—the Guardian Goddess who guards Loved ones keeping them safe and spiritually protected.

Vaqueros Riding Club

THE GYMKHANA REGIONAL EVENTS—rodeo competitions for the riding clubs are held at the school throughout the year. The winners awarded belt buckles and ribbons to the first four places in each event. Brother Daniel ran the program, the monk who busted me in Jack's room over Thanksgiving break. I keep an eagle eye out to avoid him.

Jack invites Cha Cha and me to our first Gymkhana; *"We'll be doobie, doobie, doing, behind the barn,"* he joked. I drive the car, a mammoth party wagon that fits eight boys plus. We pick up Mac hitchhiking on our way to Sacred Heart School. He jumps in the back seat and hangs his arms over the front seat leaning in close to Cha Cha. He's sweet on her.

"Can I drive your car?" he asks. Jack and Caleb are at the Gymkhana watching the barrel races.

"Sure, why not." He can take a quick spin down the dirt road to the alfalfa fields.

We drive up to Jack and Caleb sitting on the rock wall of the corral. Caleb's in-between events, he'll win a Horsemanship award later. I slow down and yell out the window, *"Oh-lah* Jackie, we'll be right back." Jack waves, and we fly past the Gymkhana toward the lush green, alfalfa fields.

Parked on the frontage road in front of Sacred Heart School, Don peered through binoculars. "There's Rosie's car, heading past the corral toward the alfalfa fields, what's she doing?" He mumbled, fussing with the focus on the binoculars. "Hmmm... Maybe they're going to get high. Shit, do I move closer? Oh, for crying out loud, *she's letting one of those creeps drive her sweet, classy car!*" He bellows.

"WOO-HOO—the boy is about to become a man!" Cha Cha cries. I pull over and open the back door. "She's all yours, *don't wreck my car*," I say in a firm tone and slide in the back-seat. He jumps over into the driver's seat behind the steering wheel.

"Now what do I do?" He looks at Cha Cha.

"Damn, *pendejo,* it's an automatic, slap her in D and *Giddy-up."* She braces herself against the dashboard. He's timid at first, going too slow and jerking our heads back and forth while he taps the brakes too hard. He gets the feel of the gas pedal then with an abrupt jolt, we stop. He dropped the front, right side of the car into an irrigation ditch two feet deep.

"Holy SHIT—Oh no, CRAP! *We aren't moving."* He shouts.

I jump out, "Yep, we're stuck and will need some macho muscle to pull us out. Cha Cha, go get Jack and a couple more guys to help us." I fight off a panicky tug.

"Damn... ¡Cabrón! He dropped it in the ditch. I've got to help her." Don wings the binoculars into the open window of the car and jumps in. "I'll blow my cover but I don't care, I've got a tow rope in the trunk." His heart thumps against his chest as he races toward them.

Cha Cha and Mac run toward the corral. Between gasps, Mac asks, "This is kinda forward, but do you have a main squeeze?" He sideway glances at her.

"Nope, and I don't want one. I'm *Stone Free,* like the Jimi Hendrix song. I'm a wild chingona-on-the-loose, I'm a boss ba-dass bitch, that's me." She twirls in the dirt road.

"Would you like to go to the Prom with me?" he asks softly.

"Oh...*out-of-sight!* Whoa, how COOL!" She exhales, re-lieved that's all it is.

"Prom is on May 19th, right before graduation, we can go to *The River,* smoke a doobie, then, boogie to Miles's band." He holds his breath and waits for her answer.

"YES! I haven't gone to the Prom, do I wear a fancy dress and corsage?" She's digging this unknown dance thing.

"Yep, and I'll rent a tux. They stop running; he turns to face her, and they share a luscious first kiss. Excited, they both re-sume running toward the Gymkhana shouting,

"We need help here!" They wave their hands for attention.

A month before graduation, we finished building the Labyrinth it commemorates the meaningful times and highlights the two-year odyssey of the *River of Love.* Oliver designed the Labyrinth.

Jack, Caleb, Oliver, Gonzo, Mac, and Martin arrive early and pick the best spot for the Labyrinth in an area near the fire ring but far enough from *The River* to avoid flooding.

"We need to clear this down to the bare dirt," Jack explains. They raided the school janitor's shed of shovels, picks, axes, rakes, and hoes. So, the day wasn't a total, sob party, Jack offered a large amount of reefer to a band of schoolmates to play music during the construction.

"It needs to be level," Caleb yells over Led Zeppelin's *Communication Breakdown*. The band jams loud and with fervor. Cha Cha and I arrive and cause a hubbub of the working crew.

"Here comes double trouble." Oliver frowns, pointing his shovel at us.

Cha Cha roars with force and abandon: "*Are you knobs really going to desert us?*" Mac sashays up to her and wraps his arms around her. "Never, sweet thang."

"*Somebody, please light up a joint!* I realize it's early, don't judge me." Oliver scuttles up, with a lit joint.

We focus on the work for a couple of hours. We clear the area and gather the river rocks to construct the bones of the Labyrinth. Each rock needs dowsing to determine its proper energy placement.

Cha Cha and I rest on a large flat rock by *The River's* edge inhaling the red dust. We're rocked by the jarring hard sound of tools hitting rock and scraping gravel. Sadness overwhelms us, reality sinks in—*it's almost over.*

No more parties at *The River,* Gymkhana's, barn dances, Proms, plays, intramural football and basketball games, bowling alley hangouts, and joyous into-the-early-morning telephone conversations with Jack—*no más mi amor.*

"What will we do when they're gone, possibly, forever?" I plead with my prima.

"*We'll still have each other!*" Cha Cha cries and slings an arm around my shoulder. We catch a glimpse of the Great Blue

Heron, downriver on the opposite bank, watching us. The bands' rowdy wall of sound calls to us; we dance over to the lively thrum of music.

The Sacred Heart boys know each other in ways no one else did. Friendships eminently spiritual, a pit crew of misfits and outsiders that fate mashed together and with the townies form a connected family. Home is not where you're born—it's where you become yourself.

They figure out in life *you don't have to navigate The River for you're already flowing in it*. It's pure, *simple Grace* and *Divine symbiosis*. They spend precious years together, during the most productive, growth-filled periods of their young lives. We honor what Franciscan priest Fr. Richard Rohr discovered: *We don't think ourselves into new ways of living, we live ourselves into new ways of thinking.*

Soul Train

Dance till the stars come
down from the rafters!
–W.H. Auden

IT'S PROM NIGHT: the corsages purchased and tuxes rented. Chavela and I buy new dresses she picks a fire engine red, backless number, mine is beige with lavender flowers. The all-girl sister parochial school, the Scholastico Academy will bus girls to the Prom. Cha Cha's date Mac counts the hours and minutes till they're together. He's been telling his friends about her.

"She's beautiful and hot, I can't wait to dance all night with her," he gushed, annoying anyone who'd listen to the obsessive ramblings. Mac's a virgin; his end goal is to get laid.

I sit watching Cha Cha at the vanity applying mascara in her small, second-story apartment near downtown. She shared it with one-year-old son, Julian. Her parents picked him up to babysit for the evening. She's a vibrant vision of young, seductive hotness.

There's a knock at the door. It's Rubin Ocho, an older, Red Cañon small-time, drug dealer her brother's friend. "What are you doing here?" She asks, surprised.

"Wow! Damn girl, *what a knockout!* Where are you going dressed like that?" He asks.

"My first Prom, probably *my only Prom,* I missed out while having Julian."

Rubin talks her into going partying with him. "Don't waste that great dress and bod on a bunch of spoiled rich boys." He said.

I'm appalled by this lowlife and quickly make my exit. "You're really going to miss the Prom to go to an old flophouse hotel turned into a seedy bar with this loser? I'm outta here." She looks away and shrugs her shoulders. I grab my purse and run down the two flights of stairs.

I park next to the theater, and Jack runs up to the car. He's handsome in a gray tuxedo. Out of breath, he bends down and pecks my cheek through the car window.

"Step out for a second." He twirls me around. "*You look beautiful.*" He scoops me into his arms and kisses me. "The prettiest girl at the Prom. Wanna do a quick run to *The River?*" He smiles broadly.

"Sure, but we can't dilly-dally. I don't want to miss a song," he runs to gather the gang. They're all decked out in black, except Oliver, in an all-white tux. I wave for them to hurry.

"AllaboardtheSOULTRAIN! Woo-Woo, WOOooOOOH!" I shout as they pile into the cavernous car. "Hey, Foxy Lady," Oliver blows me a kiss.

"Back off." Jack pushes him into the back seat.

At *The River,* we smoke and drink into a partying frenzy. A half-hour has passed since we left the school, it's evolving into the wild night we maneuvered for.

"*Oh-lah, it's DANCE PARTY time!*" I squeal and slam the Star Chief in gear, ten minutes later they pile out at the school. Jack scoots next to me, and we share a juicy smooch.

"Thanks for being such a good sport." He strokes my hair.

"We couldn't come to this shindig without a boost." I smile, reassuring him. We enter through the double doors of the small theater with the Prom in full gear. Tonight's theme— "A Night in King Arthur's Court." I'm at home here, where we spent months rehearsing and performing *Murder in the Cathedral*. A two-story yellow brick, block building, with a stage.

The building is in the middle of campus surrounded by thick, lush bushes and shrubs the monks planted years ago giving it an Ivy League school vibe. A swimming pool completes the dense oasis. A favorite spot, after Gonad football games, Marie Noonan's, classes and theater rehearsal. We would steal away behind the thick bushes and sit on the stone bench; *our Secret Love hideaway*.

We make our entrance, I imagine that we're the Prom King and Queen royalty. I hold my head up high knowing that I belong here just as much as the rich bitches from the sister parochial school. *I'm going to dance my tush off*, this is our last chance to celebrate and go out in a burst of brazen glory all starry and sublime: *Per Ardua Ad Astra*—Hard and High to the Stars.

Miles' band plays, Jack and I dance non-stop for the first hour—*every song*. The band dives into *Nights in White Satin* by the Moody Blues, a poignant, slow song. My mind wanders, while cocooning in his comforting arms. I hold tight and grip hard. *I know this is it*. The future won't be kind to us. Savor this moment; I'm swept up by a wave of belonging and Love.

Everyone's dancing—small clusters raging together, laughing, and bobbing up and down. The electric evening vibrates with bonhomie brotherhood. They're with their de facto families. The years living together fosters a natural familiarity.

Mac stumbles up to me. He's crestfallen, "Cha Cha stood me up!" He stammers. He's a disheveled, hot mess. His breath notched with liquor and pot. His bow tie unraveled, the tux shirt dangling and torn. He fell outside, and the ripped tux pants are caked with mud. *His heart's dismantled.*

"I've tried calling her apartment, many times—why'd she do this?" He slurs his words, hunches over and fights back tears. He's a sophomore; there'll be many more proms.

"I'm sorry Mac, she's made a horrible mistake and has hurt an innocent person by making wrong decisions. I'll let Cha Cha explain to you what happened." I bear hug squeeze him tight.

Jack walks up. "C'mon, it's the Who's *"My Generation."* Dancing to his favorite song, overrides any Mac drama.

"Please, go to your room and sleep," I whisper to Mac, his shoulders slumped, chin in his chest, wavering he turns and staggers toward the door.

The next day Cha Cha calls me and relates how Mac's friends had him call her while he was quite drunk and stoned. After a few rings, she answered.

"You BITCH! He slurs into the pay phone, propped up by his buddies, shouting obscenities in the background. She apologizes meekly. *"I'm SO sorry,* Mac!" She hears voices egging him on and heavy breathing—he drops the receiver and quickly, picks it up.

"Tell her Mac, way to GO!" Then click, the phone went dead.

A half-hour later still drunk, but feeling awful, he calls her back.

"I'm so sorry for that phone call Cha Cha, my friends made me do it," he explains.

"No Mac, *I'm the one that is deeply sorry.* You didn't deserve what I did. *I made a horrible mistake.* Somehow, I'll make it up to you," she promises.

For many years, Cha Cha received Christmas and birthday cards from Mac. It was an honor to have known him and often thought of him and how poor judgment can profoundly hurt those you care for. The first of many contributions to her "grist for the mill."

Cha Cha never makes it to the Prom.

Trust The River

*Leave the past to God's mercy,
the present to God's Love, and
the future to God's providence.
Then you will be free.*
–St. Augustine

JACK AND I ARRANGE A NIGHT TOGETHER at *The River*—
one last celebration of *bonding* under a silver spring solstice
moon. I tell my parents I'm spending the night at Cha Cha's.
Sleeping bags, camping stove, and tent are stashed in a secret
location. He calls a week before the special night.

"I'll bring drinks, cookies, and sandwiches from home," I
offer.

"Let's stack a pile of firewood and make sure there are no
surprise visitors," he said.

The barrage of Mom's lectures about not trusting men
works as a twisted type of birth control. I set an appointment
with Planned Parenthood. The nerve-racking visit introduced
a woman's most dreaded torture tool; the speculum. *What we
do for Love.*

On a warm May evening, a bright moon showers a gossa-
mer glow on our transformation. We meet at *The River's* entrance and kiss tenderly. *First Love,* what a sublime marvel.

We've shared so many first blush experiences together. Spent hundreds of hours talking, exchanging ideas *learning and growing.* His patience beyond exemplary, *he's proved Mom wrong on so many levels.*

We're giddy and nervous. Jack's sky blue eyes brim with excitement, he's squirrelly and talking fast and ready for me to lead the way. We have complete trust and the other's best interest at heart. I want this to be the happiest day of our young lives. *Our hearts bound together.*

He understands my difficult, bi-cultural existence: *Chicana in a white world.* How I shift without missing a beat. A hybrid creature that fits in—he admires my versatility with a *smile that sets the world on fire.*

"Let's put the tent up and make a fire while we have light. Oliver sent a pre-bonding gift." He took a joint out of his shirt pocket.

"Hmmm…something to smoke, what a surprise." I giggled.

"Super potent doobage from the Hill. Via alumni friends from Boulder, it's called *Joaquín.* It's sold in tobacco cans instead of a three-finger lid. Ollie referred to it as *muy primo.*"

He puts up the tent, I grab the sleeping bags, camping stove and slip in Martin's tape in the portable cassette player. The mellow acoustic guitar melody riffles through the campsite. We built a fire together and sit opposite each other. We watch the sudden crests of flame; our excitement building equally. *Un Fuego.* He stokes the fire, our eyes lock in the pale, gold campfire light. We're intoxicated by the luminous beauty and waves of euphoria that surround us.

I'm in a turquoise, peasant dress with a white, lacy shawl wrapped around my shoulders staving off the cool night air.

He begins: "The moment I saw you... I'm so grateful for it all. I've experienced such joy and happiness, *at this Tranquil River flowing through our lives.*"

I take a deep breath and squint at the sparkling surface of *The River* just beyond the campsite—the gentle sound of water lapping, rushing over the rocks, beating against the shore like a heartbeat.

"Our Love is an eternal embrace with beauty that ebbs and flows and nurtures us. You and *The River* are the most profound miracles that opened up a new world to me."

He's off to Tulane University. I have another year of high school. Sadness about to blanket the intimate mood, we rebound quick. "Wanna seal it with a smoke and a glass of Blue Nun?" He prompts cheerfully and pours us two glasses of wine. I force a weak smile through tear-filled eyes.

"Let's move over to *The River.*" The large, full moon hangs over the glittering water and springy waves. The gurgling, slop, slop, the sound of energy rushing, *flowing like my life at this moment.* I inhale the soft breeze of green woodsy and apple blossoms. I glimpse upstream, and on a rock: the *Great Blue Heron our avian witness,* on this monumental night.

With our glasses of wine, we relax on a large, flat granite boulder close to the riverbed. Jack lights up the joint and passes it to me. "I don't have to worry about getting too stoned and fumbling my way home." I sigh. He takes a hit. "Don't you pass out on me." He said and smiles.

"Fat chance, I'm enjoying every second with you." I drink in the way he looks at me as if I'm the brightest dancing star.

A wistful song hovers above *The River's* slapping sounds. It's Martin's—*Answer Silence with Silence,* a tender melody.

Full of the long Knowing of Love, *as if written for this exact moment.* I jump up, "Please, dance with me." He puts his glass down, stubs out the joint, envelops me in his arms as we float in the warm blanket of *Grace.*

A rush of coolness blows past and gives me goosebumps. Jack rubs my arms. "Finish your wine and let's go to the tent." I slide into the unzipped opening and jump into his sleeping bag. Mine is next to his. I'm about to give a gift that can't be given back or undone, *so precious and sacred.*

I've learned to trust *The River, the Flow, the Lover.* It takes immense confidence in God's goodness. I accept the risk—to be in the present, to *try not to make* things happen, *to not push The River.*

He slides next to me in the sleeping bag. "Are we both going to fit?" He kisses me tenderly. *He is such a good kisser.* Small things matter and enable Love to thrive—warm vibrations fill the tent.

He slips the dress sleeves down my arms and kisses my breasts as his hands fill up he cups and nips gently. He moves slowly like the earth's rotation while this profound moment unfolds.

He takes off his jeans and helps me with the rest of my dress. We lay next to each other in our underclothes—so near I feel the bold beating of his heart. Our kissing turns passionate and fervent, about to cross the threshold... the *Power of Love,* the Spirit comes from an uncontrollable place.

He slides down in the sleeping bag, removes my panties and kisses me down there. He inhales a sublime wisp of musky, amber-vanilla, sweetness *sending a quiver through him.* While kissing the hollow curve of my stomach, he realizes I'm not moving. "Are you, OK?" He whispers. I cup his head in my hands and laugh, "Yes, I'm so relaxed, I forgot to breathe." We're grateful for the comic relief—I kiss him with permission in my movement. I'm untrammeled by fears of being used, pregnancy, inferiority, and self-doubt. *I finally, do the most authentic and nourishing act, for, in the end, I answer to no one but my own desire.*

He slides on top and with gentle precision enters me . . . In one vast, thousand-fold flashback of every kiss, touch, hours of sharing walks, talks, and laughter-we meld in gladness.

"I'm sorry it took so long to do this," I confess in the dark.

"Nothing to be sorry about, I wanted to be with you, it's all that mattered, everything else was a bonus." A delicious, calm settles over us as we slept in each other's arms. Our bodies fit perfectly, wrapped together.

The next morning, streaks of warm gold sunlight streamed into the tent. Because we waited, planned, and chose with deliberate precision, we were rewarded by *Love's Larger Knowing* that holds everything including freedom from the need to know. It will give us the strength to live with uncertainty—the very definition of *Faith*.

I'm awake before him, my mind races. How can I be this happy at such a young age? I'd relive *this moment and yearn* for the naturalness of his physical affection. I lie at his side, cradled and protected in his warmth *next to his heart, so Loved.*

We're up early to see the rising of the daybreak star. Wrapped together in a blanket we sit on the same rock as the night before. Our lips raw with Love after giving *everything* to each other. We watch the orange-streaked, burgundy aurora, welcome the day. The sunrise splendor is the final blessing.

God is in The River, he holds us in the calmness of the morning light. We cocoon in a blanket, Jack's arms around me. We breathe in the cool, fresh, river scent with hints of honeysuckle, and watch the drifting mist bring forth the morning.

I Love You (Pantoum)
Six Indian Languages
(Apache, Cheyenne, Hopi, Mohawk,
Navajo, Ute & Spanish)

Shill nzhoo
Nemehotatse
Nu' umi unangwa'ta
Avor anosh'ni
Nemehotatse
Te amo, te quiero
Avor anosh'ni
Konoronkhwa

Te amo, te quiero
Tom ho' ichema
Konoronkhwa
Tom ho' ichema

Shil nzhoo
Tom ho' ichema
Shil nzhoo
Tom ho' ichema

Memories, Dreams, Reflections

I know there is another way to live.
When I find it, the angels
will cry out in rapture,
each cell of my body
will be a rose, a star.
–Morgan Farley

I ARRIVED EARLY TO MARIE NOONAN'S Humanities class. It's almost graduation time; teachers are grading final papers and clearing out classrooms. We're tackling Carl Jung's memoir, *Memories, Dreams, Reflections*.

"Can you and Jack help me after class? I need to bring boxes to my house, and I have a gift for you." Marie's smiling eyes glisten.

"I don't know about Jack until I ask him, but I'm good to go. I'll help load up and follow you in my car." I'm honored she asks us to help.

"Thanks, dear, the year flew by, as they always do." The boys file in; Marie hands out graded papers. The bottom row of the metal-framed windows is cranked wide open. The warm spring breeze infuses the room with change and anticipation.

I see Jack across the street in the Quad throwing a Frisbee with Caleb. I'm *in paradisum* with these *Dreamy Divine Beings*. Marie's voice halts my reverie.

"I want you to understand Carl Jung's ideas on the psyche and collective unconsciousness. Also, the dark shadow, archetypes, and anima/animus. These are fascinating concepts he discovered and championed, that are still used today. He writes about a constant Damion. Do you understand what he's referring to? Do you believe this concept?" She scans the room a brave senior raises his hand. "Is it like an alter ego?"

"No, this man of science and religion believed there is a spirit, an inner attendant, a guiding inspiring force. I want you to examine your lives and project the value of such a spirit. Please write a three-page paper, and we'll discuss this subject next Thursday. One more concept: Jung believed spiritual experience is essential to our well-being. A quick housekeeping item: There's a box of old handouts and Psychology magazines after class help yourself and take whatever looks interesting."

During the spring session, the school provided mini-college courses. They bussed in the Scholastico Academy girls creating an exciting party-like atmosphere and electric buzz on campus. We hear a loud commotion going on outside. Most of the classes have ended for the day and the students line up for an activity about to happen.

A boy jumps up. "Marie, looks like Father Joseph has an event going on outside, can we check it out?"

"Oh, why the hell not, I won't be able to refocus you again." She playfully waves the boys out of the classroom.

"Marie, I'm going to ask Jack if he can help us, I'll be right back." I load up my backpack.

Outside, it's *mayhem*. Basketball hotshot Mason Giles and class clown, Fast Freddy James wanted to shock the Scholastico girls sitting under a tree. So, *they dared each other to streak.*

They ran hurly-burly completely naked with "Go Bare's," (school mascot—Bears) in black paint across their ghost white chests.

Sprinting at dazzling speed through the Quad to the far end, they ran right into Father Joseph and two monks who corral them. He gives them two options: swats with the wooden paddle or streaking in front of the entire student body, the length of the Quad, roughly 200 yards.

On this golden, luminescent, Colorado spring afternoon, roughly seventy students including the girl's lineup parade style along the football field. They wait in anticipation for the streakers to run the gauntlet. They're blasted with catcalls, whistles, and clapping. Mason's whacked in the crotch with a football. I see Jack across the street, "*Oh-lah,* Jack!" I shout. He gallops over to me.

"Hiya, did you enjoy the show? Aren't you in Marie's class today?" he asks.

"She cut it short. Nope, too busy looking for you. We need help loading up boxes." I smile.

"Lead the way." We head back to Marie's class.

We fill the backseat of the baby blue, Chevy Nova with boxes of books and papers. We follow her to the elegant, old Victorian, brick house with elaborate turrets, impressive library, a beautiful stone fireplace, and overstuffed chairs.

We unload the boxes into the foyer. I offer to help unpack them. "Goodness, no. I don't know where half this stuff is going until I make lesson plans for next year. But thank you, dear. Here's the gift I mentioned." On the foyer table is a book, Carl Jung's memoir, *Memories, Dreams, Reflections.* A pristine hardbound edition, not the dog-eared paperback we used in class.

"I didn't know if you had a copy, I wrote a special note inside. I relish introducing him to my students. You were a joy to have in class. What are your plans, Rose?"

"Thank you, Marie, *I will treasure it*. Next year I'll apply to the University of Colorado in Boulder." I hold up crossed fingers.

"That's fantastic, dear—and Jack, where are you off to?" She turns to him.

"Tulane University, I'll spend the summer in New Zealand with my family. When my dad retires at the end of the year, they'll move to Dallas. The Dillon's will finally all be in the same country." He grins. He's grateful to the teacher who made such a difference in my life.

"These will be sweet memories for you, no matter what happens. The bond and belonging experienced these last two years, will be your foundation." She said. Back in the car, we ride to school in silence.

Years later Rawleigh shared in a phone conversation a touching story about Marie. She worked for another five years before retiring. After Rawleigh retired, he'd check on her, two to three times a year when visiting Red Cañon. During one of these visits at her stately, Victorian house over a glass of whiskey, she asked him for a favor.

"Anything, Marie just name it." He said.

"I'll know when the time comes for me to die. Please take me up to the mountains with a bottle of my best whiskey, pea soup, my favorite books, and leave me," she said.

"Marie, are you serious?" Rawleigh asked.

"Yes, I am." She assured him with a nod.

A few years passed, Rawleigh Rio came to town, stopped at the school to visit with the monks, was leaving to go to Marie's. They tell him she now lived at a senior assisted living facility. She watched him walk through the door and held I-give-up hands in the air: "A lady has the right to change her mind." She laughed.

Brother Owen officiated at her graveside funeral with her two sons in attendance. She's buried next to her beloved sister in the same cemetery not far from my mother and Cha Cha's parents, Uncle Julian and Aunt Lucy.

The truest gift I received from Marie *was how to learn.* She taught me the difference between education and learning. Education is what others do to you, and learning is what you do for yourself. She fostered brilliantly, *the Holy Curiosity of Inquiry.*

When I returned home, I opened the book's cover to read Marie's inscription in her elegant handwriting. "To Beloved Rose: *There is no right and wrong, there is only interesting, and less interesting." –Marie Noonan.*

Cosmic Coyotes

Shawnodese, the Spirit Keeper of the South, whose animal and Spirit manifestation is Coyote. This is the time of late childhood and early adulthood. These are times of rapid growth- on many levels. Coyote is the Teacher, guiding us through many lessons during this time. She has to trick us into learning what we need, but would rather lead us. The animal, coyote, is a wonderful mother, teaching her offspring what they need to live in harmony with their environment, and so with Shawnodese, include the Spiritual lessons/gifts of Growth, Trust, and Love.

–From the Sun Bear Medicine Wheel

I SPEND A LATE SPRING, Sunday afternoon bowling with Jack. A pleasant switch from *The River.* We drink Dr. Pepper and poke fun at the old drunks at Star Bar—a jukebox, dive joint tucked in the corner of the bowling alley.

Our time is coming to an end. We drum up new environments and experiences to distract us from the inevitable. Most Sunday nights, we park behind the barn at Sacred Heart School. We climb into the bedroom-sized backseat of the car and lay in each other's arm. We talk and kiss for hours; intimate, joyful, ephemeral moments *spent hiding in plain sight.*

I offer to drive Jack to school, less than a mile away, down a frontage road, and across U.S. Highway 50. I'm luxuriating in the last, delightful gasp of the weekend. He glances at his watch. *He does need to go.* There's a curfew on Sundays and this close to graduation, he can't afford any trouble.

We kiss and hug, "See you soon, Jackie boy. Call me tonight, and we'll discuss your lack of bowling prowess," I tease. As he's leaving, out the corner of my eye—I see my cousin Don, so damn handsome. He sticks out in this sea of crotchety, old men, stomps, and greasy gearheads. I ignore him because if I don't, he'll ask about Jack and I'll have to lie. I'm tired of all the fibs and fabrications. He's about to graduate and leave this place—*we can't be busted now.*

Later that evening Jack calls and describes the incredible walk back to Sacred Heart School. Half a block down the frontage road, he sees two, light brown, with white spots, medium-sized dogs. They're 50 yards ahead of him, running side by side, down the middle of the road. He's not alarmed, they're two pals out for a trot. He walks another couple blocks; they're still ahead of him, looking back with watchful eyes. The neighborhood is a mixture of old railroad row houses and small businesses.

"I thought if this was closer to *The River,* they might be coyotes. From a dark junkyard, a pit bull rushes out of a driveway, right at me, barking and snarling. Before I react, the brown dogs charge the pit bull, herding it back into the yard. I look closer at the two dogs and freeze. *Damn, they are coyotes!"* Adrenaline surges as I sprint away quick. It's a half-mile to the highway, and across the field to the cafeteria. They flank and then run past me, trotting 50 yards ahead. They pace and keep close tabs on me.

"I'm awestruck! They're protecting and escorting me to my destination. I wish you could've seen this. *I got such a kick out of my pup posse procession,"* he said. "I wait at the crosswalk for the traffic light to change. Down the road, the coyotes frolick in the ditch, catching field mice, gophers, and moles. Coyotes mate for life; they've been together for a long time. The light changes, and I ran across the four-lane highway." They wait until it's safe and follow me.

"I stood at the corner of the field where you used to hide your bike in a ditch, across from my dorm room at Hedley Hall. Many heart-wrenching goodbyes with tears, hugs, and kisses took place on this sacred spot. I watch the coyotes saunter down the block in the opposite direction." He sighs. "They pause and look back at me, one last time, *their job accomplished."*

The coyotes were about a mile down the frontage road. Running side by side, the slinging race of their movements full of beauty and robust wonder. "Happy Trails, my supernatural, cosmic doggies," I whisper.

"I linger at the corner, thinking about us. We occupy such different worlds. I want to be in your life after I graduate and go away to college. You still have another year of high school to finish. *It's so unfair we have to separate.* After college, I'll settle in Texas where my family lives. My father is about to retire. I can't see you living in Texas; it's even more conservative than Red Cañon." His voice trailed off.

I'm stunned, I don't know how to react; I just keep repeating, Hmmm..."

He came across a relevant quote: "If you have chemistry, you only need one other thing, timing. *But timing is a bitch.* There's a proper time for everything, no need to rush things before conditions are right, so many lives lacked balance and timing. I want to tell you to keep the faith, to hold on, Love like ours will overcome distance and time. But I won't make promises I can't keep and be responsible for your happiness; it doesn't come from outside of us. You're not going to be what the person wants you to be. Our meeting was not a random event but part of an unfolding plan." He said.

The Profit Peacemaker

Indians believe that something lives as long as the last person who remembers it. My people have come to trust memory over history. Memory, like fire, is radiant and immutable while history serves those who seek to control it and douse its flame to destroy the dangerous fire of truth. Beware of these men for they are dangerous and unwise. Their false history is written in the blood of those who might remember and seek the truth.

–Floyd Red Crow Westerman

CHA CHA AND I STRATEGIZE in my room about a weekend blowout party at *The River,* three weeks before Sacred Heart School's graduation. We'll invite Sadie, Scarlett, Jenny, and Meg. Cha Cha's in a feisty mood.

"Let's do a snipe hunt. That'll freak those flatlanders right out of their crazy *cabezas*!" she said mischievously. "I've got to pay my sister extra because it's overnight, which sucks because Julian is so easy to watch." She frowns.

"*¡Ay, Chavela!* Let's teach them some NDN ways, we'll bring sage and smudge everybody. Let's ask Oliver to score some peyote buttons. We'll build a huge campfire and sing sacred peyote songs. In a perfect world, we'd feast on the delicious tamales your mom makes. *Putting the extra Ka-Pow! in this celebration.*" I playfully punch the air.

"Yeah, but I can't ask her to fire up the tamale factory for a River farewell party for the preppies." She smacks down the unreasonable idea.

"I want to bring *something special* to graze on. Jack and his friends eat horrible cafeteria crap and Kwik Stop munchie junk food. *Jack's so thin.*" I plead, and take a deep breath.

Cha Cha's eyes widen, "Let's make a huge batch—four dozen Queen Alma-style tortillas thick and fluffy, toasted to perfection and a *HUGE pot of high-octane, green chili* thick with homemade pinto beans. We'll prepare it after school before Auntie Alma comes home and store it at my house. Slap dat pot of chili on the fire ring for an hour and serve it with mouth-watering torts after pigging-out with enormous, full bellies, *they'll be putty in our hands.*" She let loose a deep, diabolical laugh, and burst into a frenetic happy dance, arms flailing, and hips gyrating.

That night, during our marathon telephone conversation, I ask Jack to keep the invites to a minimum: Caleb, Oliver, Gonzo, Martin, and Mac. If the party's too big, the noise might attract the fuzz. Twelve people total—six girls, six guys—sweet, round numbers.

Jack and I hadn't returned to *The River* since our bonding night together. It'll take the pressure off being with the others. They'll want to party hardy, before leaving Red Cañon.

It's a freak-a-delic Friday at *The River*. A flawless, spring evening with a cool but high-energy charged breeze. Led Zeppelin's song *Thank You*, blasts from my car, six girls jammed in with camping gear, guitars, and food. Everything fit snug in the Titanic-sized vehicle. A wave of patched, faded blue jeans, gauzy peasant shirts, and Vibram stomper hiking boots, slowly spill out of the cavernous coach. Punctuated by patchouli and musk oil that hypnotize the party animals, downwind.

We unload and hoof down the path to *The River*, tripping over ourselves with excitement. Mooing at the cows, howling like she-wolves, laughing and singing in Munchkin voices; *"Follow the yellow brick road."* Silver bracelets jingling, echoing down the path, announcing our arrival. How would Jack and I be like now? *We've entered brazen new territory.*

We roll into the homey campsite, complete with tents and a crackling roaring campfire. The smell of smoke and heat whips up to welcome us. The Sacred Heart boys are *chillin' with chelas*—beers in hand, tootin' on fatty doobies. All smiles and ready to party with the townies. This is *our very own, River retreat* of water-smoothed rocks, rustling cottonwoods, and rings of fire.

Cha Cha's outstretched hands proclaim: "Behold, ye preppies, *this is off the hook FAR-OUT!*" She gives a hardy, two thumbs up, and bursts into a twirling, mad dervish dance. Her bright red, green and blue, Indian blanket jacket, flapped in the vortex. Flying beaded braids turn into jutting projectiles.

"*Oh-lah* River Gang, who's hungry?" I drop the large, pot of green chili & beans in the middle of the campfire ring. I take a quick inventory of the campsite, six tents dot the area, everyone had a place to sleep. Feeding everyone took over an hour, the large pot of chili took twenty minutes to heat up. We need to eat dinner before the sun sets, while we have light.

"The sun's down, and the bad moon is rising, time to PAAARTAY! *Let the games begin!*" Cha Cha announces. I'm relieved there's just enough grub—time to let my hair down. Jack wraps me in a warm, tight squeeze, *no trace of weirdness, we're intact.* Solid as the river rock we're sitting on. Oliver yells from a distance, "You two, get a tent!"

"Look, the Great Blue Heron!" Martin points as he glides overhead. Everyone's milling about by the riverbed. It's my favorite time of day—the Golden Magic hour, right before sunset, when daylight's a soft, red, and golden hue.

A scented willow and cherry blossom wind swirls through the camp. Large, black and white Magpies perch on telephone wires waiting for the show to begin. Cha Cha calls everyone to come and sit around the campfire ring, waving her arms exuberantly.

"We brought sage to smudge everyone. An Indian custom used to purify and cleanse yourself or environment of any negative feelings and thoughts. It opens your heart, allowing sacred spirits to enter the realm. Smudging is the common name given to the *Sacred Smoke Bowl Blessing.* The smoke attaches itself to the negative energy and removes it to another space," Cha Cha explains.

"Ollie better hold down Gonzo," Jack whispers in my ear, I smother a giggle.

"It's far out to apply this shift in energy from negative to positive and to a peaceful state. It's used to cleanse objects, a place, *your spirit,* mind, or body. Smudge when feeling depressed, angry, resentful, or after an argument. Clean house whenever you fight with your ol' man or ol' lady!" Cha Cha laughs.

She holds up the Eagle feather, takes the small, tight roll of sage, and lights it. She blows it out, leaving wispy tendrils of smoke used to whip and waft with the Eagle feather around her head and all around her body. "Into the smoke, I release all negativity. I release all fear holding me back. I release all energies that do not serve me. I pass positive energy to those I cherish." She ends the Smudging Prayer and hands the lit roll of sage to me. I wave it over my head and around my body, then pass it to Jack. We're sitting in a circle, it passes completely around the campfire with a few awkward handoffs.

I stand up. "We burn sweetgrass, also known as Seneca grass, but we don't have any tonight. One important rule to remember when doing these Holy ceremonies sweetgrass is burned after sage and cedar, to drive out the negative influences.

The four original medicine plants given by the Creator to the first peoples are sweetgrass, tobacco, cedar, and sage. Sweetgrass brings in the positive influences and teaches kindness. The holy smoke used in ceremonies cleanses the soul. When sweetgrass is walked upon, it does not break, it bends. So the lesson it teaches is, when someone hurts or does an injustice toward you, you're to return it with kindness. Bending, not breaking, like the sweetgrass. It's often referred to as the hair of Mother Earth. Pick it in August or receive it as a gift to use, don't buy it for yourself.

"We're Jicarilla Apaché, Navajo, and Ute. Or, as my grandfather called us, 'Uta.' The Spanish named our people Jicarilla which means, 'little basket makers.' Apaché is derived from the Zuni word that means enemy." I pause to catch my breath.

"Our creation story: Black Sky and Earth Woman bore anthropomorphic Supernaturals who dwelt in the body of Mother Earth. In the underworld, they used Eagle plumes for torches. Black Hac'ct'in, the first offspring of the Supreme Supernatural, created the first ancestral man, woman, animals, and birds out of clay. They needed more light, so he created the Sun and

Moon. Evil shamans attempted to destroy the Sun and Moon. Angered by this, Hac'ct'in allowed the Sun and Moon to escape to Earth. The people needed to restore the only source of light. The solution was to follow the Sun and Moon. Thus, the Jicarilla united as a people. They emerged from the underworld." I look at Jack, he shoots a big smile.

"The four sacred rivers are Arkansas—The Quapaw Akakaze (land of downriver people), Canadian—The Kiowa gúlváu (red river) The Rio Grande, and Pecos. Included in all our ceremonies are the Sun, Moon, Wind, and Lightning." I have everyone's attention, it's completely still, on cue—a loud splash from *The River* receives a big roar of laughter.

Chavela continues, "There are Indian prophecies, the Hopi claim that the Four Corners area—Colorado, New Mexico, Arizona, and Utah, is a sacred place. This area is bordered by our four sacred mountains: Mount Blanca—Tsisnaasjini or White Shell Mountain in the East, Mount Taylor—Tsoodzil or Turquoise Mountain in the South, San Francisco Peaks—Dolo'ooslid or Abalone Shell Mountain in the West, and Mount Hesperus—Dibé Nitsaa, Big Mountain Sheep or Obsidian Mountain in the North. These holy sites have a special purpose in the future for humanity to survive. We need to take care of the earth because it takes care of us. We destroy it and kill ourselves. We must pray, perform ceremonies, and fast. Our spiritual elders hold the land in the Western Hemisphere in balance." She takes a drink of beer.

"Our greed, materialism, and blind ravaged path of independence deplete our planet. We're at a crossroads, but it's not too late. We must live in harmony with natural laws and protect Mother Earth. Environmental issues must become a spiritual thing, stewardship of the Earth from a spiritual perspective. This is not rocket science people. In Native languages, there's no word for nature. We don't see a separation between Mother Nature and us." Cha Cha bows her head, signaling she's finished.

Caleb clears his throat, "Speaking of prophecies, did you know that the Indian prophet The Peacemaker, Hiawatha, and Jigonsaseh, of the Haudenosaunee created a confederacy that is the world's oldest continuous democracy? It is the most democratically advanced societies the world has ever known. The model influenced and prompted Benjamin Franklin to borrow from it to build the U.S. Constitution. They don't teach that in history class. It's shameful that they are unknown and uncredited for their contribution to America." He said.

"No, shit!" Cha Cha blurts out a bit too loud. She looks at Caleb cross-eyed.

"You're the pow to my wow!" She purrs.

"How many beers have you had?" I whisper and nudge her with my elbow.

"Look it up, if you don't believe me." Caleb chuckles as if poked with a stick. Martin breaks into a hearty belly laugh. One by one, they erupt into a choir of side-splitting laughter. A tsunami of giggles fills the campsite.

I'm on the verge of freaking out when Oliver through chortles explains how he got a great deal on magic mushrooms and slipped them into the chili pot while it was warming up.

Martin and Scarlett attempt to play a song but can't figure out how to get the guitar straps over their heads. Martin's burst of laughter sprays a fountain of beer. The whole group is laughing, some rolling around, holding their sides.

I tend to the fire that is almost out. I stoke it with a large piece of rotting oak the warmth licks my face. I let out a long, anxious sigh. *Why didn't Oliver ask and give us a choice to take the mushrooms?*

Jack's sitting quietly, so is Jenny, I realize they've never done mushrooms. I kneel down beside them and grab Jack's hand. "Hey, don't fret, I didn't eat the chili. I waited to make sure there was enough and then it was all gone. I'm straight and don't mind being Party Mom. My car is on the road at the entrance, ready to go if anyone needs to go home or back to Sacred Heart School. Buckle up kids and enjoy the ride." I talk them off the ledge. They breathe in deep and exhale to chill-out status.

"Snipe hunting is definitely out of the question. Cha Cha lay some Goddess wisdom on us." I said. If engaged in conversation, maybe the laughing will subside.

Cha Cha bows her head: "I feel the spirit of Ixchel—Medicine Woman. *You're a channel for Divine healing power.* Possibly, because of the intense Indian vibe. *Qué chido*—how cool." She belts out a loud, Indian war-whoop; "Hey-a-a-hey! Hey-a-a-hey! Hoka hey!" She tries an Indian dance, stumbles but steadies herself before she falls.

Gonzo jumps up, teeters, find his balance and zombie marches over to *The River.* One by one, they head toward him the human magnet standing at *The River's* edge. All with spaced-out expressions slowly walking mesmerized by the glittering water and roaring river wall of sound. A full moon provides a bright spotlight in a soft burgundy sky.

Blissfully still, no one speaks, *it's so calm.* The only sound is the rushing water and the plop, plop, plop, hitting the rocks on the shoreline. We hear the hooting of a barn owl. I pray no one falls into the freezing, snowmelt runoff, water.

Sadie wanders back to the fire ring, now, a big fire is blazing. She squats down, much too close. I rush to her side. "Sweetie, please, move back." I gently push her away from the camp-fire. A rocketing cinder spark shoots ash right into her eye. She screams: "Ow! That hurts!" I grab a canteen of water and try to rinse it out.

"No, don't touch my eye!" She's almost crying and refuses to let anything near her eye, being high only exacerbates the situation. She's blinking wildly, willing it to come out. I stand back helpless, not knowing what to do.

"Can I just take a look? I'll try to dab it with a tissue." I see a red fleshy, irritated, and inflamed eye.

"You need to go home and let your mom flush it out. Let's grab your things." I see disappointment in her face but also, relief. Eye injuries are beyond the realm of my young skill set. I don't want to be responsible for any harm coming to my friend.

I make the announcement: "OK, goofballs, everyone main-tain, and behave yourself. I've got to run Sadie home. I'll be back as fast as I can." Groans fill the air. I ask Jack to keep an eye on everyone. He's the least affected by the mushrooms.

Chimera

1975 - 1983

"You remember too much," my mother said to me recently.
"Why hold onto all that?"
And I said, "where can I put it down?"
–Anne Carson

To remember is holy.
–Anita Diamant

Clean Getaway

Falling in Love is not a choice—
to stay in Love is.
–Anonymous

G RADUATION AT SACRED HEART is a pain riddled and heartless joke. Four seniors party all night and make it within minutes to the ceremony. Tequila and Mescaline almost come between them and a high school diploma. The seniors march to the podium to the strains of Kenny Rogers song *"The Gambler."* Joints discreetly passed in the back row.

Esteemed Headmaster Rawleigh Rio delivers his canned graduation speech given since these seniors were freshman. "Four years ago, you handed over your children and asked me, will you be there for them when they're sick, lonely, homesick, and full of problems? Now, I give them back to you—will you be there for them?" He glances at the first row of graduates who are reciting the speech with him. He almost lost it.

He had a ring the school presented to him as a gift when hired as Headmaster that he took off, fiddled, and played with. Middle of the year, he lost it and missed it dearly. While handing one of his *"Rice Christians"* (seniors bribed with brunch at the next-door hotel restaurant to attend Sunday mass) students his diploma, the boy drops the ring into Headmaster Rio's hand.

"We saved it. You took it off at brunch and left it on the table." He winks.

Jack didn't want his parents at the ceremony. Fernando Fernandez is the class valedictorian. A contemptible, pissant, fizzled-out *Pfffttt, firecracker-dud-ending* to two splendorous, mind-blowing years. He's gone, pulling off a cold-blooded, Irish goodbye. *He makes a Clean Getaway.*

Life without Jack is like waking up to no more color, no shimmering, ineffable light, *nothing to look forward to.* I'd experienced my surroundings reverently, since meeting him. Now, I'm stifled and shut down. The *goodness glue* has *vamoosed.* I'm hard and fucked, six ways to Sunday.

The days turn into numbing loneliness. I spend the first week in my room listening to records. With the right music, it's possible to either forget or remember everything. Music and I move into the eternal, hidden heart of time.

Listening to albums is a sacred act. Music is the sound wave of the soul. The Cherokee call it *di ka no gi dv,* the music of the spirit—in the Turtledove, in the Mockingbird, in the gurgling stream. Sound evokes memory stronger than a photo.

I pull out an album and shake the round, black disc out of its cover and paper jacket, into the palm of my hand. I balance it like a plate, holding it only by the edges, not touching the flat surface. Oil from the hands gunk up the grooves of the vinyl.

I place the disc on the turntable and do a circular swipe with the velvet cleaner. I pick up the needle, and gently set it on the blank edge it rolls into the groove's sweet first note. The *pièce de résistance*—to devour the liner notes, photos, memorize the lyrics, and to decipher the artist message.

Scouring the pictures, lyrics, soothed by the *tactile nature* of the liner notes. Feasting on the lavish layers, textures, dynamics, and *emotional depth of the sensuous, storytelling of music.* The bold, intimate sharing of the essence of spirit and soul.

Artists express feelings we don't know how to verbalize. Art has the power to make ideas known. Joni Mitchell set the bar with her honest, raw, lyrics, and sings our secrets out loud. Emotional calligraphy balances narrative with musical complexity. She inspires baby boomers to pick up their pens and write, to be vulnerable, to question, to doubt, to push the limits of independence, ambition, and creative fulfillment. I luxuriate for hours with music *that melds with my soul.*

Forty years later, I'm still listening to the same albums. The beautiful ambiance and powerful emotional resonance still reverberates like the clear ring of a bell. I cherish the wear on the covers. My two, grown sons enjoy the albums I fancied as a teenager. I still yearn for the satisfaction of buying an album *for one great song,* hoping all the songs soar and am thrilled when not disappointed.

"Rosie, please, PLEASE, *please* come out with me today, *let's doooo something!* I can't live like this, staring at these four walls," Cha Cha pleaded with me daily. Our house is next door to a gas station. The neon sign has a Pegasus logo, she lays on the bed and fantasizes about flying away on the winged red horse. Silently, *cursing Jack: "¡Pinche cabrón!"*

Mr. Eddie's is a favorite family restaurant on the corner of our block and a second home. We spent many afternoons after school scarfing down fries and chocolate dipped, swirl ice-cream cones. Cha Cha offers me a bribe: "If you agree to go to Mr. Eddie's, I'm buying, but you've got to leave this room to collect."

All I want: Cha Cha, books, music, my dog King, and to read Jack's letters, *over and over*. I keep them bundled together, tied with a red ribbon, in case Mom burst in without knocking. I'd tuck them underneath the blankets or books. I dutifully, retrieved the mail every day. She's not seen the baby blue, striped, international airmail envelopes that arrived weekly from New Zealand. The sight of one sends my heart pounding.

How is reality suppose to be without Jack? Everything is backward and upside down while sitting at a three-legged table. His absence becomes a presence and portend of squandered Love. We continued to write but *our numinous time at The River of Love* vanishes into thin air.

Dear Rosie,

Always strong emotions when I leave Red Cañon. Oh, yes, and mostly a pleasant sadness.

To see that heartfelt smile beamed at me... It lights me up. I'll miss that smile with all its wattage that shares every bit of you.

I have not known anyone who can look cute, intense, and happy at the same time.

When I return I'd like to go to the drive-in in a certain Star Chief with a dark-haired beauty.

I Love you, Rose Carol Ramirez.
Jack

After the Sacred Heart School boys graduated; it was never the same. The sacred communion and togetherness evaporated with them. I bump into Martin and Mac, occasionally, *but I don't ever go back to The River*. It turns into a constant battle between remembering and forgetting. I'm too immature to put the light and dark together, which is the heart of Wisdom and Love.

My unconscious buries it deep at the tender age of seventeen: *I'm not worthy of Love*. Faith, goodness, and belief were more active verbs than stable nouns. I shut down my emotions, better to numb out, and *not feel anything at all*.

I stroll with my dog King through Rio Vista Park on a resplendent, Colorado late summer afternoon. I breeze by a hippie, sitting cross-legged playing guitar under a giant oak tree. He has a Jack Kerouac, beat poet vibe with a lit Marlboro cigarette, hanging on his bottom lip.

"Hey," I nod and shuffle by.

"Wanna hear a funny song? You look like you could use a laugh." He grins.

"Geez, is it that obvious? Hmmm... *This is the summer of Eeyore.*"

I sit down on the grass across from him and let King off his leash to roam freely. I scan quickly for other dogs. He doesn't play nice.

His name is Nigel; he strums a children's song, *The Teddy Bears Picnic*. Quirky and cute and gets a giggle out of me. Twenty years later, Jerry Garcia and David Grisman include this song on their album, *Not for Kids Only*. Quintessential Nigel.

He plays Led Zeppelin, Neil Young, Cat Stevens, and a couple of unfamiliar songs. It's near dark; I'm about to bid goodbye to my new friend, who looked about twenty-four. I'd like to meet up again; I patiently wait, no pressure, no effort required. He has a Zen-like calmness.

"He's a beautiful German Shepherd. Did you buy him from a breeder?" he asks between songs, lighting up *another cigarette.*

"No, when I was in second grade, he followed me home from school. We posted "Lost Dog" signs, and asked around, but nobody claimed him. He's smart, Loving, and obedient— except around other dogs, so he's kept on a leash.

I show him a nasty, burn scar around my right wrist. King ran after another dog, unwrapping the leather strap with such force, it burned. "King freaks out when he sees a broom the previous owner's abused him. We're pals; he's my dog, sleeps with me at night, and doesn't leave my side. Do you have any pets?" I ask, trying to switch the focus off me.

"No, I just moved from Denver, I barely have furniture, but I grew up here. See those handball courts across the street?" He points with his nose; he hasn't put the guitar down since I walked up. "Finn, my best friend and I, play handball during the summer, we come almost every night. We usually end up here, tossing the Frisbee. Wanna hear another song?" he offers.

"Sure." I smile. I'm relaxed for the first time since Jack left. Has it been three months? *Seems more like three decades.*

"Wanna come to my place and get high? Then you can stop by anytime to hear music. I play electric guitar in a band; we practice at my trailer. I'll give you my phone number." He said in a measured tone, trying not to appear too eager but excitement dances in his blue eyes.

He's sweet, shy, and harmless. I whistle for King to put him on the leash. We'll slip him into the fenced backyard. Mom will bring him inside with her. I'll call and say that I'm with Cha Cha downtown shopping.

"How did you know I smoke pot?" I ask, which sounds ridiculous, it's harder to find people in this small town *who don't get high.*

"You've got cool taste in music." He winks.

At Nigel's dingy trailer, I run in to call Cha Cha; I need her protection. My heart says he's safe but can't risk *becoming entangled in knots of my own making.* Cha Cha arrives at warp speed and is a bundle of nervous energy, bouncing off the walls of the tiny trailer. She's encouraged by the color back in my cheeks and *my smile...* It's been months since she'd seen it. We spot crates of record albums in the corner of the small, dark living room, we rifled through them.

"Oh damn, he's got a bootleg Neil Young with *Sugar Mountain* on it!" I beam, hugging the plain, white album, it's like Christmas morning.

"He has Hendrix, Santana, CCR, Yes, Eagles, Jethro Tull, Rolling Stones, Robin Trower, Traffic, The Who, The James Gang, Cat Stevens, Moody Blues and Ten Years After and so much more. *What a collection!* I hope we can chill here and listen to music. Wish he had some furniture and it wasn't so creepy," Cha Cha adds under her breath.

Nigel sits on the hideous, orange shag rug. He leans against the flimsy wood paneling in the cramped dark, living room. It has a chair, loveseat and a messy coffee table covered with empty soda cans and ashtrays overflowing with cigarette butts.

He sits crossed-legged in a blue work shirt, Levis, and heavy-duty mountaineering-hiking boots. Thin, petite in appearance; he feels our eyes on him. He has coarse, wavy, chin-length dirty, blond hair with piercing, blue eyes. His grayish, pale skin has splashes of light brown freckles on his face and arms.

Cha Cha breaks the awkward tension and silence: "All right, Wilson, pick it!" She howls. He plays three songs with a few brief pauses; chain-smokes a slew of Marlboros and downs, two cans of Dr. Pepper. It's late; he offers to give us a ride to my house. Cha Cha nods with approval.

We plan an outing the next weekend. Cha Cha, chock-full of surprises, suggests going to Tunnel Drive. He writes down his telephone number, and we pick Saturday to meet.

I'm Lazarus rising from the dead, three months and counting time to return to the living. Mourning, melancholia, and acute nostalgia almost ripped me apart. I start senior year and must focus on attending a decent college, the golden ticket out of Red Cañon.

Santo Niño

If the only prayer we ever say
in our lives is "Thank You,"
that will be enough.
–Meister Eckhart

CHA CHA AND I PREPARE DINNER AT MY HOUSE on a blistering, hot August evening, in the midst of a heatwave. We're sweating and suffocating in the stifling, hot kitchen. The old house has no air conditioning, and the kitchen window doesn't open.

Little Julian, now enrolled in great Auntie Alma's Head Start class, watches television in the living room with her. The open windows and front door provide a fresh, cross breeze in this part of the house.

"What's going on with you tonight, *why are you so uptight?*" Cha Cha notices my edginess. A large mound of red potatoes sits on the table to peel.

"They're making me go on a pilgrimage to the Santuario in Chimayo. Every five years, Dad takes Grandma Grace to this holy church in New Mexico. It's a four-hour drive; we pray in the church, grab burgers, and drive home. We go and return the same day. Under normal conditions, it's a grueling trip but right now—*I'm just not up for it.* The itty, bitty, shitty committee is still in charge." I hint at my foul disposition since Jack left.

"Back up girl, what's the Santuario and why do you have to go, if the pilgrimage is for your grandma?" She turns down the blaring radio.

"Haven't I ever told you about the *Lourdes of America?*" That's what the locals call it. Grandma prefers Dad because he drives the fastest. She hunkers down in the back seat and prays the Rosary. I'm the human radar detector for the State Patrol and referee for my parents.

El Santuario de Chimayo is a modest adobe church built in 1810. A *Penitentes* priest roaming the countryside, while whipping himself, (a self-flagellation form of penance) spots something glowing on the mountainside. Digging in the soil, he finds a crucifix. Three times it's moved to neighboring villages only to reappear in the same hole. Finally, the people build a chapel over it in Chimayo.

Miraculous healings begin to happen. The villagers figured out, it's not the crucifix *but the sand* that has healing powers. It's the *tierra bendita* of—*El Posito* the sacred sandpit. Grandma always brings home a small plastic container of the Holy Dirt. The healing properties when ingested cure a variety of ailments. She takes it for debilitating arthritis in her hands." I sip a glass of soda on the table.

She peels the potatoes and listens attentively. Her eyes light up: "Ha! *I crave and Love eating dirt.* Do you feel the power when you're in the church?" she asks.

"Yes, but this trip, my heart's not into it, I can't endure eight hours of my parent's bickering." I shoot her a frown.

"It might help you heal, prima." She peels the last potato and stands up for a quick stretch.

"I'll feel like a hypocrite, and I'm afraid Grandma will see right through me."

"Keep the faith, baby. Tell me more about this fascinating church." She pulls up her chair closer to mine.

"The legend goes that the healing soil springs from an Indian shrine. The curative powers come from the sandpits dried remains of the original hot-springs." I move over to the stove to stir the big pot of beans about to boil over.

"Dat's COOL!" she hollers.

"Wanna hear more?" She nods her head excitedly.

"Catholic is a word that came from the Greek—*katholikos* which means universal and inclusive. In the early days of the church, Roman citizens referred to it as the upstart religion that followed the ways of Jesus. Among the members, it defined the very nature of the church, in that it was universally for everyone. No exclusions according to nationality, race, economic, or social status. Our ancestors wanted this religion to be universal and diverse." Cha Cha's father is divorced and the family doesn't go to church.

"Christianity was meant to be the non-violent message of Love. The Lord works in all sorts of service to be done, in different ways, in different people. We see this beautiful diversity and unity in the universe—from Latin, unus+versus, *"to turn around one thing."* Not tribal and exclusive for members only, that it has evolved into. When everything becomes about *"belonging"* instead of a transforming experience, people live in a world of shared illusions. Republicans versus Democrats, Nationalism, and Xenophobia. This type of thinking makes us incapable of depth or truth.

Tens of thousands of people make pilgrimage walks each year on Good Friday. Some walk hundreds of miles, carrying crosses to the Santuario. It's a beautiful story about a child, faith, *thanksgiving,* and the perfect intersection of Spanish, Mexican and Indian cultures." The beans simmer and potatoes fry to a crispy brown.

"It started in seventh-century central Spain in a field where a statue is found of Mary holding the baby Jesus. Miracles in the area are attributed to the Virgin Mary, a chapel is built and destroyed by war, rebuilt and again, destroyed by war. Finally, another statue was assembled with a detachable, baby Jesus in 1162. They remove the child, Jesus keeping him near when women are in labor. It becomes standard practice that Mary statues are made to include a detachable, baby Jesus.

Wars break out against the Moors. A story about a young boy that nourished the Spanish prisoners is told. He slipped past sleeping guards or walked by them unchallenged with a gord of water and loaves of bread. The boy is Jesus, also known as *Santo Niño.* By the end of the war in 1492, tales of the Santo Niño prevailed.

Fast forward to Mexico, in 1540. While building the city of Fresnillo, in North Central Mexico; the Spanish general overseeing the construction, orders a statue of Mary and baby Jesus from Spain. Shortly, after its arrival, an explosion erupts in the silver mine and traps several miners. The women gather around the statue and pray for the *Intercession of Our Lady.*

They notice the detachable baby, Santo Niño is missing. The miners escape the mine and describe a young boy who appeared to them. He offered water and led them to safety. People return to the church to discover the Santo Niño statue back in the arms of his mother with *soiled clothes and worn shoes.*

Santo Niño finds his way to New Mexico and *works many miracles.* The Santuario keeps a room off the altar where the sacred pit is, it's full of crutches, body braces, and testimonials from people healed and cured. Among the wooden Santo Niño statue are shelves of children's shoes left by the faithful. Some as thanks and offerings to the Holy Child and *a perpetual supply of clean shoes* for future journeys helping those in need." Dinner is ready.

"Can I go in your place? Will you teach me how to spot State Patrol traps?" Cha Cha asks eagerly.

I'm exhausted from reliving the past and fearing the future. When would it sink in that *the present is truly the only place we exist?* I'm in a no man's land holding pattern, waiting for my life to jumpstart when reunited with Jack, which isn't anytime soon. I repeated my mother's mistake by believing that I had enough Love for both of us which was a fool's errand.

I go on the pilgrimage. I'm alone praying in the old wooden pew of the rustic adobe church. *"Hail Mary, Queen of the Holy Rosary, I offer you these petitions. I lay red and white roses at your feet..."* I feel a light touch on my shoulder, I turn, but no one is there. I close my eyes, and there's a soft hum in my ear: A rush of pure Love fills my body, rejuvenating every cell lifting the maelstrom of sorrow. I receive my blessing from the Holy Child, Santo Niño. *The whole pilgrimage was for my sake* Grandma instinctively knew.

Tunnel Drive

The one who gives would never remember.
The one who receives would never forget.
–Jewish Proverb

NIGEL MEETS CHA CHA and me at Murphy's Poor Boy Drive-In on Main Street. *The best burger shack in town* with its quick bag of cheeseburgers, fries, and banana milkshakes. It's a crisp, end of summer, Sunday afternoon. We cruise to Tunnel Drive, a four-mile hiking trail down a dirt road of an old train route with two man-made tunnels inside of a granite mountain. The working train tracks run along the road above the breathtaking, Arkansas River.

We're at the entrance when I gasp, "Please, pull over, *hurry.*" I point at the mountain above us. Nigel parks the white, 1968, Volkswagen camper van on the shoulder of the road. We jump out to look. He emits a sweet, chuckle/snort, "A herd of Bighorn sheep! Wow! All the years I've spent mountain climbing and skiing, I've never seen them." He smiles broadly at me and pinches his pale arm.

"My dad told stories of running after Bighorn sheep as a boy when my grandfather was a ranch foreman at Taylor Ranch in Texas Creek. I didn't believe him—*till now.*" We watch the sheep in silence. They grazed gracefully on the side of the mountain. Cloaked in luxurious thick white fur with their curled, horned heads down, unaware of their adoring audience.

Nigel's nervous and pulls a cigarette out of the top pocket of his blue work shirt. His shaky hands are a side effect of all the nicotine and caffeine he consumes. He's still unsteady around the strong, Chicana chicks but is quick with a shy smile, a sudden laugh, grateful for the *serendipitous meeting* in the park.

We continue up the steep dirt road, breezing through the first tunnel, only 80 feet long. Rolling down the windows in the white, Volkswagen camper van, Nigel slows to a crawl. Cha Cha sticks her head out of the window and shouts: *"ECHO... ECHOO... ECHOOO!"* The sound bounces back; we laugh in unison. He hits the horn, equally as funny—a tinny sound like a high-pitched, burp.

We enter the second longest tunnel, a quarter mile long, around mid-point it's pitch-black, and Nigel stops the van. "Do you know the heartbeat story?" He whips out a flashlight from under the seat, turns it on and holds it under his chin creating a scary face. I'm sitting in the middle, I turn to Cha Cha, and we let out ear-shattering squeals. He assumes *we're game*.

"Two high school couples go parking at the local cemetery. They're necking and steaming up the windows. They hear a light tapping, (he taps on the dashboard) then, it's louder (balls up fist, pounds harder). They're freaking out; BOOM! BOOM! BOOM! The deafening sound is like a heartbeat. They wipe the fogged up windows to see where it's coming from...."

"Stop! I don't want to hear any more." I shout in a firm, serious tone. "Please, drive, I want out of this freaky, TUNNEL!" I'm breathing heavy. Cha Cha's laughing hysterically; she can't believe what a baby I am. He drives to the end of the tunnel and pulls over to the side of the road. Our eyes adjust to the light we look down at *The River.* A group floats by in an oversized, floppy boat, and we listen to the rafter "keets" echoing up from the canyon.

Nigel pops-up the camper shell and pulls out the padded benches and table to sit more comfortably. We have a cooler full of sodas, and for snacks, there's Doritos and M&M's. I hand out drinks and candy. Nigel opens the windows for cross ventilation. Sage and red dust blow in with the breeze.

We sit in silence for a few awkward minutes. Nigel's eye twinkles. "What gifts we've stumbled on today. Wanna play a game, listing what we're grateful for—it can be a favorite food, movie, song, artist or moment. Rose, want to start?" He looks at me.

"I'll pass—Cha Cha, got anything?" I don't want to open up.

"Right-on, funsies. Hmmm... I'll start with easy ones: Carlos Santana, sleepovers at Rosie Posie's, Jimi Hendrix... Sunsets on Skyview Drive." She takes a pull off her Dr. Pepper. "Gardening with pop's, killer mota, late-night horror movies with Auntie Alma. *Tortillas hot-off the-griddle* and Grandma Grace's lemon meringue pie." She licks her lips loudly. "Long road trips, poetry, *dancing, dancing, dancing!* The birth of my son. That oughta do it." She crosses her arms and nods.

Nigel goes next: "My Fender guitar, climbing Venable-Comanche Trail, the most stunning spot in Colorado, cross-country skiing on the Sangre de Cristo Rainbow Trail, Murphy's Poorboy cheeseburgers, Skyview Drive-In, the Beatles *White Album,* and Rose's smile." Nigel ends with a bold flourish.

"Awww...Rosie, he's sweet on you," Cha Cha teases.

"You cross-country ski?" I ask with a wild look in my eyes.

"Yep, I got six sets of skis, boots, poles, and wax. Everything needed to take a van full of people to the mountains for a day of fun." Nigel said.

"Hot damn, when are we going?" I flash a sparkly smile.

Pésame

Mother said, "Go and give
sympathy—condolence
comfort the grieving"

Never imagined, pésame would be
given to me

Tears flow... ache of abandonment
seared in the memory and bones

The seventeen-year-old psyche
doesn't understand
what she did or didn't do

The pain fresh embedded deep
in Forever's Bedrock

How to let go?
Buried truths burst forth

Blast it with Freedom

Resurrect—like the Child
of pure Love

O N A BLUSTERY, October afternoon, my senior year, I co-
vertly slip onto Sacred Heart School Campus. I'm missing
Jack and thought being here might help me feel close to him. I
park in front of Hedley Hall, and walk to the theater where we
used to neck behind the thick bushes. I sit on the stone bench
and feel the stabbing pressure of tears. This was a bad idea, I'm
a ghost visiting a past life. I limp back to the car to *leave this
place forever.*

I hurry across the street and skirt the front of the Star Chief.
Ravishing guitar riffs ring through the air. Martin's perched on
the front steps of Hedley Hall. A troubadour in a white puffy
shirt, his long, wavy, black hair ripples in the brisk breeze of
the fall afternoon. He's ten yards away playing with his head
bent down. *It's awful being here* without Jack. I scoot around
the ginormous grill of the car to disappear before he looks up.

My hand's on the driver side door handle: "Hey, Rosie!"
Martin bellows from the steps. Stealth mode blown, I lumber
toward him. He looks older and more mature. How does a
teenager age over a brief summer? I wondered, already knowing the answer.

"*Oh-lah,* Martin, that was beautiful. Is that a new 12
string?" I stumble up the steps.

"It's Ralpharoni's—my best friend. I borrow it when I write.
Where have you been, Rose? How are you?" There's a glassy,
emptiness in the dark obsidian eyes. The Martin sparkle's gone.
"What's wrong, Martin? You're not your usual, chirpy self." I said.

"I had a bitch of a summer. My mom's got stage four breast
cancer. She's battled it for over a year, this summer, she took a
turn for the worse." He winced.

"How horrible, *I am so sorry*. I lost a gorgeous, young
aunt to breast cancer. She looked like Elizabeth Taylor." I don't

mention the awful way the doctors butchered her and the horror of her suffering. "Why didn't you stay home with her?" I sit next to him on the cold, cement stairs.

"I'm on full scholarship, she insisted I return and didn't want me to watch her die. If she holds on till I graduate, I'll postpone college." His voice cracked, he puts the guitar down, covers his face with his hands, and breaks down and cries. *Sadness washes over us.* "Come, let's ditch this wind and sit in the car." I hit his leg and stood up.

The sun's setting I don't want to get him in trouble but *who cares?* Death puts perspective on such mundane matters. We slump down in the front seat of my boat-of-a-car and push the leather bench seat all the way back. I turn on the radio, set at whisper low.

"I feel numb," he said turning his face toward me leaning his head against the back of the seat. Strangely, up close, he's manlike now, not the boy I spent the last two years partying with.

"What a grief-stricken, sloppy mess we are. *We've both lost so much.* I'm the last person you want to hang out with." I glance at tree branches whipping in the strong wind.

"Rosie—*look at you.* You won't be alone for long. You're the smartest, hottest, little firecracker in this godforsaken, hillbilly town. Jack's a complete moron for leaving you, the *dickiest of dick moves*," he shouts.

"I don't know how to square this, but I'll either die of him or be cured." My voice falters, and the tears fall. He slides his hand between the car seat and behind my neck.

"Don't fret why give your heart to someone who doesn't cherish it? Jack's desertion had nothing to do with you. He's a shitheel. And he won't be the only one, trust me. We learn the

most about Love by those who never Love us. *Move on, Rose.*
I bet if you bumped into him twenty years from now you'd
receive the same result. Hot for a spell, then a cold fish, breaking your heart once again. Why torture yourself? Wait for that
special soul that will *Love you completely and make YOU a
priority."* He looks over at me.

"So harsh, Martin—I'd like to defend Jack, but his coward-
ice is my living hell." I cough back a sob and pull a tissue out
of my jacket pocket and wipe my eyes.

A rigid torso in a red and green plaid flannel shirt, tucked
into Levi's, bends down outside of Martin's window and in-
spects the inside of the car. In an instant, I recognize the scary,
black beady eyes framed in Buddy Holly glasses. Brother Daniel
is in Martin's face: *"What's going on here?"* he demands.
Suspicious eyes scan the front and back seat of my car.

"Nothing, Brother Daniel. Rose bumped into me playing
guitar on the steps. We haven't seen each other since last May.
She's helping me deal with my mom's breast cancer." Martin
plays the sympathy card.

"Oh, very well, wrap it up she can't be here, I don't want
any trouble. If Father John sees you, he'll be very upset." He
glares at me. I spent the last two years dodging this terrifying
man after he busted me in Jack's room.

He stomped off, glancing back at us before he rushes
through the double doors of Hedley Hall. "That's right Mr.
Bespectacled, Beady-Eyed monster, *Keep on Truckin'*—no exchange of body fluids going on here. He hates me. I bet he's
glad Jack's gone. I don't belong here, Martin. You better go
before I start crying again." I crack a weak smile.

"There's a barn dance next week. Sam Tootman's band is
playing, wanna come and party with us lame seniors? You did

Murder in the Cathedral last spring, some of my friends were in that play." He auditioned, but Brother Owen didn't like his outspokenness, so he wasn't included. Oliver's influence got Rose & Company cast.

"If the barn dance is on a weekend night, I've got to cheer at a football game. Can I listen to you play sometime?" I grab a pen off the dashboard and write my phone number on his hand.

Grief shared is grief lessened. Sharing our sadness is what my mother called *Pésame: to comfort and offer sympathy.* A sacred, Catholic ritual practiced in Chicano cultures. It helps souls heal when they're sad, cut down, or lose someone dear. Practiced at funerals or in any grieving situation. Martin and I hug and promise to see each other soon. I'm relieved-his overall look is improved, he flashes a quick smile, and waves wobbly as I drive away.

My days at Sacred Heart School are over. Martin's as miserable, scared, and lonely, as I am. We're *the Island of Misfit Toys* no one wants or cares for.

Two weeks later, I'm driving home from Grandma Grace's house. Half a mile past Sacred Heart School, Martin's running across U.S. Highway 50, he sees my car and waves wildly.

"Rosie, pick me up!" he yells. I pull over onto the frontage road. *He's so happy to see me.* He tugs on a large, bulky looking, army surplus duffel bag.

"Can you give me a ride to Sacred Heart?"

"Chore, hop in." I lean over and push the passenger door open. A vast improvement from the last time we were together, actual color in his cheeks and a sharp glint in his eyes.

"How ya doing?" he chirps.

"I'm OK—you seem happier."

"School keeps my mind off Mom, I just got a shitload of laundry done, thanks for picking me up." He adjusted the duffle bag against the bench seat. It's cruel the school didn't provide laundry facilities, forcing the students to use the rundown Laundromat. I pull into the main entrance of Sacred Heart School, in front of the monastery. It's a Thursday, late afternoon; I've no cheerleading practice, and no homework, a rare occurrence.

"Want to go for a walk? You can park behind the barn, and we can meander over to the alfalfa fields," he suggests. My common sense screams, *NOOO! Don't lead this poor boy on,* but his eager eyes entice my big heart—*why not?* I've nothing to go home to. He's surprisingly witty, smart, and fun to be with.

Martin is sitting in the front seat and *appears as a small child.* I blink hard and look again. There he is, a robust, seventeen-year-old with rock star, jet-black hair cascading around his shoulders and pleading, dark, almond-shaped eyes.

"It's only a walk, Martin friends listening and crying on each other's shoulder and nothing more." I give him a *don't-read-too-much-into-this* look.

"Yes, ma'am, just a simple walk," he mimicked in a slow, Southern accent. "The lush, alfalfa fields before the first frost are velvety green and smell *divine.*" He waxed eloquent. I park behind the barn and scan for Brother Daniel. This is his territory: horses and Gymkhana. There's no sign of him.

We head east on foot toward the alfalfa fields. My last memory here was of Mac dumping my car in a ditch during a Gymkhana competition. After the crowd cleared, Jack and I slipped into the barn with the double-wide doors, a twenty-by-thirty footer with six stalls. We climbed up to the hayloft for a smooching session. Sweet, delicious fun, high up, looking down at the verdant, alfalfa fields with the purplish Wet Mountains as a backdrop. We were alone in a safe and warm place. *A mini-miracle for us.*

While kissing, we listened to the horses in the stalls below. We laid on a bed of hay for hours in each other's arms. We cuddled, kissed, talked, and laughed. I wanted to give myself to him that day, and now, I can't remember why I held back. *Catholic guilt and fear of pregnancy.*

That constant, damn nagging Alma voice in my head. Her moral brainwashing a cunning mixture of good and evil with a strong grip of control. I marveled at his patience, his unselfish giving, thoughtful and Loving ways, *so what happened, why did he choose to leave me?* Our unraveling began with the negative pushback of doubt. Tears well up, but I fight them off. The sadness still flows in waves, even months after his departure. The pain remains, but the tears lessen. *Grief is the price of Love.*

We stroll toward the alfalfa fields. I've no idea what the hell I'm doing. Running into Martin a portent of my purpose here. We look for *The Great One* outside of us, but *the Spirit is always in here and in between everything.*

"Rosie, what's that heavenly aroma in your car? Did it come like that? It smells of delicious fruits, flowers, and warm, female scents." He said and catches me off guard.

"Um, I'm... not sure. I transport lots of female friends that wear patchouli, musk, vanilla, sandalwood and the ever-present Baby Lotion that *we slather our bodies with.* My mother is an Avon junkie and wears powders, sachets, and perfumes. I'm a devotee of Mother Mary, who's known for the scent of December Roses. There's a visual—Our Lady of Guadalupe riding shotgun with Rosie Ramirez. Hmmm..." I crack a grin.

"It's *FANTASTIC!*" he shouts. "If only you could bottle it. *I Love riding* in your car. I'm swept into another dimension, into a sweet smelling, portal undreamed of. Jack's one lucky guy." He glances at me. The sound of his name jars me back to harsh reality.

"Please, don't talk about him, *it's too painful.*" I lower my eyes to the ground, signaling this subject was off limits.

"Rosie, stop doubting yourself. You're a deep, innate, sensitive person, and wise beyond your years. Some milquetoast white, suburban boy, unless he's much older, isn't going to know how to handle you. Your help in dealing with my mother's illness, I have so much respect for you. I've found a kindred soul. I'm not in Love with you in a carnal way, but *I do Love and care for you*, do you understand?" He stops walking and turns to face me.

"I too, feel a strong emotional bond." I nod. His reassuring words calm me.

We're almost to the dirt road that runs through the middle of the alfalfa fields. He grabs my hand; I'm startled by his forwardness.

"I promise not to ask you again, but since we talked in your car, *I've wanted to kiss you.* This one time, a kiss between friends." He leans toward me.

"Won't it make it weird between us? You won't misconstrue it?" I ask.

"Never seemed possible that this could happen but please— *just one kiss,*" he pleads.

I take a deep breath and exhale. He watches me. I've no reason not to trust him, he's the gentlest and most honorable of souls. The sunset turns amber, honey-gold, pure as the sensation warming my heart. I don't want to betray Jack.

We veer off the road, toward a big rustling cottonwood tree. He leans me against the rough tree trunk. We watch the autumn light cast a golden overlay on the tiny alfalfa plantings. The large, orange orb drops behind Star Watcher Mountain, a mound west of town, named after a tragic, Indian princess. Martin's still holding my hand.

"I'll do it if you don't tell a soul and Jack must never know." He takes a quick, large step toward me; this is a pure expression of affection. He gathers me in the warm circle of his arms, soft as a plush blanket on a winter's day. No one's touched me since Jack left four months ago. I close my eyes and let Martin kiss me—unaware if he's *ever kissed* a girl. I purse my lips, he presses his against mine.

My mind wanders to Jack and what a great kisser he was. No need to tutor or instruct him, it flowed naturally. I'm brought back to the present by the sheer length of this kiss and how we're breathing in sync... inhaling, kiss, exhaling, more kissing, together as one breath.

At this moment, we don't feel separate and share primal and deeper levels of consciousness *with the Breath of Divine Love blowing in, swirling around and through, uniting us.* Children experience this at a pre-rational level. So do mystics on a universal level, a unitive consciousness.

The kiss restores, heals, and strengthens me. It fills me with bold grace and performs the same miracle on Martin. I silently pray and make a wish. *He goes for it* with a wave of lips melding, arms untangling, and we separate. I take a deep breath and study him. He's stunned with eyes wide with profound gratitude.

"Oh man, Rosie, *did you feel that?*" He raked his fingers through his thick hair.

"Thank you, I'm.... awestruck." He said.

I'm relieved there's no awkward residue. *We never talk about it again.* During this encounter, Martin appeared first as a child and then, switched back to a young man. In the Bible, the *Child is a symbol for miracles,* as soon as the Child is born in your consciousness, the miracle will happen, if you believe and are willing to recognize the power of the Holy Mystery and call upon it.

I drop him off at Hedley Hall with the overstuffed duffel bag of clean laundry. As I drive away, I honestly see him as a radiant spirit with a Loving and giving heart. *God's Love knits us together so completely;* that all may be one, you in me and I, in you. Today, we *Danced with the Divine* and was filled with *Holy Gratitude.* Martin and I are SS—Still Standing, we pull through our sorrow and grief together. *We are held above the dark waterline.*

In the Spring, his mother leaves this earth. I don't receive the miracle I prayed for, but forty years later, *my wish is granted.* Everything exists as a connected whole, through Jack, Marie, and Sacred Heart School at the east end of Red Cañon *I'm connected to Martin.* The flotsam of misery that flows in our lives aligns concern for the other's well-being.

We sporadically bump into each other during senior year. His beautiful, healing, acoustic guitar-instrumental music is a gift from a higher power and a glorious expression of truth. An enormous talent and caring friend that I'm blessed and grateful to have in my life.

Love is the faithful heart of the cosmos. What if caring for each other is the summit?

Manitou Falls

*Only those who will risk going too far
can possibly find out how far one can go.*
–T.S. Eliot

I WAIT FOR JACK at the mothball smelling Old Victorian St. Claudia Hotel/bus station on Main Street in Red Cañon. It's week of Thanksgiving, my senior year of High School and his freshman year at Tulane University. Jack's first visit to Red Cañon since graduating last May. I'm nervous and anxious.

I watch him gather his suitcase from underneath the cargo bay of the Greyhound Bus. His thick, chestnut, glossy hair falls over one side of his face. His focused, elongated, strong body moves quickly he sees my car when the bus pulled up.

The initial greeting will set the tone for the entire week. I didn't want it to be awkward or uncomfortable. *What is it about him* that keeps me so crazy in Love? This isn't puppy Love or teenage infatuation and more difficult now; he's a thousand miles away at college.

Our inchoate Lovemaking is complete and genuine regardless of the lack of experience. He takes the narrow, soft side of his hand and brushes lightly against my lower stomach above the pelvic bone: a feather brush of Love so perfect. *The lightest*

RIVER OF LOVE   237

stroke draws out the deepest desire. This tender image grounds
me and loosens sorrow's grip.

He struts with his bag, toward the car. I take a deep breath
to steady my nerves: "To all that is holy, please let this week go
without a hitch. Guide, direct, and protect us." My heart jack-
hammers. I jump out of the car and run to greet him.

"Hello, handsome, *come here, and give me some sugar.*" I
reach up and wrap my arms around his neck. He drops his bag,
lifts me off the ground, and twirls me in the middle of the side
street off Main Street.

"Hey, we don't want to call any unnecessary attention to
ourselves." I go from bold to suddenly shy.

"Damn, I've missed you." He whispers and nuzzles deep
into my hair.

We walk hand in hand, over to the car; he opens the driver's side door, I jump in, he leans down and plants a steamer
kiss. All tension and anxiety evaporate with the departing bus.
That kiss wipes away six months of overthinking, doubt, and
misery.

I reserved a room for the week at the Spanish Inn in Manitou
Falls, a small mountain town, 50 miles west of Colorado City.
"My parents think I'm at a cheerleading clinic," I tell him. The
Sky Chief's gassed, oiled, suitcases secured in the trunk. A cool-
er of his favorite Michelob beer rattles in the backseat.

"Let's get out of Dodge, pronto before we're seen." I pull
out the knob on the headlights.

"Still have the ol' bomb. Will she make it to Manitou Falls?"
He stretched out his legs; it's a four-hour bus ride that stops at
every small town between Stapleton Airport in Denver and Red
Cañon. He had to cool his jets for two hours in Dallas, the connecting flight from New Orleans. He's exhausted.

"I don't take her on long hauls often. Cha Cha's on red alert with her brother's car if we need help. No surprises will ruin our week together. The Spanish Inn is ideal it's quiet, and within walking distance to restaurants downtown, but there's no reason to leave the room." I throw him a sultry smile.

"No argument, here." He leans back on the soft, leather bench seat, reaches over and slips his hand into mine, where it stays for the hour-long drive.

"You cut your hair!" He gasps, finally figuring out what's different. The black, thick Indian mane that flowed down the middle of my back when he left is now chin length, curled under.

"Feels like cheating with a sheila with a cute bob!" He teases and pokes my side.

I glance down at the speedometer. I've got to watch the speed; U.S. Highway 50 is deer country. I click the high beams on. This relationship is like driving a car at night: one can only see as far as the headlights shine (one week). There's no roadmap but as I look up at the bright stars beaming down—*Happiness*. Darkness is needed to see the stars.

It's pitch black when we arrived at the quaint, red adobe, Spanish Inn in Manitou Falls. A picturesque mountain town west of Colorado City, nestled in the grandeur of Pikes Peak. Founded in 1872, by a doctor as a scenic health resort. He discovered the healing powers of the mineral springs which now flow from an iconic Indian statue fountain at the end of town. Tourist filled up jugs with the delicious carbonated mineral water.

When we lived in Colorado City, my family took lazy Sunday afternoon drives to Manitou Falls to fill plastic jugs with the bitter, salty tasting water. Ute Indians thrived on it for many generations. Manitou is the indigenous word for Spirit.

I check in at the Southwestern style motel office. The property has five small log cabins. Our cabin has a round white Spanish fireplace that greets us with crackles, pops and a warm, welcoming glow. The monster pine four-poster, king-size bed, was turned down, and primed to swallow us up. The setting so perfect my soul relaxes, adrenaline letting down.

Jack flips open his suitcase and pulls out a bottle of Beaujolais wine *to beat all beyond comparison.* The specialness of the occasion made it so memorable.

Watching the fire calms me. Everything's in place, *at this moment.* We create our paradise as we've done since we met. I throw a split log on the fire. He pours the dark, garnet elixir into wine glasses and hands one to me. I whiff its mineral fragrance and sip, its smooth raspberry flavor has the *tart sweetness of Love* and bitter aftertaste of uncertainty.

I want to dive into that luxurious bed, burrow deep, and not resurface. We embrace, tumble, and roll, into the inviting, four-poster bed.

"My life is empty without you." He lingers, breathing heavy in my ear then sliding over to my mouth, kissing with convincing pressure that melts the fear and sadness. The kiss fires me up. I pop out of bed and run over to the glass of wine. I sit naked on the overstuffed, Indian blanket covered chair, in the gold whipping firelight. I sip the wine, a soothing remedy for a ragged heart. He's crushed by the pain on my face.

"Is everything all right?" He stretches his arms out toward me.

"Everything's perfect. *I'm just savoring it.*" I close my eyes and draw in a deep, calming breath. These overwhelming bursts of happiness occur at the margins of the unbearable.

"Please, come back to bed." He tugs at my leg. I grab our wine glasses. I pause: *How many times will we make Love this week? Then, he'll be gone. When will be the last time we make Love forever?* As usual, I'm overthinking, getting ahead of myself, projecting into the future, not being in the moment. I flip it, *what if he never returns, what if this is it?* I glare at him and *turn Apache in this perfect Indian setting.*

I run to the wagon wheel end table, deposit the wine glasses, and jump into bed. I pin his arms against the bed's wooden headboard and roughly kiss his neck and shoulders. I convince myself not to be angry, it's not his fault—*there's no one to blame.*

His hands are on my hips; he softly moves them over my buttocks. I slip him into me. We glide in slow motion. The college FM radio station plays a mellow, jazzy tune. I keep time with the undulating beat. In his caressing, warm sky blue eyes, I see the burst of aggressiveness pleases him.

We make Love throughout the night with pillow talk filling in the gaps of time we've lost. I'm encouraged by the easy and fun conversation, similar to the courting ones while we walked in the dead of Colorado's coldest winters. The long period apart has not diminished our strong emotional bond.

I stir the fire and retrieve from my purse a Goddess card with the Goddess Guinevere on it. "Cha Cha asked me to give this to you—Guinevere is the Goddess of True Love. *The romantic stirrings in your heart have propelled the universe to deliver great Love to you.* Guess we're bound by Guinevere." I shrug with mock indignation.

"That Chavela's one smart chick. Thank her for me. I hope her and Julian are well. I've got a gift for him in my bag. I'll take Guinevere back to the Big Easy for a Bloody Mary at my favorite watering hole."

Around 4 a.m. we doze off; something wakes me up. I'm grateful for the chance to watch him sleep. He's almost smiling with a content look on his boyish face. I'm filled with joy and crystallize this in a storehouse of precious memories to replay when averting the muddy river of reality. Annoyingly remembering, what I want to forget, and *tragically, forgetting what I want to remember.*

Overthinking will dog me my whole life. The next couple of years will be like pulling a rabbit out of a hat. Now you see him, now you don't. We can't get enough of each other, and leave the room only for meals and long walks in the crisp mountain air, along the winding, mountain creek that ran the length of Manitou Falls.

The Holy Longing

Tell a wise person, or else keep silent,
because the mass man will mock it right away.
I praise what is truly alive,
what longs to be burned to death.
In the calm water of the love-nights,
where you were begotten, where you have begotten,
a strange feeling comes over you,
when you see the silent candle burning.
Now you are no longer caught in the obsession with darkness,
and a desire for higher lovemaking sweeps you upward
Distance does not make you falter.
Now, arriving in magic, flying
and finally, insane for the light,
you are the butterfly and you are gone.
And so long as you haven't experienced this:
to die and so to grow,
you are only a troubled guest on the dark earth

–Johann Wolfgang von Goethe

Get Back on the Horse

There is no remedy for Love,
but to Love more.
–Henry David Thoreau

C HA CHA HANDS ME THE GODDESS OONAGH card: "Prima, isn't she right-on? She's the Goddess of Easy Does It— *There is no need to hurry or force things to happen. Everything is occurring in perfect timing.*"

Along with us for the adventure in the Volkswagen camper van is Finn, a friend of Nigel's. An ebullient, fresh-faced, fellow mountaineer and "day hopper" at Sacred Heart School. They've been best friends since serving in the Civil Air Patrol rescue cadet squadron now disbanded. It's how Nigel acquired the old army surplus, cross-country ski equipment.

We're tooling southeast on Highway 69, heading to Rainbow Trail, which is at the base of the iconic, Southern Rocky Mountain range of the Sangre de Cristo Mountains— *The Blood of Christ.* The trail runs 110 miles along its eastern edge from Salida to Westcliffe, Colorado. It's a gentle hiker's trail with spectacular views of the Wet Mountain Valley. Starting at the elevation of 7800 feet to 9400 feet at the top. The tallest sand dunes in North America glinted at its western base.

Father Francis Torres, a missionary, named the range during an exploration of the area. He died from wounds by native slaves he mistreated. While he lay dying, the alpenglow of the sunset hit the snow-capped mountains in a burst of red. He exclaimed, "Sangre de Cristo, Sangre de Cristo! The Blood of Christ." This area attracted a spiritual community. The Ute shamans called it *"Bloodless Valley"* because of its sacred space of peace, spiritual power, and prohibition against warfare.

Nigel grew up in Red Cañon after he graduated from high school, he moved to Denver. He worked as a mountain guide for four years and returned a couple of months ago. His parents still live here. He's downright giddy—it's a windless day, topped off with a clear, cerulean sky. The weather feels like an affirmation: *perfect conditions for cross-country skiing,* the kind of day people move to the mountains for. He plans to win me over with his guitar skills but to share cross-country skiing together *was pure gift.* A sliver of good fortune after a string of bad breaks.

We went to Rainbow Trail on family picnics but no one we knew cross-country or downhill skied. Both are rich peoples' sports that require expensive equipment.

My Grandfather Frank was *a true vaquero,* a third-generation Colorado rancher and *one of the last real cowboys.* He worked as a foreman nearby for the Taylor Ranch in Texas Creek years ago.

Cha Cha's adorable in her army jacket with snow bunny earmuffs. We wear blue jeans with long johns underneath. *Denim is the worst gear* for skiing because it takes forever to dry. *If you're wet, you're cold.* By next trip, we'll borrow ski gaiters to wrap around the bottoms of our jeans.

"Is cross-country skiing hard? *I'm a-scared,*" Cha Cha jokes. Finn's in the backseat. He leans forward so he can hear.

"It's a piece of cake. Are you athletic?" he asks. We both cackled.

"In junior high, she used to beat the goat ropers in track, football, and basketball. She'll slay it," I boast.

We have lunch and canteens of water in our backpacks. We arrive at the Alvarado Campground. Nigel jumps out of the van and says he needs to wax skis. It could take awhile.

"If you want to stretch your legs, take a bathroom break, or smoke a joint, feel free," he suggests while lighting up a cigarette.

"Not a chance—won't get high while attempting a new sport," I said.

"Who brought the dope?" Cha Cha asks.

The skis look like 2X4 boards, the equipment is ancient, but I don't care, it's thrilling to try something new, and to get out of Red Cañon. I grab Cha Cha's hand and pull her to the campground bathroom. We breathe in the tingling piney air.

"Nigel's cute in a gnomish way," I sigh. She follows me into the thick stink of the drab cinderblock outhouse.

"Rosie, let's get loose-goosey and have fun today, when we reach the top, we'll get ripped. How hard is gliding downhill?" She grins.

"I feel disingenuous with Nigel like I'm leading him on. I only want to be friends."

Cha Cha waves her arm over her head, like a cowgirl at a rodeo about to rope a calf. In her best John Wayne voice: *"Just get back on the horse, little lady!"* She sways back and forth.

"*¡Ayyy, Chavela!*" I blip—pinch her *chiche*—breast. We almost didn't hear Nigel calling us above the squeals of laughter.

Nigel had all the skis laid out. "We're ready to rumble, only one set needed wax. I want to be at the top of Hobbit Hill by lunchtime, so we can make it down before dark."

"Yes, Capitán, *Hi-Ho Silver. Exit stage right.*" Cha Cha salutes our fearless leader.

"Whoa! Am I going to be able to maneuver these 7-foot-long boards?" I guffaw at the length of the skis. I'm all of five feet tall.

He helps us put on the odd leather shoes. Lacing up and sliding them into the steel bindings on the skis. Then hands us our ski poles, his focus is meticulous and methodical.

"Glide around and find your balance, while I put my shoes on," Nigel said.

Finn's ready to go, he checks a light meter for the 35 mm camera he brought to take photos of the pristine Alpine mountain lake at the top of the trail. They've hiked this trail many times and climbed Lake of the Clouds, Crestone Needle, and Humbolt Peak. Nigel is a skilled and experienced mountaineer.

"Is it OK to shove off? I'll forge a path for y'all to follow." Finn said.

"Perfect—we'll see you up top." Nigel waves. Finn glides away and quickly slides into a smooth rhythm, back and forth in the deep, glittering powder.

"No one's up here, there are no tracks. We usually don't bring girls on ski outings. Hope they can cut it." He ruminates when Cha Cha blasts past him.

"Hey, slowpoke Rodriquez!" she taunts.

Nigel signals for me to go ahead of him. I'm cruising at a fast clip until one of the ski tips bogs down in the deep, powdery snow. It pitches me forward and lays me out flat on my

face. I'm laughing too hard to be embarrassed. After he wit-
nesses a few more humiliating falls, I turn to him. "You go
ahead with Finn and Cha Cha, I've got this." I wouldn't feel
abandoned if he skied with the others.

"No Rose, I'd rather stay with you. I'm savoring the view."
It is breathtaking between the Aspen groves of shimmering spun
gold, the pop of green sagebrush, and the spotty Junipers. The
Wet Mountain Valley spell broken only by the dusty, snake-
like country roads, and intricate patchwork of compact home-
steads, down below. In front of us looms a panoramic view of
a magnificent series of snow-capped vistas.

My soul is receiving a profound psychic scrubbing. The intense burning of my thighs during the gradual climb surprises
me. I delight in the small stream that runs along the trail with
its soothing babbling. Finn and Cha Cha are long gone and will
wait awhile for us at the top.

"Sorry, I'm so slow," I shout over my shoulder. I'm discouraged and mask my frustration and impatience with myself. I
look up, and he's waiting for me—*again.*

"Give yourself a break, *it's your first time.*" He's thrilled
to have me all to himself. A jackrabbit scurries alongside us,
itching to race. "Not a chance buddy, you'd beat me, hands
down." Two-thirds up the mountain toward the crest, I turn
around.

"I need to stop for water." I'm so thirsty.

"Of course, I'm sorry, cross-country skiing is a vigorous
sport. Keeping hydrated is vital. This is Hobbit Hill," he said.

"No, this is a lame excuse to give my legs a rest. I'm experiencing a new kind of thigh burn. I'm going to be sore tomorrow." I'm shocked *how this is kicking my ass.*

"It works all the core muscles." He affirmed. We sit next to each other on a hollowed-out log, sharing water from his canteen absorbing the astounding grandeur of the Wet Mountain Valley on a south-facing knoll. A Hobbit might jump out from behind one of the stunted trees.

"Nigel, thank you. *It's flat-out magical.* I'm having a blast." My flushed cheeks are carnation pink, and my forehead glistens with beads of sweat. He wants to kiss me, but something stops him.

"Rose, I overheard you and Cha Cha, are you getting over a breakup? If you don't want to talk about it, I'll understand," he said.

"No, I'm relieved you asked. My boyfriend of two years left in May, he's going to college in Louisiana. We're in contact and still together. Nigel, *all we can be is friends.* I should've told you sooner." I look over at him.

"I get it, everything's topsy-turvy. I'll be your friend, Rose." His downcast eyes register deep disappointment.

"Shall we, I'm sure Finn thinks we abandoned him with Cha Cha." I'm uncomfortable.

The trail flattens out at the summit. *I'm stunned*; the small, pristine Alpine lake makes me gasp. The glass-like water mirrors the majestic beauty surrounding us. There are lush, green, pungent, sagebrush, Ponderosa Pine, and Douglas-Fir trees surrounding us. It smells of pine sap, fresh lake water with musky, earthy, red clay. *A nirvana place for the replenishment of the soul, body, and spirit.* I haven't experienced this Holy Wholeness since sitting on the riverbank watching the sunrise with Jack... *A lifetime ago.*

"Awwwmazing! Finn, did you take some beautiful shots of this heavenly place?" I ask, huffing out of breath.

"Yep, it's gorgeous, isn't it? So worth the workout, I forget how it feels to see it for the first time," Finn said. Content with our achievement, we eat lunch, and Nigel smokes a cigarette.

I don't want to leave and concoct ways to homestead and live forever on the Rainbow Trail. Chipmunks in the brush argue over a crust of bread. The mountain air wind melody lures me sweetly. *The pines in the wind sing your name.*

"This meadow in the springtime is full of wildflowers. Waves of cornflower blue Columbines, did you know its the Colorado State flower? We've seen a family of beavers up here." Finn's talking in fast spurts.

"Did you guys get high without us?" I ask.

Nigel gives me space to *just be,* the most generous gift as I worked through stages of grief. On some days I rose above the sorrow, on others sadness gripped me; only activity and movement released me from this dark radiating place.

Nigel the Angel, an apt nickname, is the purest, kindest soul. *Blessed are the gentle, they shall have the earth. Blessed are the pure in heart: for they shall see God.* When I listen to his music, or we just sit and talk, I'm healed by such natural peace, like at *The River*—cleansed of life's irritants.

Nigel is accepted in our circle. We hangout at his place and on weekends and go to the band's gigs. I receive a sliver of sunlight, a breakthrough after a lively night of music. He's rehearsing with his bandmates while I read a book of poems. A veil lifts and I cross over to the other shore. I yield to, rather than oppose the *flow of The River of Life.*

I stop stewing in the sadness and the illusion of Jack... *I'm finally cured of.* His passive ways and family loyalties help me concede that I would never be a priority. I push aside purblind stubbornness. *I must move on,* let him go, rewire my brain. Above all, I want to stop missing him. I call back all my energy and release the past—so to live in the present.

Nigel's alarmed by the odd look on my face. "Are you OK?" He asks during one of the breaks of the rehearsal. I didn't want to disrupt the harmonious jamming.

"I'm fine," I assure him. My ego hijacked my body creating an anxiety gap about the future that took me out of the present moment; *it robbed me of my joy.* Just watching the ego creates consciousness and cycles of success.

Nigel holds it together, excitement building, but notices a distinct change in me. This *new Rose blossoms in full splendor.* Nigel, my emotional healing Band-Aid, pulls me through the school year, graduation, and into a new life. I abandon him as abruptly as Jack did me. The universe needs kind, Loving souls like Nigel to heal the broken parts that are abused and hurt. *He was the purest of gifts.*

At the end of the summer, Nigel drives me to Boulder to the University of Colorado.

Dad and Nigel sit hunched over in the dark Ramirez living room with *their hearts dismantled.* He stops by after returning from Boulder. Mom told me later that she stayed in the kitchen and cried alone allowing the men to share their grief.

Don knocks on the door. She let him in. "Is Rosie gone?" He finds a chair in the tiny living room. He knows of Nigel, but they've never met.

"Yep, she's moved to Boulder. Nigel, this is our nephew, Don. Nigel just took Rosie to University of Colorado," Blaze said with tearful eyes cast down. "I can't believe my baby girl is gone forever."

"Tío, is my job done?" Don asks jokingly to lighten the mood.

"*You did an excellent job* keeping our beautiful Rose safe. Thank you from the bottom of our hearts." He stands and gathers Don and Nigel in a group hug, and chokes back the tears.

Crash & Burn

What cannot be said
Will be wept
–Sappho

M Y FRESHMAN YEAR AT UNIVERSITY OF COLORADO in Boulder was a dangerous blur of *self-destruction*. I was like one of the corralled wild mustangs my dad wrangled at the Taylor Ranch in the Sangre de Cristo Mountains—*running free with the gate left open*.

Combine excessive partying with extra difficult classes: Philosophy, Biology and lab, and a senior level Creative Writing class. I was *doomed to fail*. At the end of the school year, I returned to Red Cañon defeated and broken. *The only bright light in my life was Jack*. We're still writing and calling infrequently. He had transferred from Tulane University to Texas A&M.

I moved back home, after a few weeks we we're invited to Grandma Grace's for dinner. My first cousin Pearl and family are visiting from northern California. Pearl is my dad's niece; the daughter of his sister, Trish, the oldest and only daughter of the Ramirez clan. Trish married a man from the Bay Area years ago and they lived in San Leandro, California.

Pearl married her high school sweetheart Geo, a robust, handsome Italian. They have three, gorgeous children, two boys, and a girl, under the age of ten. This is their first road trip vacation and visit with their great grandparents and relatives in Colorado.

A typical family dinner at Grandma Grace's consists of crispy, golden fried chicken, mashed potatoes, green chili with chunks of savory pork, homemade pinto beans, thick tortillas and her signature dessert of lemon meringue pie.

Uncle Bernie claims Pearl and I are identical, because we have similar features. She is fetching with thick, black curly hair, coal black eyes, and a bubbly personality. The comparisons stop at the physical. She's content being a stay-at-home Mom and housewife. My ambition skyrockets into the stratosphere but temporarily the firepower has fizzled out.

During dinner, Pearl asks the question everyone is curious about: "Rosie, are you returning to CU in the fall?" I want to jump into the vat of mashed potatoes Grandma Grace so graciously placed in front of me.

"No, I'm not sure what's next except that I want out of Red Cañon," I said.

"I may be getting ahead of myself because I haven't discussed this with Geo, but you could return with us to San Leandro, spend the summer helping me with the kids, then find a job. If it doesn't work out, come back home." She had the glimmer of a dare in her eyes.

"That's a tempting and generous offer. Let me know what you decide." An exhilarating idea, I can barely sit through dinner, the timing so perfect, *a fresh, new start for me.*

One week later, June of 1976—I moved to northern California. *Go West, young woman.* The second that tricked out party van crossed into Golden California *I tumbled, steadfast in Love with the most thrilling of Lovers.* What's not to Love—the perfect weather and the progressive lifestyle. Time to reinvent myself from the ruins of my choices. *I'm all of nineteen years of age.*

The summer whips by, and I start a job as a bank teller. Pearl and I are at a softball game, and she introduces me to an old high school friend, Evan. He's a ceramic artist. I'm eager to meet anyone outside of Pearl's suburban neighborhood. He's totally wrong for me—a quiet and shy introvert eight years older.

At first, he impresses me—pulling out all the stops. We see the art house films in Berkeley, dine at a favorite crepe shop and browse Cody's Books, the legendary bookstore. We attend his famous artist friends art shows at galleries in San Francisco. He maintains this level of excitement for a year.

I battled with Aunt Trish about spending nights at Evan's. She didn't approve of our having premarital sex. I lived under strict rules all my life; *no one is going to dictate to me.*

Evan barely survives on art installation work when his brother offers him a sales position at a building supply store in the Sierra Nevada foothills. He asks me to move with him. Aunt Trish almost blows a gasket when I tell her. She rails about *living in sin,* and how her brother would blame her when he finds out. My response: "Who's going to tell him?"

We visit Evan's brother in Pleasant City during the holidays before moving there. An adorable town near Lake Tahoe, where the oaks turn to pines, with towering redwoods that challenge the imagination in the Sierra Nevada Mountains. A friendly area with a rural flavor, surrounded by picturesque vineyards known for its exceptional Zinfandel grapes.

We rent a two-bedroom duplex, and for the first year, it's comfortable and steady. Alas, Evan reveals his true nature; moody and indolent. He goes to work, watches TV and to bed. Every day's the same, rinse and repeat, including weekends. I turn into an old Hausfrau at the age of twenty.

Jack's still the one, and *he is always in the periphery*. I write and call but can't muster the courage to invite him to California. Every conversation, I describe how beautiful, fun, and exciting, it is to live here. I thrived in the make-believe land of Rose and Jack. I call him one spring evening after Evan goes to bed and we talk for hours; finally, *what the hell*—without thinking it through, I invite him to visit.

"Why don't you come out?" I ask.

"I'd like that," he said with enthusiasm.

He's to fly from Dallas to Sacramento, I pick him up at the airport, and we'll go camping in Lake Tahoe. It'll be heaven. I mention a roommate *but don't tell him that he's my boyfriend*.

I attend the community college and work as a teacher's aide at an Elementary school with first-grade teacher Viv, we become fast friends. I also work part-time as a teacher's aide at a preschool.

When not at work or school, I jog, play tennis, and check out books from the public library down the street. I'm euphoric, living in this beautiful town but barely have enough money to live on. My goal is: *"Once Jack's here, life will fall into place."* He's the only missing link that my heart pines for and my soul desires.

If only I'd explained to Jack how unhappy I was with Evan. I didn't trust him to have that uncomfortable conversation. Evan maintains the perfect poker face, but deep down, he knows.

Jack comes in July for a week-long visit. I can't contain my excitement, and it hurt Evan. Three years of smoke and mirrors, it's like acting in a movie in the wrong part. Jack arrives at the airport and is blindsided by my living with a boyfriend and is furious I misled him.

My initial plan was to pick up Jack and go straight to Lake Tahoe for the week. I didn't want them to meet. Evan convinces me that I'm not capable of going to the airport to pick up my friend. He wanted to check out the competition. During the hour-long drive to the foothills, I'm wedged between them in my 1965, Chevy Nova. Jack drapes his arm over my shoulder. Evan seethed.

The next three, long, torturous days I juggle Jack's hurt feelings while appeasing Evan. I learned from Evan that *change is painful, but nothing is as painful as staying with someone you don't belong with.*

Jack enters our stark but homey, bright yellow, duplex in downtown Pleasant City. He plops down on the maroon corduroy, floppy, beanbag couch with a perplexed frown on his face.

"So, what's the story with this Evan character? He acts as if he owns you. Do you want me to clean his clock?" Evan's in the kitchen making a sandwich and can hear Jack's every word from the attached room.

"Jack, I'm sorry, I didn't tell you I was living with a boyfriend. I was afraid you wouldn't come." I look down at my hands.

"Damn right! I wouldn't have come. Why did you trick me?" I've never seen him this angry. We sit and stare blankly at the television till Evan goes to bed.

Evan's bedroom door closes, I lean toward Jack and kiss him. He's still fuming, but my warm kisses melt him. Our high school bodies reconnect with our adult ones. It's every bit as wonderful if not better than in high school. I let Love lead the way. Jack responds to my kisses, and we lock in a tight embrace, laying on the couch. We're tumbling into the familiar passion of the past when we hear a loud, forceful shout from Evan in the bedroom: "Rose come to bed!"

Jack grabs my hand as I got up to go to the bedroom. "Figure out a way for us to be alone, I can't be with this asshole my whole trip. I may do something I'll regret," he warns.

"We'll camp at Lake Tahoe and sort this out. I'm so sorry," I whisper and hug him.

It's a bright, perky summer morning and Evan goes to work like he does every day. Evan goes to work as he did every day. I make Jack breakfast, and we pack for our camping trip to Lake Tahoe. I follow him into the guest bedroom that has a single daybed, bookshelves, full of books, and a desk. I reassure him how much fun our trip to Lake Tahoe will be.

"*Work with me, here.*" He's not even listening.

"Fat chance, is there an airport in Tahoe? I'll catch a plane there. I can't wait to get the hell out of California," he said.

I'm crushed, and about to cry. He spins me around leans me over the daybed, slips off my running shorts and enters me from behind. I don't resist, I'd fantasized about this moment, and while it was happening, I'm numb.

After the brisk and dismissive encounter, it's as if a door clanged shut; he doesn't touch me again. He forgets it as soon as he's gone.

That evening Evan returns from work, we go to dinner at a favorite Mexican Restaurant. They glower at each other over the red and white checkered tablecloth. I don't know what possesses me to play the song *Torn Between Two Lovers* on the jukebox. Jack's red-faced and about to explode. He shoots eye-daggers at me. I've lost him forever. One misstep after another.

"To breathe the air the angels breathe, go to Lake Tahoe," Mark Twain once wrote. It's a favorite and magical place that I'd looked forward to sharing with Jack.

We pull into the campsite, the sun is setting, and we're running out of light. We set up the tent, and build a fire. The tension is so thick we need to talk this out, *but I'm frozen with fear.* Why didn't I beg forgiveness and promise to do anything to fix this? We hear barking, howling, *it's so close.* A pack of coyotes surrounds us.

"Just fucking, *RICH!* What's next, swarms of locust and lightning strikes?" He scowled. Only by the Grace of God, we weren't ripped apart by wild coyotes. There's no way to fix this shitstorm. I've broken his heart and will never see or hear from him again. *It's all fun and games till someone gets hurt.*

The next morning after a scary, sexless, sleepless night. Coyotes yelped and cried all night long. We silently broke down camp. I drive him to the small airport a few miles down the highway. He boards a puddle jumper to Sacramento and vanishes from my life without a peck on the cheek or an *au revoir*. The man I had planned to spend my life with, seven years blown to smithereens.

He was meant to be mine.

I severed a sacred cord, so in Love, with him, it hurt, pain so deep and real. *Dread and bliss, two faces of the same divinity.* At twenty-two, I lacked confidence, courage, and strength of will to demand his whole attention. Add *his lack of conviction,* and it was the death knell to our relationship. I questioned if Jack ever Loved me.

I lost him and my other significant Robust Love—*California.* The enchantment shattered. Leaving would be difficult but staying would be worse. I retreat to Colorado bumming a ride with a hippie couple driving to the East Coast. I split from my beloved, California, *for now.* I'll be back because I belong here; *this is home.*

I failed at college and now, at Love. I crashed and *burned twice by the same flame.* I have learned now not to go back or retrace steps wishing it to be as before—it never is. Many years pass before I transform the errors and illusions of the *tenaciousness of Real Love* and how it prevails over obstacles of time, space, and place. The breakup is a salient point in my life. All things happen for the best, for a beautiful and *Divine reason.* Grace builds on Grace. (John 1:16).

There is such a joyful look on my father's face when the hippie van pulls up with his baby girl, safe inside. So grateful for a family and home to return to, even under such sad circumstances. *Home is what catches you when you fall—and we all fall.* I lived in northern California for four years.

Star Watcher

River Dance

Migrating to Manitou
biting wind on cheeks
glittering snow crunched
squeaky underfoot

Dance to the wind's melody
rippling rush of The River
trill of the songbird

Moment of presence
You flow in me like a riverbed
receiving and letting go at the same time

Joyful at what was... what is
nurture what will be
Grace forms a void—
then fills it

River of Holy Mystery
exist as it is
hands and hearts wide open

Love—Ever Present
Love—Evermore

THE UTE INDIANS wintered in Red Cañon every year, since 1300 AD. The visiting clan from the eastern plains called them the *"Blue Sky People."* The even blue sky was perpetually overhead. This area served as a war line between the mountainous domain of the Ute and territory of the eastern plains Indians. Sporadic tribal fighting kept settlers away until the early 1800's. The gold rush of 1859, brought them to Red Cañon.

The Ute stop at a pristine, hot springs 10 miles from the Arkansas River. The natural hot springs with its bubbly sulfur magic cast a spell on the weary travelers migrating many miles from the higher regions. They relax for two days soaking in the hot volcanic pool. Located on a flat, high red desert plain of sagebrush, with Whitetail deer, antelope, possum, and rabbits. *An endless horizon full of promise*, with its bluebird sky and wave-tilted clouds.

Upon arrival, they thank The Great Spirit for safe passage by smoking the sacred pipe, burning sage, sweetgrass, and doing the *blessing of the four directions.* They drum, dance, and sing songs about Manitou, the name of this precious paradise. They feast on roasted prairie dog and juniper berry mush, with *piñones* fry bread.

After the celebration, they move into Red Cañon to set up winter camp near the rich refuge of the Arkansas River. This area teems with wild game: deer, elk, wild boar, and fish. Also, beaver, rabbit, squirrel, porcupine, prairie dog, and chipmunk supplements the food supply. *The ideal, bounteous, safe place to spend the winter.*

Under a cloudless cobalt sky, Grey Wolf, Chief of the Ute sets out on a hunting trip, with his sons and best braves. He leaves two braves behind for protection of the women and children at the camp. Nearby, the Blackfoot, also, settles in the area for the winter. They're on the verge of starving, lacking the hunting prowess of the Ute. Blackfoot braves sneak into the Ute camp after everyone goes to sleep. They steal their meat, pemmican, (dried meat mixed with melted fat, flour, molasses, and suet) all provender stockpiled for the long, harsh winter.

Grey Wolf spots a Red-tailed hawk motionless still balanced in the air and has a premonition of the wrongdoing. They track the Blackfoot thieves to their camp and kill them. Grey Wolf spares one baby girl, after stabbing her mother. He picks up the baby admiring the exquisite, beaded belt wrapped around her. He brings the infant to his wife to raise.

Little Petra, grows into a stunning, smart, Indian princess. Around the campfire, they told a legend about a courageous Indian warrior who died and turned into a star. Intrigued, Petra gazed at the pulsing stars for hours on the razorback ridge, the (hogbacks) earning the nickname, *"The Star Watcher."* Forty billion stars kept her full of wonder.

The Blackfoot vow revenge and wait for the perfect opportunity to attack the Ute camp. It came twelve years later when the Ute return to their favorite encampment by the Arkansas River. Blackfoot Buffalo Chief and his band of braves wait till nightfall and attack the Ute camp. During the relentless slaughter, Buffalo Chief kills an Indian maiden crawling toward him. A moment after, he recognizes the beautiful intricate beaded belt *made with Love* by his dead wife for his child. He realizes he just killed his daughter!

Heartbroken, he buries her on the side of the mountain. As Buffalo Chief rides away, he stops to look back and watches the grand mountain morph into *"The Star Watcher."* Petra's

soft, silhouetted shape against the dark sky, worshiping the
stars she adored.

◄────────•────────►

Skyview Drive is *breathtakingly beautiful...* At its highest
point, the panoramic view of Red Cañon is spectacular—being that high made you feel *so ALIVE.* The road's a two-mile,
scenic drive across a razorback ridge built in 1903 by convict
chain gangs in Red Cañon. Free labor enabled city planners to
complete challenging projects. Red Cañon's first prison was the
Colorado Territorial Prison built in 1871.

Skyview Drive is on the outskirts of Red Cañon it runs parallel to U.S. Highway 50. The Fred Flintstone-like rock arch-
way entrance starts with a gradual incline up a razorback ridge.
It climbs like a roller coaster ride, falling away 800 feet on both
sides. A one-way, one lane, 15 mph speed limit, a narrow road
that fits only one car, no Recreational Vehicles allowed.

Sagebrush dots the dry and dusty landscape with large
limestone boulders jutting up from the ground. Skyview Drive
was a jovial, exciting, thrill-seeking party place for the younger crowd. One side is the cityscape of Red Cañon and the
Arkansas River Valley. The other side is an exhilarating view
of the mountain peak known as *"Star Watcher."* Named after a
slain Indian princess, a legend we're told by our parents.

Negative karma from the prisoners seeped in during the
construction of the road. Horrendous accidents and suicides
occurred on Skyview Drive. Tragic car wrecks by young people
under the influence drive up to park or as a dare, and end up
plunging down hundreds of feet into a washout.

Running parallel to the road are three, large earthen humps
called *"hogbacks."* Smaller razorback ridges that locals frolic

on sleds and inner-tubes during the winter in an ethereal snowy wonderland.

My friend Buck tells of when in high school while delivering newspapers in a neighborhood at the base of the hogbacks he's startled by a massive fireball bursting on Skyview Drive and rushed to the accident. The firemen and police discovered a man who came up on a parked car in the middle of the road and didn't have enough time to stop. He shoved his young boy and the dog out of the car, saving them before plunging to his death.

Another tragedy involved three brothers celebrating one of them graduating from high school. They ran off the road and were all killed. A recent suicide occurred when a teenage boy overdosed, his body found by the hogbacks. Allegedly, a woman caregiver had molested him.

Cha Cha is fortunate she isn't a Skyview Drive statistic. A crazy, Inuit, boy named Chino moves into the house next door when she was thirteen. Cha Cha recounted the time he picked her up in his old, white truck, "Let's go for a ride." At Skyview Drive's entrance, he jumped out, forced her over into the driver's seat: *"Time to learn to drive!"*

She inched up the steep incline road, not daring to look over the side of the car. A quick glance over the edge *totally freaked her out;* she stared straight ahead. There's a horrific, hairpin curve on the decline that frightened her; she took it extra slow. One night that nutjob Chino shut off the headlights while she's driving. She screamed, pulled over and refused to drive. She heard that he was killed in prison in a fight over a pack of cigarettes.

My most poignant memory of Skyview Drive is from my early twenties when I return from living in Northern California after a clusterfuck of failures. I found a temporary bartending job, in a fake Western town (tourist trap) next to the world's largest suspension bridge, 10 miles outside of Red Cañon.

The only highlight was the comedic outlaw gunfighters, who put on hourly shows for the tourist. They loitered in the bar to harass and tease me. Also, the river rafter guides rolling in cash. Money flowed from the hoards of tourist who came from all over the world to raft the wild, white water of the magnificent, Arkansas River.

One slow Monday, early evening at closing time, a foreign exchange student from France wandered into the 1800's style, Western bar. I serve him a draft beer. I'm tired and want to clean up and go home to rest my achy feet. None of the usual suspects drop in the first part of the week. The coast is clear for a quick getaway.

He has long black, hair and soulful, blue-gray eyes; he tries to rope me into a conversation. I go about wiping tables and wash the huge beer mugs piled up on the bar. *"Please, drink your beer and hitchhike into town while the cars head that way."* I murmur under my breath at the backpacker whose on the hunt for a place to sleep tonight. I have no intention of playing *Hostess with the Mostest* to Mr. Frenchy.

"What's it like growing up here?" he asks in a soft voice, as I breeze past him.

"Freezing, arctic cold in the winter, spectacular in the summer, friendly people, like any rural town. I just returned from northern California, near Lake Tahoe. I can't wait to return. I'm burnt-out on Red Cañon, *too many ghosts here."*

He traveled all through the states and is at the end of his trip. Weariness oozed from him. I sympathize with how exhausting to go from each location not knowing a soul or where to sleep.

"I've seen the Royal Gorge, Denver, Pikes Peak, Colorado City, Garden of the Gods, and the Air Force Academy. What else is there to see? What's Skyview Drive? I got stuck standing by the sign, hitchhiking here to Buckskin Bart's." he said in a sexy, French accent.

I look at my watch. "If you wait till I close up, we can catch the sunset on Skyview Drive it's quite the scenic spot," I offer.

"Sure, is there a youth hostel in Red Cañon?" he asks.

"No, but we can drive by the Lazy Daizy Motel on Main Street and find you a room."

We drive to the top, middle section of the sky-high, narrow, one-way road of Skyview Drive. I park by a small, old, wooden shack used at one time to sell drinks and tourist tchotchkes. Behind it, drops a narrow path worn by years of kids using it for a private place to party and watch the sunset. Huge limestone boulders jut up on the side of the hill. I jump from one to the other, full of nervous energy.

We settle on a comfortable flat rock to watch the rosy, ocher streaked, end of summer fiesta sunset. I'm so bereft, empty and lost, back where I started. Colorado is my motherland but Northern California is my home; *my heart cries out for you— California!* I'll find a way back.

"What's the name of that mountain?" Frenchy points across from our perch.

"She's called *The Star Watcher.*" I tell him the story about the Indian princess. I'm exhausted with the weight of the maiden's stone heavy misgivings on my broken heart. *It hurts deeply when you can't Love the man you want.*

I'm sitting on the same rock, and look up at the same massy, star-speckled sky. Her world perfectly suited her needs: mine uncertain and lacking. I imagined the Indian princess Petra lived a full life, and when killed by her father, didn't know it was him. I need a wholehearted soul-clearing cry. I disliked how these minor distractions drain me. I frittered away most of my twenties *on all the wrong people.*

The calcium in our bones, iron in our blood; humans built from exploding stars from the big bang explosion. *We are stardust; Joni was right-on.*

I beg the brightness of the stars to burn away my sadness and wail at the ancestors to heal my broken heart and help me break free from this cruel chimera... I reach into my pocket and pull out a cigarette, unravel the paper, and lay the loose tobacco at the base of the limestone rock. *La ofrenda*—an offering for Petra to escape this *Ghost Town of Squandered and Lost Love.*

"Great Spirit, I offer myself to Thee to do with me as Thou wilt. Relieve me of the bondage of self, that I may better do Thy will. Take away my difficulties, that victory over them may bear witness to those I would help of Thy Power, Thy Love, and Thy Way of Life. May I do Thy will always." I recite the Third Step prayer.

"*Happy counting, Star Watcher.*" I stare at the dark purple sky to see the slow dance of the infinite stars; the biggest watch me with your eyes.

———— ⚓ ————

Before & After

1984 - 2016

———— ⚓ ————

There comes a point in your life when you realize:
Who matters,
Who never did,
Who won't anymore,
And who always will.
So, don't worry about people from your past,
There's a reason why they didn't make it to your future.

–Adam Lindsay Gordon

Diamond Among the Rocks

Altar de mis Amores Preciosos

Between the rational spaces of the brain
they camp out like demanding children—mewing
"Look at me!"

Resigned. Stuffed down. Pushed away.
Hiding underground waiting for eons

Time doesn't obey our commands

Tenderhearted memories conjure up
and mold into flesh and bone
Connect and communicate
Soar like Eagles

Years trailing backward—forward

Words fetched you back,
fountain of tears wept
hearts cracked wide open,
poked and prodded
Mine the garden of sorrow

Past ~ Present ~ Future

The Holy Trinity of Regret
If Only's
What If's
Could've Been's
Nostalgia's False God's
refuse to be inconsequential

L OVE 101: *To know how to Love is the supreme work of our lifetime.* I hightailed it back to Colorado at the tender age of twenty-three, leaving northern California in 1979. I entered into a five-year dark place of sorrow. A barren passage of long-ing and regret, awash in guilt for opportunities squandered. I connected with men, now known as "friends with benefits" (not coined in 1979). In hindsight, *there were no benefits* just the occasional warm body to stave off loneliness. Afterward, the emptiness boomeranged back, with intrinsic worth taking a major hit for the Rose Team.

I kept an exhausted squad of angel guides scrambling on their toes—*so grateful for my safekeeping.* A secure time before statistics of between one in five female college students will ex-perience rape or form of sexual assault. One in three women suffers sexual violence, which is systematically underreported.

Jack used to tease me that I totally ruled when it came to our sexuality. Girls growing up in the seventies, on the cusp of the sexual revolution, were sexual pioneers pushing into unknown territory. During this period and into the eighties, *a woman decided whether a guy got to first base, second base or went all the way.*

A paradigm shift happened in the eighties-nineties, where a woman saying no or taking the lead was ignored. Aggressive men snubbed past societal rules. The wave of Consent Laws will help change the landscape, swinging the pendulum back to women's protection. Males need to understand that they need to hear 'yes' before proceeding with a sexual encounter.

When choosing a "boyfriend or girlfriend worthy" partner, a criterion of quality is essential, allowing only the upper eche-lon to *bestow upon the most, extraordinary, rare, mysterious, sacred of gifts given,* and shared with another person.

Crucial elements must come together: mind, body, emo-tions, and soul, *to give your heart to someone.* The utmost, profound, and transcendent, of experiences requires care, thought, and caution. *The goal is pure physical resonance with our inner being, to experience total rapture and the beauty of being alive.* Joy balanced with responsibility.

Entitled reciprocity and the ability to express one's needs and wants will deter from unsatisfying relations. Shrewd judg-ment is needed when deciding who to make memories with—they can leave permanent scars like an invisible emotional tat-too that doesn't go away.

During this five-year period of numbing despair, I received my share of scars. The *Boyfriend Bermuda Triangle* was a looming lacuna after Jack. An aggregate of characters that ar-en't list worthy. I'd like to scrub all the dufus moronicus' from my memory banks. I feared to be alone but not until I realized my worth did I stop giving discounts. Not everyone lost is a loss.

One ginormous frog, the ultimate Jabba the Hutt of Bad Boyfriends, was extra abhorrent. I'm ashamed *I wasted my precious youth, beauty, and Love, on him* but learned an in-valuable lesson of life—Maya Angelou: "Believe people the first time they show you who they are."

He ended the era of shitdom. If they claim to Love you, but raise a hand and strike you, *it's a deal breaker*. Actions roar volumes. He pushed me to a point where I no longer feared being alone and broke a wooden tennis racquet over his fat, Humpty Dumpty head. After you mister, *Hell would be easy*.

And then.... there was Hunter Lane. I meet him through Chavela who snags a primo research assistant job with him. He's a renowned writer of Indigenous Peoples' History books. His father was a past mayor of Red Cañon, a historian, and preservationist. A confirmed bachelor, who lives alone and is five years older than me. *The quintessential, Colorado mountain man with good looks, charm, and brains.*

I pick up Chavela from his office on a Friday afternoon. I work at a television station in Colorado City and come for a weekend visit. He stands next to her desk going over manuscript notes. I breeze in, what catches my eye is the shoulder length, chestnut brown hair, and a bushy, Civil War style, mustache.

"Hey, Cha Cha—ready to go? Hi, I'm Rose, Chavela's chauffeur." I laugh. He reaches and extends his hand, "I'm Hunter." He shoots me a beaming smile as wide as a valley and holds my gaze with big, sparkly, russet eyes. My heart flutters, like a flurry of small hands.

He shuffles around the desk to get closer. I'm excited by the direct laser beam focus.

"Where you girls headed?" He asks.

"The nearest happy hour." I flash a million-kilowatt smile and take note of his demeanor: an intelligent, relaxed, hippy vibe.

"Hoist one for me." He gives me a buoyant wink.

I'm light-headed. Steady sister, I take deep breaths to steel myself.

Cha Cha jumps in the front seat of my car, "Ouchie, WAWA. My boss is smitten with you! He sure fills out those button-fly Levi's. *What an amazing ass.*" She sighs.

"He oozes skirt-chaser, *not interested.* I lived through that nightmarish hell with Mom." I clench my jaw and shudder.

"So, if he asks you out, you'll reject him?" Cha Cha leans in to see my reaction.

"Don't get ahead of yourself," I warn.

Midweek, I receive a call from Hunter Lane.

"Would you like to come to my place for dinner? I'll prepare my special Marinara sauce and introduce you to Buddy, my best friend." We settle on Saturday night. He ends with a *"Bah-Bye,"* in a clipped, cowboy accent.

What's the harm—to be feted by a gorgeous Renaissance Man? I'm cautiously curious. I drive to an area tucked away in the foothills of the Wet Mountains. A shire-like community, the small house is made of straw bales, solar-powered, with well water from a pristine underground stream. I'm greeted at the door by Buddy, an adorable 120 pound, Newfoundland who steals my heart within seconds.

The house smells of Dr. Bronner's peppermint soap, wood smoke, and fresh ground French Roast coffee. My nervous stomach clenches all through dinner. After a spread of spicy, Italian Sausage Marinara, salad, garlic French bread, and an expensive bottle of Cabernet Sauvignon—we smoke a joint. *He smoked prodigious amounts of pot.* We sit on the couch in the dark living room and he describes his current book: a compilation of Colorado creation stories. He gushes about Cha Cha.

"Best thing—*she introduced us.*" He slides next to me and plants a luscious, first kiss. Puffy soft lips, with a cool, minty taste, protrude from under the thick mustache.

He writes on a grand old oak Craftsman desk in a small office off the living room. The room decorated with Indian artifacts and blankets, and a small daybed which *we fly to another cosmos on.* I held back fervent tears, when making Love, not wanting to freak him out with excessive emotion. A long period had passed since sharing the precious gift of my body.

It was hard to leave this fantasy life after being with him. Elegant in a natural élan way. Driving away from his place, I soaked up the splendor of the lavender-tinted, Wet Mountains in my rearview mirror. Diminished by my black-and-white landscape after the spell of his Technicolor world. It harkened back to Darby Dawn days, optimism that evaporated when I return to the bleak realities of my life.

We share one last, enchanted weekend. Hunter plans every detail creating a Cinderella-like 48 hours. A spring snow fell lightly from a light red sky on a Friday evening. I experience a new level of nervousness when his blue pickup pulls in front of my cottage in Colorado City.

I open the door; he greets me with that effusive, mustached smile. The lion mane of wavy brown hair frames an ebullient face beaming with excitement. I'm bombarded with burgundy, bluegrass bolts of melody, and ribbons of poetry furling, a stirring of hope aches deep... until *I return to my senses.*

"Are you prepared for a kick-ass fun time?" He hands me a heavy, grocery bag of alcoholic spirits, leans in, and gives me a warm kiss. I've planned an elegant dinner, and in the morning we'll drive to Denver to the Colorado Museum of Natural

History to pick up research material. We'll stop at an exclusive liquor store that stocks all his favorite wines.

I prepare a Gorgonzola, clam linguini dish which he pairs with a citrusy, Pinot Grigio that compliments the pasta perfectly. An exquisite, caring Lover but his lifestyle, intelligence, and sublime Lovemaking aren't enough to convince my heart that he's safe. The rewards-to-costs-ratio: too risky—albeit, he's an astonishing rich respite, I desperately needed. *Candy for the soul.*

I adopt the negative worrywart, fretful mindset that plagued my mother. I studied at the feet of the master. Finally, after my twenty-seventh birthday, I stop living in my head. Overthinking leads to *"fearful thinking."* Fear is a thief—it robs you before you can even begin. *I stop letting the past steal my present,* and quit holding onto, what is meant to be let go.

What seems like an abyss turns into a foundation. I hand it all over to God—the negative narrative I'd wrapped myself in, and start attending mass, and praying, which helped to move beyond judgment. To sit silent, let Him speak to me through my thoughts, to free fall into the arms of God, *the only true solid security.* I desire Grace, Mercy, and Forgiveness—*His very name.*

I often visit Grandma Grace. We'd sit in her sunny, big kitchen with the dark purple African violets lining the windowsills, and the wafting of coffee, boiling pinto beans, and tortillas that lulled me into a comfy zone of well-being. We have long, easy conversations that meander to the subject of my finding a mate. She explains in sweet accented English that sounds like Spanish: "I pray the Rosary every day *mi'jita,* and I ask Santo Niño to please find you a Loving husband." It takes five long years but as promised Grandma Grace with her undying faith and constant prayers manifests a life partner for me.

A resplendent diamond among the rocks. I desire an honorable and trustworthy man. I relinquish control and let Divine Flow guide me, *simply by saying Yes.*

A coup de foudre—an arbitrary event that divides my life into the *Before and After.* I go for a run along my *beloved, Arkansas River* in Colorado City on a blue-tinted winter afternoon with Valentine's Day looming... and bump into the man I'd share my life with.

Luke runs toward me and tries to pass on a hilly, narrow section of the path, we dodge the same way and nearly knock each other over.

"That was a close call! Are you OK?" He reaches for me, laughing and a bit dazed.

"We both guessed the wrong way, how amusing." I grin. He's tall, blond, and tan, like a California surfer. He lives in my neighborhood and has spent the winter skiing. He moved from New Zealand landing there while on a globe-trotting trip after graduating from St. John's University.

"Can I run with you?" He asks. The Great Spirit has such a sense of humor: *pure, sweet, unmerited Grace.*

Leap

Old Love, leave me alone,
Old Love, just go on home
It's just an illusion
caused by how I used to feel
and it makes me so angry
I know now that I'll never learn.
–*Old Love* by Eric Clapton

L UKE AND I SPEND SHIMMERY, bluebird days courting on the ski slopes of Breckenridge, Copper Mountain, Keystone, Monarch, and Vail. He's an expert skier, who honed his technique in New Zealand. He's patient, considerate, and kind.

During the off-season, we bike, play tennis, hike, and camp. We go to football and hockey games at the Air Force Academy. We dine on calzones at a hangout pizzeria near the private college where we met on the trail that skirts the bank of the Arkansas River.

A month into our relationship, his father dies from heart failure, he returns to Minneapolis for the funeral. His mother and two younger sisters come to Colorado for a vacation. His tender attentiveness with them convinced me that *I'd found my man.* My mother claimed: "You can tell what kind of person a man is by the way he treats his mother."

It's the first time since moving back from northern California, that *I am truly happy*. I'm keeping the Distress-O-Meter at bay, *barely*. I have hives on both arms and average four to five hours of sleep a night, *a genetic gift from my mother*. I've the constitution of a skittish racehorse, but need to rustle up badass fierceness to transform my life with Luke. *Courage is being afraid and saddling up anyway*. Fake it, baby, till you become it. I've met the man of my dreams, at twenty-seven, I again, reinvent myself. *Time for California Dreamin'—Golden Pony Boy take me home*.

I didn't know what Love was until I knew what Love was not. I asked for what I wanted, stood steadfast, and believed in my intrinsic worth. Dawdling and weakness ruined it with Jack. *When True Love appears don't hesitate: jump in with both feet and ask questions later*. Most people don't find one great Love in their life; I'm blessed with two. I have a premonition after an unusual night of restful sleep. I wake up and see Luke and me in a sunbathed large kitchen, happy and surrounded by Loved ones.

I take him to meet Grandma Grace—she pulls me aside: *"Mi'jita, he's the one* I prayed for." Her tear-filled eyes light up as she squeezed my hand.

We share an overwhelming year of new experiences. He lands a lucrative sales representative job with a major pharmaceutical company and asks me to marry him. He's from a large, Irish Catholic family in Minnesota. He's dynamic, wicked smart, and adventurous. A free spirit who lives life full-tilt.

After a year engagement, we're married in a stone chapel nestled at the base of Pikes Peak on Fourth of July weekend. I found my place of belonging with Luke, and I'm *homeward bound*.

In our mid-thirties, after six years of marriage, our family expands to four. We have Emmet, a chubby, beautiful, baby boy, eight months old, and Richard, a gorgeous son, four years old. We pick Pleasant City to transfer to in 1990. The same town I lived in early twenties.

I'm juggling two boys under the age of five. Oldest son Richard is the best big brother, he goes to preschool half days. Baby Emmet nurses and wakes up in the middle of the night. I have few friends, no family nearby, and little relief. Luke, is an enormous help, but travels for work.

I'm blocked and dream of drowning in mud, sludge, and tar. One recurring nightmare I'm swallowed by quicksand. *I'm in a full-blown spiritual crisis.* The daily grind chips away at the translucent brilliance of living. I hand over the Keys to the Kingdom—my freedom, essence, and mystery for a secure life. The classic abrupt and unexpected rupture that occurs, in a comfortably, numb life, which blocks happiness. My desire to please resulted in high psychic costs. Denial is where the birth of rage ignites, under the guise of a *"good wife" and "good mother."*

My friend Viv, who I worked with as a teacher's aide in 1978, still lives in Pleasant City, and welcomes us with open arms. She teaches elementary school and attended the Psychic Institute receiving training in healing and psychic reading. I go to her for readings. She starts up a weekly women's healing group. We meet every Monday night, 5:15-6:15 p.m. for one hour.

Ten women gather at Viv's a comfortable house with adobe-colored walls and wooden floors. A mix of teachers, a veterinarian, a winery owner, a writer, and two retired ladies. Viv's a peaceful, calm introvert who *exudes sereneness.* She has short brown hair and warm, Loving eyes. For the first six months, she teaches us the basic aspects of healing. The group thins to five, loyal participants. Every week we learn about different levels of spiritual knowledge: chakras, grounding, protection roses, Cosmic energy, and mock-up screens.

Viv leads us in meditation for about 45 minutes; then we discuss what happens during the session. She ends with a light grounding and sends us home by 6:15 p.m. She teaches how to heal ourselves and to share the training with others. She offers this freely.

A steady, rhythmic pattern emerged over the next two years. Every week we're enlightened by her wisdom and by specific guides that help us along our spiritual path. During one of these meditations, I find myself at *The River.* I float above the small pasture where the black and white cows grazed.

I hear Viv's soft voice guiding to put up a protection rose above our aura and send grounding cords down to the center of the earth. "Feel the energy from Mother Earth come up through the feet chakras, through the ankles, legs, to the solar plexus bring cosmic energy through the crown chakra. Open up your chakras to receive the Golden Sun cleaning throughout your whole body, send it back down through your grounding cord," she instructed softly.

Hovering, I'm excited and curious why *I'm here of all places*—am I dreaming? Was I sleeping? It happens all the time; we poke light fun at the droolers and snorers during the session. One sweet, co-worker of Viv's, Patty, is a frequent sleeper.

I see the Labyrinth! Its as we left it. The clarity and realness overwhelm me, I choke back tears. I am comforted by the mountain wind song roaring through the trees. I didn't return to *The River* after Jack graduated in 1974. I was overcome with sadness and abandonment.

I'm flooded with emotions-possessed by FOMO, (fear of missing out) even before the onslaught of social media. I thought everyone lived in the crotch of the pleasure principle except me. The picture in my head *of how life is supposed to work out* constantly derailed me.

Viv gently brings us out of the meditation, "Reground your grounding cord, take a deep breath, reach up, and stretch." The meditation went longer than usual so I don't share the surprising River visit. Viv began her special prayer that ended each session. "As we meditate, we open the doors through which we increase our communication with the God of our heart. May it be with the blessings of the Supreme Being." It sounded similar to the one Caleb said at the christening of *The River,* some twenty years earlier. I gasp—a lone tear rolls down my cheek.

Viv ran quickly through the closing meditation. I delight in her grounding our beds, where we sleep, and the silver cord connecting our physical bodies to our astral bodies. Thrilling to visualize my soul wandering through the astral plane doing what it can't do in ordinary life.

Returning home, I write down every detail of *The River's* meditation visit. If it was a dream, why did it appear so lucid and vivid? I write an outline for this book. I'm inspired and *meant to do this,* the conditions are always going to be impossible. Since marrying Luke and having our beautiful sons, there was no time to be creative or so, I'd convinced myself. I still kept a journal and knew someday I'd find the time, and the discipline, *just now wasn't that time.* I cheated myself in the worst

284 AIMÉE MEDINA CARR

way. What I didn't realize, it's possible to write anywhere, any-time. *All that's needed is the desire, passion, and will to make it happen,* and to grant myself permission. It takes a kind of genius to save one's own life.

Viv told us how spiritual guides wait for us to ask for help. Our free will requires that we ask for their assistance. My hectic schedule with all its demands and activities was an excuse to stay in the muddled quagmire.

Fear of failure had a vice grip on me. I preferred the comfort zone of a self-imposed confinement. Standing in the doorway—half in, half out. Luckily, we *come to the Divine not by doing it right but by doing it wrong.*

Ten years turned quickly like a page, my boys are in college. Our destiny seems hidden but flows from one circumstance to the next. *Providence the divine thread, weaving through our lives.* The Supreme Being is the ultimate recycler. Nothing wasted, in the economy of Grace, *not even our worst sins, she uses them to soften our hearts toward everything.*

Viv resumes our Monday healing group—this time it's a perky psychic blond, Alana, from the old group, and Patty, now battling stomach cancer. Right out of the gate, I sense something different. It's Michael, my spiritual guide. He's a strong, unsettling presence, but my heart assures me, he's safe, and the protector of our family.

Viv introduces Michael the Archangel to me, adding that he chose me at birth. Archangels are powerful non-denominational angels who watch over earth's inhabitants. Michael, whose name means *He Who is Like God,* is the angel who eradicates the effects of fear, proving protection, courage, and backbone in the face of taking intimidating action. He believes *Love is the*

Power beyond Power.

Viv starts the meditation: "Visualize a line of energy from the base of your spine to the center of the planet. Chose a visual that suits you." She pauses. I imagine a thick, white rope with a large, metal hook, clicking into the center of the earth, that's my grounding cord. She continues, "See the Golden Sun above our bodies. Call to all, and ask for your energy back. Gold Sun's energy shines down on us cleaning out every cell, throughout our body. Continue to ground, release what's not needed down your grounding cord, refill with Golden Sun energy. Receive the healing energy. Go to the center of your head—the mind's eye releases any interference. Clean out the private psychic sanctuary behind the eyes. Relax—shoulders, face, and jaw, continue to ground and release." Her voice trails off.

I'm drifting—the first thing that appears is the sparkling cottonwood trees, they're shedding their "cotton." Small, white fluffy seeds blanket the ground. I'm relieved and delighted to see the Shangri-La of my youth isn't destroyed. My ancestors protect this sacred, hallowed ground. *I'm floating over my beloved River of Love in Red Cañon.*

I'm mentally ready: opportunities open up to allow the Goddess Aine, *Leap of Faith* to lead the way. *This is a sign—*I'm tired of spinning my wheels and desire to break free, stop the human doing and be the human being. Living Large people don't hold onto their opinions. They don't live in a world all or nothing, black or white. There's *a third way; not just flight or fight but hold the pain till it transforms you.*

I've returned to *The River*—there is only the *now*—you can't GET there; you can only BE there. Mercy must be part of the equation. My head and heart collaborate like a sacred circle

286 ÁIMÉE MEDINA CARR

dance, *receiving Love, allowing Love, and giving it back.*

I have immense guilt about the rift between Jack and me when he came to Pleasant City in 1978. How do I ever make it right with him? He cut me off, *so much time has passed.*

I hear Viv's faint voice; "Open up the chakras for a thorough cleansing, self-will lives in the chakra of the solar plexus. Trust the will of the Universe. Bring up Earth's energy to clean out all these energy channels—release all that's not needed, down the grounding cord to the center of the earth to be neutralized. Bring in the Golden Sun energy washing through all the body channels. Open up the crown chakra, direct cosmic energy to flow back of the head, neck, down the spine, and down the grounding cord."

I collapse in the grandma-like, rocking chair, my favorite spot to sit during meditation.

I can stop trying so damn hard. All those years of willing myself into being happy. *All I had to do was relax and let in the flow of life itself.* The simple lesson we learned *at The River.*

"Listen to the indwelling witness, the spirit that guides you. The wisdom and guidance you'll need to cross this chasm will be like Charon ferrying you across the river Styx, or Hermes guiding the soul across all scary boundaries. These are authentic soul friends and spiritual directors or elders. Celtic Christianity calls them *Anam Cara,*" whispers Michael.

I float over the riverbank and look across the welcoming water of the Arkansas River with its fast-moving waves and *wake-the-hell-up sound.* I'm so grateful for this revelation; a veil's been lifted. Downstream; twenty feet away, on a rock, sunning himself—the Great Blue Heron, with his slate blue-green puffy chest and perfect fanned feathered wings.

I wouldn't redo or take any of it back—*I'm so grateful for it all.* Even the messy bowl of spaghetti parts, the missed connections, the colossal mistakes that keep me awake at night and most responsible for putting me in the *flow of The River.* Such is the pattern of the soul, a progress of sorts, three steps forward, two steps backward which isn't a disaster—it's a Cha-Cha-Cha. *I didn't have to worry, He's been here all along,* watching over every misstep, stumble, and mistake. To go into my mistakenness *is to find God.* Through wounds, He opens up the heart.

I must not push *The River, trust that we are already in The River and the Creator is the certain flow and current.* The Divine Image is planted inherently and intrinsically within us. Divine is your secret name. *"I am my beloved's and my beloved is mine."* (Song of Solomon 6:3)

I commit to begin my book. It's early April, I call Cha Cha the next day and explain.

"Cha Cha, how are you, *comadre?"* I begin.

"So nice to hear your voice. What's up, Sis?" She knows something's different.

"I visited *The River* at healing group last night, and I want to start a book. Will you come to California and help me? I can rent the Dillon beach house for two weeks in July." She teaches poetry in schools for the Colorado Arts and Humanities program and has summers free.

"Hell, YEAH! We'll do a two-week writing workshop."

Intention is a powerful force. *Divina Providencia*. The freedom to create, no wimping out, or turning back.

Leap and the net will appear…

Doppelgängers

In youth we learn;
in age we understand.
–Marie Ebner-Eschenbach

CHA CHA ARRIVES AT DILLON BEACH after the long train trip on Amtrak. She drops the bags on the worn, wood floor in the small living room and announces curtly: "Let's go for a walk, *gotta see the ocean now,*" and beelines for the door. I grab my hoodie, phone, (camera) and a baseball cap. We follow the narrow, steep path down the bluff to the water. Three minutes from the front door to the waves—*pure bliss.*

We shuffle slowly on the beach, gathering our souls, allowing them to catch up to our bodies when *we see them coming.* They're right in front of us. A wavy, floating mirage of future, present, and past merging onto the cosmic beach highway of the Universe. Goddess Aphrodite, a mini look-alike of myself, and Goddess Rhiannon, a mini look-alike of Cha Cha, are walking toward us. It's like looking into a mirror of us thirty-five years ago: *the years shuttle backward.* They have the same wide-eyed gaze of teenage wonder we had at that age. These young beauties exude more confidence and poise, but still display eagerness and vulnerability.

Bronze with bikini tops and sarongs casually wrapped around their slim, petite hips. Effortless and no fuss beauty— *the best kind*. Their thick, long, black hair ripples in the beach breeze. Strong, toned, legs with barefoot springy steps in the soft, glistening sand. They're oblivious to their shimmering beauty and divine magnificence.

The beach is a frozen tableau lulled by sweet ancient ocean music. The Goddesses are swept up in their world. In a dance of talking, gesturing, and smiling, sharing every intimate thought, and feeling. A whirlwind of grace, beauty, and joy.

We act nonchalant as they float by, listening to their chirpy chatter. They don't look at us. We hold our breath, wait a couple of beats for them to walk far enough away. We turn and look at them longingly, one last time: our fresh-faced, supple, younger ravishing, doppelgängers.

"We're in an episode of the *Twilight Zone*," I said.

"*That was super freaky*, like looking at a mirror image but when we were in high school! We couldn't sell this to *Ripley's Believe it or Not*. What kind of sorcery is this?" Cha Cha's eyes widened. "Little bitches didn't even notice us. Find me a flat rock; they're still within beaning distance," she said miffed.

"¡Ay, Chavela! Look at them. They're a gift—what would you tell your younger self, if you had the chance?" I look over at her as she flashes me a big shit-eating grin. "Let's head back to the house. I need a drink." I said and linked my arm through hers, turning us back toward the gray weathered beach house above us on the barnacled bluff blanketed in yellow and orange ice plant flowers.

We dodge past the hoards of visiting dogs; Dillon Beach was a rare, dog-friendly beach. We see babies playing in the sand, older couples and families strolling. Clam diggers bent down, hard at work. A bright, multicolored dragon kite high above the beach dipping, diving sharply, then rising high, and twirling in the wind. Its long tail snaps with serpentine beauty.

At the beach house, I go into the kitchen, and open a bottle of my favorite jammy Syrah from a neighbor's winery. I pour a full, round, plump glass, and collapse in front of the large, picture window. I look out at the baby blue, Pacific Ocean in spectacular, panoramic view. Cha Cha's a recovered alcoholic, so she cracks open a pouch of medicinal Cannabis prescribed for insomnia. She had trouble sleeping after writing her memoir.

"I've got herbal raspberry ice tea—want some?" I offer.

"I'll sleep like a baby tonight." She sank into the chair beside me, we look like we're on the steer of a large boat in the ocean. The naked eye has a crystal clear view of the bay to Tomales Point, an enormous, tree-filled, green chunk of an island, across from Dillon Beach.

It was breathtaking.

"To answer your question, what would I tell my younger self? I'd advise young Cha Cha to stay away from Sun-In, it won't give you sun-streaked highlights. It turns black hair an ugly, brassy red. Remember, how pissed Auntie Alma was when we did it the summer before Junior High's school pictures?" She giggles.

"I'd tell mini-me to have confidence and trust in LOVE, that is our very being. The be all, end all. We are Love, plain and simple. *Trust the benevolent Universe.* Surprise of surprises— you come to wholeness not by doing it right but by doing it wrong. You learn more from mistakes and failures. *Wounds become our glory.* Let them teach you while releasing ego boundaries and keeping a watchful eye on awful pride. *Believe in the religion of nature, not of man.*" She pauses to take a sip of her ice tea.

"Don't let others determine who you are—don't fall for who's worthy and who's not. Have the inner freedom not to obsess over what society tells you about wealth, celebrities, social status, and power. Live simply and do what you *Love*. Find what you were put on this earth to do and *SOAR* with your given gifts. *By doing what you Love, time stops, life flows, and you don't work a day in your life.*

Go and teach others how to give, and meet with all walks of life, not just your kind, right, *comadre?*" She points her chin at me to signal my turn.

I hold up my glass of wine ogling the dark burgundy color in the alpenglow.

"Love is the beginning, Love is the middle, and Love is the end, we will be judged *only by how much we Loved* in our lifetimes. *Love gives life its meaning.* Life gives us this one chance to Love.

Joy is another emotion. She uses it to delight in herself, through us, in us. *Joy is it: be led by it.* You cannot choose it; it comes through unsatisfied desire while you are relishing the perfection of a moment. It's an inherent, *inside job* determined by the eye of the enjoyer. Joy is entering into the clearest insight and perception into the Eternal. *Joy is the utter reality.*

Saint Francis believed we are troubadours, minstrels for God. Don't be afraid to be a fool or be too serious. I'd tell my younger self to pray for the connections that allow her heart to grow. Find out who you are, your deepest desires—this will lead you to express your true self, the reason and purpose you're here. We all have one or two unique gifts to give the world.

Our doubts are traitors and make us lose the good we oft might win by fearing the attempt.—William Shakespeare. Fear is lack of faith, don't be a victim of it. *Try new and scary experiences* cultivating growth that pushes you out of comfort zones." I sipped my wine.

"You can't pay me enough to be nineteen again. I've earned my scars; I don't want to go through all that pain twice." Cha Cha clenches her jaw.

This is a two-week writing workshop vacation with my soul & heart sister, poet, writer, and theater performer. I'm beginning my first novel; she's working on a One Woman show for theater. I reserved the dates in April from the owner, a church friend. A recharge our batteries place. To write, read, listen to music, savor old notes from high school, and do Goddess card readings. Walks on the beach collecting shells, starfish, and heart-shaped rocks. Rejoicing at the pelicans, sea otters, and all the species of birds that live here. Long stretches spent on this beach and I become a bliss ninny.

The best thing—the solar-power quits around nine o'clock which forces us to go to bed early. I'm a habitual night owl so this alters my routine. Also, the spotty Internet allows for *real connections.*

"I got an idea while writing my memoir. I want to contact the old high school friends that we partied with at *The River.* The forty-year Sacred Heart School reunion is next summer. Let's organize our own reunion for The River of Love Gang. *Whaddaya think?*" She asks.

"Wow! That totally came out of nowhere. Hmmm... It's a fantastic idea. Is *The River* with the fire ring and the Labyrinth even still there? I haven't gone there since my mid-thirties.

"Oh yeah, it's there, no one knows the Labyrinth exists but us. We hid it well, down the thick deer path. The city built a nature walking trail on the other side of *The River,* so there's no traffic in our area. I double-checked before I left; it looks like the day we built it.

"It'd be fun to have them all back in Red Cañon and have a picnic. There's a hot-air balloon festival on Memorial Weekend, the same weekend as the reunion. My hubby can get the old dormitory to stay in. It will be like a big slumber party except now, we have diabetes, gray hair, and arthritis." She rubs her sore knee.

"Speak for yourself, *vieja*—my hair is colored every six weeks.

"Qué, Qué, say that again?" She feigns being hard of hearing.

"I do have Martin's contact info. He found me on Facebook last year, and we met in Santa Cruz at Christmas. He brought his guitar and played on the beach for Luke and I. We talked, laughed, and visited for hours. The veil of forty years lifted as we time traveled back to high school, as familiar as yesterday. *I Love when that happens.* He'd have some of their contacts. Sure, why the hell not? Let's shoot for Memorial Weekend in Red Cañon. I'll have most of my book done; you can help me edit it after they leave." I get a rush of excitement.

She pops up, rifles through her suitcase, and pulls out Ostara, the Goddess of Fertility card. *"It's the perfect time to start new projects, access new ideas, and give birth to new conditions.'* This card jumped out of the deck while packing, a propitious omen." She winks.

"I'm hungry, let's slap a couple of sandwiches together, and watch the sunset on the beach." I said. I'm verklempt; there's one person who won't come to our little wingding reunion. I look out at the vast, shimmering, Pacific Ocean. The large window frames the bay, I'm on the steer of a magical boat connected to the Source. "Time to throw off the bowlines, sail headlong and breathless from the safe harbor, raise the sails to catch the gale force of the *Spirit*."

The pesky questions that can unravel a life, patiently wait, urging me to be a shade braver. Neil Young's song *Trail of Love* rumbles through my thoughts: *"Sail along, sail along silver moon. Don't be blue I know in time we'll meet again. We come and go that way, my friend. It's part of me and part of you. I'll always be a part of you."*

Chavela Finds Clarity

Let us not look back in anger
or forward in fear
but around in awareness.
–James Thurber

CHA CHA CHECKS ON THE LABYRINTh before The River of Love Gang returns to Red Cañon for a reunion. She brings gardening gloves, a small trowel, a pruner, and garbage bags to tidy up *The River*.

She maintains it usually after visits to the family graves at the nearby cemetery. She spiffs up her Auntie Alma's grave with fresh flowers, feeds and prunes the radiant, red rose bush at the base of the rose granite headstone with the exquisite Mother Mary design.

Cha Cha rode her cute red Ruckus scooter with a basket for Bear, her Border Collie. She pulled and dug up weeds, re-set stones in the Labyrinth and picked up trash. She keeps a notebook and pen handy in case a poem or an idea pops into her head, for the One-Woman show. Repetitive, menial chores often jump-start the creative side of her brain and open up the unconscious. Long walks work the same magic.

The Labyrinth and campsite are on the north side of *The River* opposite side of the Arkansas Riverwalk Trail, a walking trail owned and operated by the local recreation and park district. Ten years ago, the city built a bridge 100 yards west of *The River* area an integral connector route for drivers to avoid downtown traffic.

She's a natural comic, with one-liners and funny phrases that flew off the pages of her notes from junior high and high school. Our favorites and most used were: "Wise-out! Wish me lucksies, Put that in your Funk & Wagnall, Dat's cool, Rap on, Oh Shorts! Who axed you? Spot cha' later, Comprendo? Get it On, Honkeys eat shit, Chicanos eat beans, Funky Honky, Geemaneeze, Keep the Faith, and Crusty (dirty look). Right-on, Chore (sure), Dream on... Muchita, Brown Sugar, Throwin' a Drag, Motor Scooter (crotch), Rosca, (rear end) groovsie hap's, Sock it to me! Guffy's (boobs), 'and that's the truth pfpf!'" (Little Edith on Laugh-In).

I have every scrap and precious note of the *mini-time capsules,* even the silly and cryptic ones. We kept daily journals, wrote volumes of poetry, *our true essence revealed in the writing,* and between the lines. She drew funny pictures and quoted lyrics. We thrived on these notes, as kids do now for texts. Virginia Woolf called letter writing the Humane Art.

Notes are like photographs, returning us to that exact moment in time revealing our souls. The notes have the old book smell—lignin, a polymer related to vanilla. Paper when stored for years breaks down and smells warm and sweet.

Chavela in her fifties, after years of floundering and missteps, transforms her life through stages of understanding. Alcoholism, drug use, and hopelessness kept her off track for many years, but she held on, steadfast.

She's introduced to her husband, quits drinking, graduates from college, and discovers her writing voice. Her inner sight returns and creates beautiful poetry. Her experiences help others, her strength and power transform lives. *Nothing is ever wasted, nothing is lost.* I tease her that *we're late bloomers.* Our second act is going to be *chingón.*

The Goddess Lakshimi—Bright Future, aids her. She quits worrying which relaxes her, and the writing starts to flow. She serendipitously finds a publisher and the first book of poetry is published. Chavela lands a once in a lifetime, dream job— teaching poetry to elementary and middle school children.

The Great Spirit is more a verb than a noun and manifests her wishes/dreams/requests. Deliberate and honest work opened channels, intuition, ideas, characters, and words. It all flows—remembering our ancestors through stories, poems, and art. A form of prayer—attention—if we don't tell our stories, *who will?*

Cha Cha finished her memoirs. It resurfaced sad and painful memories that flared up her depression. A cousin molested her at five years of age; it tainted her life until she wrote about it and worked through the trauma. She exorcised the pain body to free herself from victimhood and feelings of unworthiness. Can't start the next chapter if you keep re-reading the last one.

She knew I'd like to renew old friendships and rekindle happy memories. The upcoming Sacred Heart School, joint classes reunion, inspired her. How invigorating to walk the Labyrinth again *with them.* Would the ancestors make one last appearance? If she had the means, she'd arrange for the biggest, over-the-top firework show to rival the huge professional Fourth of July celebrations.

Her perfect fantasy was to find the band that played the day we built the Labyrinth. They were Sacred Heart School students Jack paid off with Sensimilla, or Panama Red, from *Boulder on the Hill*. A dicey spot to score primo drugs, near the University of Colorado in Boulder. Drugs weren't as potent as they are today. Now, children with autism and epilepsy receive relief from CBD Cannabinoids (chemical compounds of cannabis flowers). A special song of Martin Piruzian's or from the Morgan twins would have to suffice.

I wrestled with how to contact Jack, afraid that if I called he'd hang up on me. I decided to write him a letter. On a crisp, spring morning, while pedaling up a moderate ascent on my mountain bike, *I'm given a portentous sighting*; a large, five-point buck waits for me at the top of the hill. The magnificent beast is statute-still on the left-hand side of the summit. He faces east toward the sun with his head turned in my direction, beaming intense brown eyes right at me.

I jump off the bike, onto the shoulder of the road. I freeze; I don't want to startle the vision in front of me. I stand mannequin still, holding my breath when a car comes up from behind me. The buck heads up a steep bank to the apple orchard above. He looks down at me for one, long eternal moment, and then disappears. *I know it's my dad.*

Dear Jack,

It's been so long. I see you're still in Dallas. I live in northern California. I've been working in the film and TV industry for ten years, but this year I began writing a novel. A total work of fiction, I take pleasure in letting my imagination do its creative thing.

Martin Piruzian found me on Facebook before I started this journey. I visited with Martin, and we shared fun memories about Sacred Heart School.

Chavela finished a memoir and had a great idea of gathering The River Gang for a reunion. I hope you can make it we're planning for Memorial weekend. Sacred Heart School is hosting the 40th high school reunion for the class of 1975 and with a balloon festival to revive tourism for the rebuilt suspension bridge after a disastrous fire.

I hope time has healed the old wounds that kept us apart. I'd like the chance to reconnect and begin anew.

I hope you are doing fantastic.

All the Very Best,
Rose

River of Love Reunion

Pleasure is found first in anticipation,
later in memory.
–Gustave Flaubert

It's Memorial weekend in Red Cañon, Colorado, and underway is the Inaugural Balloon Classic Festival and the 40th high school reunion, Class of 1975, at the Sacred Heart High School. I drive by and see the trucks with balloon baskets on trailers in the field. They're preparing for tomorrow's 6 a.m. launch, weather permitting. A lot of *breaking-the-fun-barrier potential,* if there's liftoff. The lush, green, Wet Mountains stood guard in the background.

I'm meeting my friends at El Martinez Mexican restaurant, a small adobe building that was a rendezvous meeting place; Jack Dillon, Caleb King, Scarlett & Sadie Morgan, Oliver Fellini, Gonzo (Gomez) Gallegos, and Martin Piruzian. We arrive in separate cars at the parking lot on the eastern edge of town.

"This place hasn't changed at all!" Caleb said. He inhales a spicy tamale aroma, as he unfolds his lanky legs, and spills out of the small rental car. The tidy cap of blond curls is a shade darker with strands of silver; his glacial blue eyes twinkle

Redford-like. He was the best-looking stunner at the preppy Sacred Heart School. Caleb at fifty-nine is still a *"stone fox."* He writes spiritual books, lives in Tibet, is married with two teenage boys.

I open the car door and shoot toward Jack Dillon. I see Jack's pupils flare immersed in the sunlit, iridescent halo of my coal black hair, and the flash of the high voltage smile reminiscent from high school.

"Man, oh, Man—*you look amazing!"* I said. We embrace. His long, glossy, chestnut, hair is now, thin and gray. His smoke-blue eyes glisten with tears. We're instantly transported forty-four years to the millisecond our eyes locked, and everything irrevocably changed. A bittersweet blast of nostalgic affection so indomitable it knocks me back a step.

He smiles warmly, "Like an instant type of time travel, huh?" I clasped my hand over my mouth and nod.

A sweet miracle that our paths crossed in the small mountain town. A cosmic accident of perfect conditions that aligned our transformation. We're part of the 78 million baby boomers in this country. Children of the 1960s, born between 1946-1964. Counterculture radicals who end up running the world like Bill and Hillary Clinton. *If you remember the Sixties, you weren't there.*

I was a wife and mother during the tyrannical 1980-90s, the *"women can do it all"* period. I'm a fair-weather hippie who traded my radical, revolutionary 1960s card for the secure life of medical health insurance and a 401k retirement. I'm a stay-at-home Mom until my sons were in middle school then went to work in independent films. I began as a property master then, producer and writer.

Jack Dillon's a computer analyst in Dallas. He is in a long-term relationship, *not married, but not alone*. He's never married and has no children. We managed a couple of short visits after he graduated in 1974, but after I married in 1986, we lost touch for thirty years.

The Morgan sisters are fraternal twins. They moved to Red Cañon sophomore year in high school. They were keen, peace Lovin' hippies. Sadie has a girlish shape with long, flowing, brown hair. Now at fifty-six, she's a straight-laced, Bible-thumping, mother of six, and lives in Colorado City. She's elegant in a gauzy, light blue sundress. Scarlett has short, flaxen hair. In high school, it was long and silky. She's single, lives in Seattle and owns a bookstore. Casual in khaki shorts and a white T-shirt, the sisters, sport silver rings and bracelets glinting in the summer sun. They jump out of the car and run over to Jack and Caleb who they greet and hug.

The last car to pull up contains Oliver, Gonzo, and Martin. Oliver's a small, wiry slip of a man with the same kind eyes and Loving spirit. I beeline into his arms. Second, to Jack, I missed Ollie the most. We corresponded after graduation but lost track of each other about twenty years ago.

Oliver was out of the closet in 1972, his schoolmates accepted him. Gonzo, also gay, was Oliver's roommate. He was a fragile and shy Hispanic boy from New Mexico, dragged to *The River* for parties. He is unrecognizable—heavyset with thin, salt and pepper hair. He's uncomfortable, *just like in high school*.

Martin is a professional musician and played guitar at all *The River* parties. A sweet, comforting soul, a year younger, and left behind after the older boys graduated and scattered to different colleges. He hasn't changed with just a few streaks of gray hair.

We stroll to the street that leads us to *The River*. The rural neighborhood is still a farming community with local businesses. A machine shop on the east side with Holstein cows fenced in a pasture, on the west side of the street.

Cha Cha patiently waits for us at the corner of the main road to *The River*. Her braided, Mestiza hair is streaked with silver. She shouts, "*¡Órale!* There you are!" A cosmic echo ripples from forty years ago. "I thought I was going to experience *The River* solo." She scolded.

"*¡Ay, Chavela!*" We yell loudly, in unison. *A spitfire* who doesn't take a backseat to no one. She orchestrated the first walk-out protest in 1970, at Red Cañon Junior High School. In stern defiance, our group demanded to add blue jeans to the strict and limited dress code of dresses and pantsuits only for females. She came up with the idea on a frigid, snowy winter Monday morning before class; we're smoking cigarettes behind the little corner store across the street from the junior high school.

"Damn, I'm freezing my ass off is this ridiculous dress!" Cha Cha clutched at her down jacket tight shaking while puffing on a Marlboro. "I want to wear warm jeans to school. I nearly got hypothermia walking that bitch of a mile this morning." She says through chattering teeth.

"Yeah, jeans would rock. What should we do?" I ask.

"Let's organize a walk-out protest. We'll get phone numbers for a phone tree alerting when to bring jeans and at lunch change into them. Stash protest signs in the bushes beforehand and march-the-fuck onto Main Street in front of the school protesting the asinine archaic dress code." Cha Cha works herself into a lather strutting cocky like Mick Jagger.

Everything went as planned. Over 70 girls participated including Ms. Wogg the English teacher, and Ms. Manray the drama teacher. They provided a white bullhorn for Cha Cha who led the cheer while we marched: "What do we want? JEANS! When do we want them? NOW!"

We didn't receive everything we demanded jeans allowed only on Fridays but set a precedent by the time we get to high school jeans are commonplace. We won, giving us a taste of power in groups (*sisterhood*) and leadership.

Life as participation, of which the sixties with its imperfect movements was all about. Lives transformed by Vietnam, Watergate, the Sexual Revolution, Equal Rights for Women, the Civil Rights Movement, including American Indian and Black Power Movements, and the War on Poverty. The epoch teemed with tumultuous spiritual and social change. The current wave of acceptance and popularity of Marijuana—is a definite echo from the Sixties.

America's forms of justice were hard fought for in the sixties, including Women's reproductive rights that have eroded steadily, an undoing of a century of progress along with anti-immigrant resentments surging. We continue today to confront and struggle with systemic racism, the most serious dilemma our country faces.

Martin Luther King Jr. marched on Washington for jobs, civil and economic rights. He called for an end to racism and appeared to raise consciousness that made inroads into fighting it. Delivered on the steps of the Lincoln Memorial in August of 1963, the *"I Have a Dream"* speech was not in the original text but turned out to be the defining moment of the American Civil rights movement.

What most remembered, wasn't planned—Mahalia Jackson called out: *"Tell them about the dream, Martin!"* A woman spoke up and made a difference. He believed we must live as brother and sisters or perish as fools. After Dr. King's assassination, it was back to business as usual for people in power. Now, Xenophobia smolders, stoked by political politics that throws raging fuel on prejudice and racism along with hatred for the poor and underclass. *These United Divided States.*

We must fight for an America that works for all of us. In a cyclical pattern of the sixties, once again our nation relies on the effervescence of hopeful youth and the wisdom of women. The goal is to *move the boulder of good forward* for the emergence into an ever-greater consciousness of an aware and renewed world.

Our high school friends paid no attention to race, class, and gender. Back then, the world was dazzling new, ours to explore, companionship thick as trees along our divine magnetic *River of Love. Flowing ~ flowing ~ flowing. "Let The River take you..."*

Hearth of the Divine

Gratitude is happiness,
doubled by wonder.
–C.K. Chesterton

THE GROUP REACHED *THE RIVER* and was shocked by the lack of change—the Labyrinth was exactly the way they left it. *"¡Ay, híjole!* Isn't it perfect? Forty years later and no vandalism or punks messin' with our sacred space." Cha Cha beams with pride.

"It's untouched—just like old Indian burial grounds, nothing disturbed them," I said.

The rush and uplift of fresh running water, the beloved elms and sacred cottonwoods stand watch with their soft, pulpy, fragrance. The afternoon light shoots through the leaves and set them aglow like shards of green and yellow glass.

The fire ring is as we left it, The Spirit illuminates us with *Grace,* pulsing, positive charged ions, that gently blankets us with energy. One by one, we walk the Labyrinth, feeling the powerful familiar flow of *boundless Love.* Forty years have passed, we're moved by the warmth, closeness, *and the electricity in the air.* I haven't experienced this since I left the inside of this soft, tender world.

"Who knew, what we stumbled upon? We were so fortunate to meet and build these wondrous friendships and experiences. *The River was the center and source of our connection.* Can you believe this power? I don't feel this in church, is it possibly because we're outside?" Jack asked.

"César Chávez said there are two types of churches—one of buildings and *one of the people*," I said.

"Grace builds on nature. Troubles appear because we refuse to sit quietly for awhile each day. Don't underestimate creative solitude," Sadie said.

Oliver is holding a large picnic basket and calls us over by *The River.* He lays down a blanket and pulls out sandwiches, potato chips and fruit. Gonzo lugs a cooler of drinks to the sitting area.

"We need to ground ourselves with food; please sit and eat. Thank you, Cha Cha, for providing all this lovely refreshment for us." Her truck is parked near the entrance of the path.

We're all gazing at *The River*, hypnotized by the slapping, flowing waves. Light bounces off the water, tossing in every direction like a sparkling chandelier.

"The biggest lesson I learned from *The River*, Scarlett squinted at the twinkling reflectors, *was to Love yourself.* Without it, you can't be happy. Learn that, and you're home free. There's an old Hindu story: Long ago all men were Gods, but it's stripped from them by lesser Gods. They try to bury man's divinity in the center of the earth, or in the ocean, finally, they hid it deep inside man, knowing he wouldn't look there. Holiness masked well. The proud won't recognize it, and the humble fall into it every day. *Jesus found it,*" Scarlett said.

"After we graduated and left Red Cañon, I didn't cope well with the emptiness." I bow my head. Oliver leans in and put his head on my shoulder. "With everything ripped away, I lost the ability to say YES to a higher power. Finally, in my late twenties, I admitted my powerlessness and asked for help. I quit trying so hard, relaxed, and let Spirit steer. *I receive the insight if it was to be, it would come to full fruition on its own accord, and if it not, grant me the light to see and understand that.*"

I swing my arms around Oliver and Cha Cha. "The Love that the Great Spirit extends covers every part of our being. If we don't believe this, we divide ourselves into good and bad, hating one another. Accepting inner poverty—*emptiness.* I had an epiphany in my thirties, looking out at the water; I asked *why am I trying to push The River?* I let go of the reins and accepted radical grace." I let out a huge sigh.

"Had you returned to *The River* before then?" Jack asks with a slight Texan accent.

"No, there were too many memories, and it made me miss everyone. It's hard for me to visit Red Cañon. Going to *The River* fell out of favor with the Sacred Heart School boys who found other places to party. It wasn't the same after the seniors graduated and left," I explain.

"Home at the *Hearth of the Divine.* The most precious lesson I learned from this place was compassion; I've made it my life's work. Just let the water flow—breathe, receive, and give into the flow." Caleb took in a deep breath and let it out slowly. He tapped into an elemental spirituality in his books after working as a freelance photographer with the non-profit group Doctors Without Borders.

"I learned not to give in to insatiable appetites and the dissatisfaction of not having enough. The more you get, the more you want. It diminished delighting in the now because we're preoccupied with what's next. *Ravenous consumption*—the hedonic treadmill we're trained from an early age, to need and want more. Hands grasping at earthly treasures too occupied to clasp *God's hands as he holds them out to us in Love*. Caleb glanced around making eye contact with each one of us.

"*I find detachment allows flow*. Constant protecting and worrying inhibits flow. *Life's not a problem to be solved but a mystery to be lived*. The more you let yourself go, it returns stronger—the paradox of flow. Detachment leads to freedom. Whenever you're not preoccupied with the outcome, you can relax," Caleb said with a broad smile. He has the same charismatic, free spirit as the early mystics, a gift only a higher power can give. He walks over to the edge of the riverbank, picks up a flat rock, and sends it skittering across the rushing Arkansas River.

We spot the Great Blue Heron downstream, preening for us on the opposite riverbank. Martin stretches out his legs. "God has three answers to our prayers—yes, later, and no, *I've got something better*. I savor solitude: it's when I write my best music. I'm awed by the generosity and care I receive when touring." Martin said.

Gonzo looks down at his hands. "I didn't understand this place. It was creepy and haunted. I came this weekend to catch up with old friends." He crossed his arms.

"Some things aren't explainable; words get in the way. You either get it, or you don't. The anarchy of the ineffable." Sadie says and smiles at him.

"It's an individual choice; you choose what to see. Our attitudes and perceptions create our reality. How you Love one thing is how you Love everything, awareness is a subtle, simple concept and hard to teach. I look at the pure presence in each moment before I label, critique, categorize, exclude, or judge it up or down. It's the key to experiencing this place." Caleb turns to face him. Gonzo's crimson red face stares unblinkingly into the distance.

"I'm thrilled for us all *to be together*, again and I'm grateful for this place and you—*my oldest and dearest friends*. Let's go to the dorms and motel and prepare for tonight's festivities." Cha Cha stands up from the cooler she's sitting on.

I stride over to the Labyrinth and slowly wander over the treasured stones that symbolize a significant time in our young lives. Everything is complete. *I'm overflowing with indescribable happiness.* "It's like this, like that." Saint John of the Cross worded how unexplainable the sheer joy of Grace can be. The force field is intact.

The guys head to the Comfort Inn motel to check-in, and to get ready for the Balloon Festival, and the high school reunion. The women luck out; we stay as guests at Sacred Heart School, in Hedley Hall, the old student dorm. Chavela's resourceful husband, Vito, was a caretaker at the winery, and made all the arrangements.

We enter the 1960 style, two-story, red-brick block structure. *I turn sweet 16, again* with a fear pang in the pit of my stomach from the terror of being caught by beady, black eyes. I've returned forty years later to the scene of the crime-Jack's old dorm. It smells of Pinesol and decades of stale air with cracked, yellowed linoleum from layers of floor wax.

I pour a large, spirit-enhancing, glass of wine. Cha Cha

opens a bottle of water. We pull chairs together and put our feet up, for a quick, relaxing chat.

"Well, so far, so good. Everyone's having fun, except Gonzo." She rolls her eyes.

"What a grand idea to reunite The River Gang—*Kick off your high heel sneakers. It's party time.*" I serenade her with the Steely Dan's song, *FM*.

The art of moving on, without letting go. The time before I met my husband Luke, was full of disappointments, and wrong choices. I'd given up hope of finding Love until renewed by Luke's kind eyes, a man with a heart of gold, whose favorite word is *"Outstanding!"*

We shape the inherent possibilities, maximize the good, the true, and the beautiful. The Infinite Source manifests *in the now*. Grace shines and transforms us if we are willing.

Love is Short–
Forgetting is Long

Never cut what you can untie.
–Robert Frost

W E MOSEY OVER TO RED CAÑON'S first inaugural Balloon Festival in the southwest corner of the old Sacred Heart School campus. Nine hot-air balloons will launch weather permitting, each morning at 6:30 a.m. Skydiving demonstrations, arts and crafts vendors, wine tasting, and live music rounded out the festivities.

We arrive early evening, food and craft booths line up in big white tents on the grassy grounds. We mull around eating sticky cinnamon buns. The white, portable stage looks exactly like the one used years ago at Chautauqua Park. A Brass Quintet plays a lively, jazzy tune.

The main event is the Balloon Glow. The pilots will light up the hot-air balloons like light bulbs. Oliver suggests checking out the Sacred Heart Wine Tasting room.

"Let's go drink the monks' Kool-Aid." He smiles squint-eyed, and sprints up the stairs, his petite, wisp of a body disappears into the crowd. The building has the look of a Swiss Chalet; it's the old nunnery converted into a wine tasting room.

It's packed making it impossible for our large group to stand together at the bar. We push Jack and Caleb up to where the tasting room hostess dribbles wine into glasses. She describes the Ascension, an exclusive American Merlot, the monks released in honor of the Balloon Festival. Caleb asks politely, "Nine glasses of the new release, please." Jack helps scoop up the glasses. We huddle in a cramped corner and sip our wine.

Now, with our wine glasses, we're free to go to the bar and try different varietals. We play wine-roulette, trading glasses, and tasting each other's wine. We're boisterous and loud, people stare and move away from us.

"Yes, move along, we're Sacred Heart School alumni royalty, we have full reign here. *Be gone, unworthy masses.* I spit in your general direction. Oops, I'm channeling Monty Python." Oliver chuckles. He pulls out a Kazoo from his lilac, Oxford shirt pocket.

"No effen way, Ollie! *That's insane!*" Jack cries. "At the Sacred Heart vs. Alamosa basketball playoff game, junior year, the illustrious Maestro Oliver organized a half-time Kazoo music performance, all in the name of school spirit." Jack bows his head toward Oliver.

"Tell us about it," Scarlett said.

"I was a team spirit whore," he quips.

"What songs did you play?" Sadie asks.

"Someone had to step up; we had no school band. The administration canned *Mad Monk,* a.k.a. Brother Owen for inciting the crowds with his rockin' organ. So, after a couple of practices with Gonzo, Martin, and Mac we put on a decent show at halftime. We played the Puffa Puffa Rice song— Tchaikovsky's *1812 Overture,* Don McLean's, *American Pie,*

The Eagles, *Take it Easy,* and Jethro Tull's, *Aqualung,* the crowd's favorite."

"We got beatdown by Alamosa like we were grade schoolers," Caleb moans. He was on the varsity team that got waxed.

"After the game, we escaped to *The River,* drowning our sorrows," Martin adds.

"A senior let me borrow his car to run to *The River,* and while haulin' ass I sideswiped a telephone pole." Jack pauses to drink his wine. "Dale Wolf's orange Bronco got crashed on a regular basis, and they'd just roll it right back on its wheels." He laughs.

"It's surreal being here," Martin said. His face brightened with the mutual warmth enveloping us. Cha Cha throws an arm around his shoulders, *"So happy to be together, again."* I grab Oliver, and Mr. Drama screams, *"Yeow!* What a death grip, chica. Nice biceps, do you lift hay bales on your farm?" It turns into a 60s style, trippy Lovefest with juggled wine glasses sploshing, shifting bodies embracing, sipping, and laughing.

"Madre de Dios, que vino!" Cha Cha squeals.

"Ollie, we live on 2.5 acres in the Sierra Nevada foothills, known for its wine and apples. I grow a salsa garden (chili and tomatoes), with my sweet dog, Sophie, and a rambunctious cat, Mimi, my muse. Mountain lions, coyotes, and bears roam the back forty. Also, red-tailed hawks, quail, hummingbirds, possums, raccoons, deer, and red foxes." I sniff the wine and upend the glass; I'm surprised by the rich and complex taste.

"I'm not a Merlot fan, but this is tasty." I lick my lips.

We inch up to the bar to try more vintages. A lively optimism hover above us. *Vino Veritas; from wine comes truth.* We're exuberant with the friendship agreement forged by solid invisible bonding threads and a robust *heart connection.*

The packed room empties out—the Balloon Glow was about to begin. We file out the door toward the open field where the multicolored, hot air balloons balanced. The pilots blast hot air, lighting them with the burners, slowly illuminating them. One by one, they gleam, and glow bright, a kaleidoscope of brilliant colors. We levitate with the balloons.

The Quintet's sturdy horns echoed through the field; the mild summer night tickles with a light ruffling breeze. The Wet Mountains surround us like Indians warriors.

Sadie's crystal blue eyes flash with excitement, "The vibrant colors make me *feel so grateful to be alive.*" I glance at Jack, and he quickly looks away. I'm not sure if he's avoiding me, or I just tasted too much Merlot.

"They look like floating dinosaurs." Caleb chuckles.

"Let's grab some cotton candy and check out the band," Scarlett breaks the spell.

We meander over to the stables and barn area where the Gymkhanas' and barn dances took place. The fence of the corral and barn are made of stone with a wood hayloft. There's a collective group sigh; this is hallowed ground for Caleb.

He hailed from Santa Fe, New Mexico, and adored horses. Growing up with vaqueros I'm aware that *Cowboys aren't born they're made.* Caleb is an animal and Nature Lover. Friends still talk about the enormous, pristine aquarium of colorful fish in his dorm room. It was the perfect bubbling object of obsession after smoking pot or dropping acid at *The River.*

How does a place after forty years, hold hearts so tenderly? I'm weak-kneed, and I didn't even go to this school. Jack bends down and whispers, "Do you remember when we climbed up there?" He points at the hayloft.

"No, was it great?" I ask.

"Ouch! My heart's skewered." He bit his lip and clutched at his heart. I shoot him a look that said—*we'll discuss this later.* He was mine when he was filled with wonder and promise.

We walk across U.S. Highway 50, to the old stomping ground: Star Bar Bowling Alley. We divide into teams and bowl a couple of rowdy games. I down two Viking-sized beer mugs and fumble my way to the bathroom of the *new and improved* neon bowling alley.

I see Jack at the bar sitting by himself. I push open the door to the women's bathroom and rehearse what to say to him. Not an ideal setting, but time is running out. He's leaving tomorrow after a visit to *The River*, where we'd all be together. What if I don't get to talk to him alone? I want assurance that we're OK. We need to talk it out tonight. I've waited thirty-six years to tackle the bugbear that's kept us apart and to *let go of the miasma of regret.* Transform the mistakes, the selfish, willful, shadow side of the psyche.

Forgiveness is an act of letting go, and the only way to be free from the entrapment of the past. Those who give and receive it become a conduit of the flow. I want to heal this unfinished business and restart a friendship (philia) with Jack.

Jack and I aren't *Free Birds,* like when we first met. Now we have partners, families, and responsibilities. I refuse to reside in this contaminated psychic field processing decades-old wounds. Our experiences need to be *experienced all the way through*, especially the most wounding ones. My goal is to make amends with him: to start anew. It's easy to let go of the past, once I realized, no matter how different it might've gone down. *I couldn't be Loved more than I am now.*

"May I join you?" I hop onto the barstool next to him. Breathe deep from the belly; exhale slow, my heart races.

"Sure, why not," he said. The smell of stale cigarettes and mildew permeates the air. The dark, neon blue and green, poor lighting, cast a cavernous pall. We focus on our reflections in the mirrored splash-back in front of us, which is behind the bar.

"I'm pleased you came this weekend. I wanted to see you." I scan his insouciant reaction—*nada*. He takes a drink. "Why is that?" His expression was cold and distant. He wasn't going to make this easy. I've never had a hot flash, but it's a burner under the hood. *En Fuego.*

"To apologize and mend our friendship which was para-mount even to being Lovers.. I thrived on the hours of talking, listening, and being there for each other. I admired your word-play and clever musings, poking fun without offending. *I miss that.*" I squirm on the hard stool, adding to my misery. He's going to say something sarcastic, or ignore it altogether, equally hurtful. Either way, I'm toast.

"*Being Lovers wasn't so bad.*" He throws his signature saucy, sideways glance that whips through my heart. I brace my hands on the bar to steady myself.

"I've missed your snarky personality, these last thirty years." He smiles. I laugh too loud; relieved he's letting me off the hook.

"So, old friend—hmmm... I like the sound of that." He looks straight ahead, not registering any emotion. "Are you happy?" he asks.

"*Enormously so,* I'm blessed beyond measure." We lock eyes in the mirror.

"That's all that matters." He drinks his beer. "It feels odd to be here, like slipping into younger skin and reliving a past life. I didn't know how detrimental academically Sacred Heart School was until I got to Tulane and was two years behind. It's strange, after living in many tolerant locales, conservative, Red Cañon was the gayest place I ever lived.

The song, *The Low Spark of High Heeled Boys*, asked: 'If you had a minute to breathe and they granted you one final wish, would you ask for something like another chance?' My answer would be no, I've had my turn. Let someone else take my place to do better. This trip down memory lane taught me that I'm damn lucky to meet such interesting people and fortunate enough to take a long, recollection of yesteryear. He flashed a smile and hollers at the bartender.

"Can you please bring this lovely lady a beer?"

"Why did you come, it doesn't sound like our memories matched up?" I ask.

"I was impressed with your letter and surprised how you still feel responsible for our demise. *We participated in it equally*, although, when you played *Torn between Two Lovers* on the jukebox during the California visit, *I almost went ballistic*. To find out your 'roommate' was a boyfriend, was equivalent to a donkey kick in the ribs.

That trip wasn't responsible for our expiration. In retrospect, the decision to leave the state weighed heavier on the outcome. I could've graduated a semester early and gone to a school nearby. Our relationship was doomed from the start and damaged further by my abandonment of going to college so far away.." He turned to look at me.

It's bell-clear, all those years; *I Loved him more*. I handed my heart to someone who recklessly discarded it. The chelas about to do the talking. Stunned, I let it sink in.

"Pump the brakes, sister!"

I recalled how the younger version of me operated: I put my happiness in the hands of others. Young Rose lacked the confidence and self-esteem to demand her needs met. *I should have Loved him less and Loved myself more.* I hadn't figured out the most fundamental law of the universe: ask for what you want.

Better to Love too much, than not eno*ugh. Everything comes back to you anyway; it's all a gift.* Let life happen, life is in the right, in any case. Looking back, *Jack was a stepping-stone to my wild and precious life.* Jack's visit to California was such a seminal event, sending me back to Colorado to meet my husband Luke.

I shrugged off what a fool I was. He just relieved me of a lifetime of illusions. I turned to face him: "I'm grateful for the insight you've given me." Carl Jung rode the torture train: *where you stumble and fall, there you will find pure gold.* Not the fools' gold I harbored all those years.

The experiences we shared, helped me grow into the woman Luke fell in Love with. It allowed me to open my heart to him and appreciate the Love he has to offer*: to trust again.* Spirit pushed me forward to the next step of my life.

"You never married or had children?" I ask. I overheard him tell one of the guys.

"I have a partner; she's an analyst at the firm where I work. We've been together twenty years." His demeanor shifts to uncomfortable. I don't know where to go from here. The bartender's impeccable timing eases the tension. He places an icy, draft Porter in front of me.

We drink in silence for a few, uncomfortable minutes. Sitting with Jack Dillon after all these years, I feel relief, closure. *Ayyy... I'm free.* A graceful, mellow ending to a fiery, teenage romance that ignited many passions, not only in us but in all that came to *The River—The Flowing Stream.* I recall the wish I made during the Miracle Kiss with Martin, forty years later, *it's finally granted*—to have Jack in my life in some form.

We're both so different. Divine Loves difference. *I want to recover and inhabit the graciousness of our relationship.* It's larger than the errors made in the late seventies.

Friendship is an act of recognition; it is most treasured as the years go by. *I believe in resurrection, reset, and second chances.* Contradictions within us harmonize and give way to streams of growth and beauty... Out of the winter and into the spring. I had to try, one last time.

He remained through the years; the idealized *lost chance*—it's far harder to kill a phantom than a reality. He's the one lost to bad luck, failed effort and the aphorism of *who not* to hand your heart to. My first glimpse of him in El Martinez's parking lot he looked tired and frail.

Jack—*the Giant Love of my life,* who I overly romanticized whittled down to a mere mortal. A real flesh and bone person who stooped passively in baggy grandpa jeans. *Don't trust your memories.* I didn't know Jack—*only the chimera of him.* Let light in through the cracks for patience and less judgment. My sin was expecting perfection. All I crave now is *Love and Union.*

This *messy art of facing things...* Pain is the price we pay for being human, but suffering caused by illusion is optional. The power is *being in the present and being connected.* To not get rid of, but *to let be with compassion.* Let things come and go on their own, *to flow like a riverbed,* which is continually receiving and letting go at the same time. Constant receptivity and non-clinging release, *no forcing or holding back.*

"No one knows this, but Chavela and I had a falling out and lost touch for about ten years. When she proposed this reunion, I'd hoped to reconnect with you." I shifted my weight.

"How did you find each other again?" He asked.

"At my Grandmother's Grace funeral. We ate together at the luncheon afterward and rekindled our relationship. Cha Cha Loved her so much. *Grandmother Grace, once again, worked Divine Love in my life.*

"Cha Cha supported me through the deaths of my parents when I needed help the most, opened her home to my family. She came to California to help me start my book. Reuniting was *a blessing of pure grace.*" I fought back tears. *This is definitely, my last beer.*

"I still don't understand why you want to re-establish friendships from forty years ago, we've all changed, and there's no chance of connecting with any regularity. It seems like a waste of time," he says. I cock my head to examine him to see if he's serious.

"If I had that attitude with Cha Cha after the estrangement, there'd been no reunion. I'd have a huge hole in my life." *I'm totally flummoxed and getting irritated.* "Man, oh man, I get it—if you don't want to be friends. I'm sorry for what happened between us. I don't know how many *true friends* you have, but these are precious people that *I want back in my life.* Friendship is sweet beyond the sweetness of life and is ultimately defined by the desire of each person to be involved. It merely needs tending, built on past experiences. It has a sturdiness Love may lack." *The wild Apache is about to rear her angry head.*

"Whoa, you're not going to punch me like your sister? *You're so feisty!*" He laughed. "I'm just pushing your buttons, Rose." He leans toward me, nearly falling off the barstool, chuckling. "I'm not that big of a hardass." He pokes me in the side, *just like old times.*

The River of Love Gang was watching us from the ridiculous, dark bowling lanes they struggled to bowl on. There's a group sigh of relief when Jack pokes me. Sadie asks the obvious question, "Why didn't they end up together?"

They're huddled around pitchers of beer, squinting in the dark. Oliver quickly explains, "He visited her in California, and it went south, and they don't see each other again."

"That's it, they just quit? Why didn't they fight for their Love? *Everything came so easy to them.* They were the epitome of happiness. We all wanted what they had. They hit a bumpy patch, and caved? I don't get it." Scarlett shakes her head.

"We can walk away from our history, but it doesn't mean it lets us go," Caleb said.

I jump off the butt-busting barstool. Willie Nelson's *Blue Skies* blasts from the jukebox.

"Before you stomp off—where's my sweetgrass?" he demands.

"Did you say you're a *smart-ASS?*" I finish my beer and rub my sore behind.

"If we're going to be friends and the jury is still out on that—*you've got to ditch the Texas twang.*" I walk over to where the others who pretend to be bowling.

"Get me out of here, before I go blind! Let's go eat breakfast at the Village Inn," Oliver barks. He turns and throws a strike down the bowling lane, pins popping up, flying wildly.

The Four Loves

philia: friendship
Eros: passion
storge: familial Love
agape: infinite Love

–Center for Action
and Contemplation

Love is My Religion

Love is my religion—
I could die for that—
I could die for you. My
Creed is Love and you
are its only tenet.

–John Keats

Jack Dillon (8:30 AM) We are waaayyy too hungover to go to brunch at Belvedines. Can we meet at the Chapel around 10:00 am? We want to check out the vineyard and tasting room before going to The River.

I RECEIVE A TEXT FROM JACK. Last night we planned before turning in around 2:30 a.m. to assemble at a reasonable hour and go to brunch at Belvedines—Red Cañon's *only premier* restaurant. Owned by an established Italian family that prepared delicious, authentic, Italian pasta dishes.

They offer a fancy, Sunday Champagne brunch buffet. Their specialty is thick char-grilled steaks, a signature salad drenched in a garlic vinaigrette dressing with big chunks of blue cheese, and bottomless baskets of sweet, Italian bread. It was the place to go for dates, to get engaged, anniversaries, birthday's, sports award dinners, and Prom. My cheerleading squad was feted with banquets three years straight for State Championship titles won.

Belvedines' bar area had barrel-shaped, overstuffed leather chairs, and a gigantic aquarium. Jack and Caleb go with Paul Rosas a friend of Caleb's from Santa Fe, and Toots Stone, one of the hell-raising Texan boys. They share a boisterous dinner when the check comes they ante up their portions of the bill. Toots offers to take it up to the cashier and then, skips out with the money! Luckily, Paul knew the waitress who put the charges on his tab.

Belvedines hadn't changed in thirty years when Luke and I treat my parents to a romantic dinner. It's during a brief reconciliation period before they divorced in 1986, *after thirty-five years of marriage*. A sad time for our family.

Dad took Mom's Love for granted, unable to appreciate its extraordinary mystery. He assumed she'd take care of him forever, forgive any misdeed, dalliance, and screw up. He shocked her by his lack of judgment and discretion.

But *Love has its limits* when the end came; he chose another woman over her. Years passed, Mom waited for him to return, the sadness almost swallowed her up, she had to let go to survive. She's the abandoned woman, but Love for him remained in her heart.

A few years before his stroke, Dad called Mom and begged her forgiveness, which she granted without hesitation. He asked to come back into her heart and home.

"No Blaze, it's too late." She still Loved him as fiercely as the day they met. It was *First and Forever Love* that she took to the grave. Catholic vows of marriage are a permanent bond. He was her one and only.

I fall in Love with Luke, my future husband during this horrible time of the hellish divorce. She relied on Lucy, Lana, and Rae through this dark and bleak period. Being around Mom was like trying to rescue a drowning woman thrashing wild: I feared going down with her.

I text Scarlett and Sadie the change of plans and roll over to savor the quiet before taking a shower. Cha Cha's still sleeping and will be bummed about brunch since she didn't drink last night and won't be hungover. I'll make it up to her after they leave.

The massive, four-story Tudor Gothic monastery is impressive, with large, stained glass windows. This site is on the National Register of Historic Places. The Abbey monastery built in 1924, all 66,000 square feet. Workers poured fittings for the foundation and by the next day they were gone, they'd constructed it on an underground river. The school opened in 1926, survived the Ku Klux Klan, the Depression, and three major wars. It operated on a pure, indomitable spirit.

The monks closed the school in 1985. They dwindled down in numbers, poor financial decisions by the Abbot put the property at risk. The last nine monks relocated to different monasteries in the Midwest and East Coast. The monks spent their lives at the Benedictine monastery; *it was their only home.* The church is no longer consecrated and the property sold to the highest bidder.

Oliver grabs my hand, and we race up the stairs of the monastery to the doors of the chapel with Martin, Sadie, Scarlett, Jack, Caleb, Gonzo, and Cha Cha following behind us making their way up the grand stone staircase.

"They strongly encouraged us to go to mass on Sunday; mandatory for the lower and optional for the upperclassman. Headmaster Rio had a group of seniors called the *Rice Christians,* who attended mass on Sundays. He bribed them with brunch next door at the Ramada Inn restaurant. The idea came from missionaries in China that doled out rice to attend services. He averaged between 15-20 boys for brunch. Miles Layton and I played bluegrass music at mass on Sundays," Martin said.

"I thought mass was for the Catholic boys and the others got to opt out," Cha Cha says while climbing the long, limestone staircase to the Chapel entrance. She's radiant with dark, tanned skin, in a white sundress cinched with a Navajo turquoise silver concho belt, and Huarache sandals.

"No opting out here, the priests were strict with us. They had to be, or it would've been total anarchy. We still, managed to raise hell." Oliver chuckles. We reach the large, double wooden doors that look like those of King Arthur's Court.

The men *(and priests)* walk in quietly, one at a time, dipping their fingers in the font of the holy water. Making the sign of the cross, filing into the pews, rote style as if in a trance, the same way they did it, every morning, 40 *(400)* years ago.

Their eyes dart back and forth, at one another. Martin sings softly, a Gregorian chant: "*Sperges me Dómi-ne, hyssópo et mundá.*" Oliver joins in, and they repeat the phrase, five to six times. Harmony of the spheres, angels swing open the welcoming gates of heaven.

"What are we here for? *Propter Chorum,* the monks say: for the sake of the choir." Oliver replies. All the sweet, Glee Club, memories wash over him. Every student was required to take Art, Typing class, Glee Club, and Gymkhana.

"Remember that a young person should "drop-in" to the world and serve as a citadel of integrity assisting his fellow man and recognizing his relationship with God," Martin recites the school's mission statement.

"How impressive!" Sadie claps, the flashback mesmerizes the ladies. Sadie's the least changed of the group. A time traveler from the 1970s. Clad in a tie-dyed blue T-shirt and blue jeans. *She still wears Birkenstocks.* Her long, waist length, thick, chestnut brown hair has shimmery, streaks of silver. She still has an effusive, natural glow.

"This brings back a flood of memories, mostly, oppressive ones." Caleb jump-starts the trip down memory lane. "The funniest I recall was the older, retired monks who slept through mass with heads bobbing and dribbling drool." He grins. Jack nods in agreement.

Caleb and Jack didn't attend mass often, but when they did, it was together. They were inseparable.

"We snuck into the monastery and raided the jugs of the sacramental wine." Jack made a twisted, sour face.

"I adored the angelic pipe organ, the vesper chimes, and the Gregorian chants sung so perfect by the monks. I saw a child run screaming from the monk's library, scared by the 20-foot cross with the tortured Jesus face," Gonzo said.

"My weirdest, hella-scary experience was walking down the hallway, just outside this door. I bumped into Father Otto, and said 'good morning,' he nodded back at me. Later, at the Community Center, I saw on the bulletin board his picture and obituary! He died three months, earlier. I was at Father Lloyd's bedside when he died—*the smell of roses filled the room.*" Oliver's eyes glistened.

The magical spell is broken by Gonzo's cell phone ringing.

"Remember the days before cell phones, before computers? Computers are addictive, habituating, and hijack the brain. I do my work, shut it off, or wander for hours. I constantly battle with the time suck entities." I crossed my arms and scoot back in the church pew.

Cha Cha shifts her body forward. "The one thing baby boomers will be known for is that we were the generation that came of age *before the Internet*... The digital revolution madness. No matter how tech-savvy and early adaptive one is; we lived in a world before it all came to be. The only fluent translators of the *Before and After,* there's a rare preciousness in that." She sighs.

Jack stands up in the pew and faces the group. "Those armed with tons of data believe they got it all figured out. Wisdom lies in the higher realm of consciousness, surrounding us and constantly recreating. It's in the mystics of all ages and faiths, in art, psychology, myth, and science. Knowledge removes us from the mythic world. Information and wisdom are two separate things. Wisdom involves that written above and below the lines; *the perfect balance between intelligence and Love."* Jack glances at Caleb for confirmation.

Caleb begins slowly, "We've confused knowledge with true wisdom for far too long. They're not the same, although, both are finally necessary. Dionysius called it *'super-essential knowing'* or third-eye seeing when our heart space, our mind space, and body awareness are all simultaneously opened up to *presence.* We flow into the naked and undefended now.

"We suffer from a nature deficit disorder and have to connect daily with nature or lose renewal. It's so necessary for survival. We need neighborhood gardens, potted plants, stargazing, and night walks. Keep close to nature's softening influence to feel beauty. Silence and waiting are how the higher power slips into our lives, and when the timing is right, *we are his instruments.* The mind is a beautiful thing but if it's truth you're seeking—*the soul reveals it.*" Caleb stands up; he senses the group's restlessness.

"It's wine-thirty! Let's go to the winery. We need a little hair of the dog," Oliver said. We stop at a coffee shop in the old Community Center. The 14,000 sq. FT facility barely completed when Jack arrived his junior year in 1972. It's where students and monks ate their communal meals. It was the student's living room: the small dorm rooms were used for sleeping and studying.

We grab bagels and coffee and amble over to the tasting room. We're passing by the barn when Jack gives me a broad smile. It was our special hiding place between the Indian Lore Building and the barn, in the old Sky Chief: we laid in the bedroom size backseat talking and necking for hours.

Caleb spells out slowly, "G-y-m-k-h-a-n-a. The coolest program the school offered. Second, to basketball, it was my favorite part of the day. I Loved riding my horse June, what a beauty. I fed her twice a day and helped Brother Daniel with cleaning the stalls.

The Indian Lore building in front of the barn was where they stored all the Indian artifacts. Including the weapons and outfits used at the summer camp held in the Sangre de Cristo Mountains. Brother Daniel ran the camp with his favorite students. Each camper was given an Indian name and taught Indian lore and ways of living in the wilderness. It was a beautiful, mountain lodge and an excellent recruiting tool. Most of the campers participated at an early age, went on to enroll in the four-year high school.

The tasting room had a few couples at the bar. It smelled of cheese and musty wood. A young man appears from a back room, greets us with extra enthusiasm when Ollie mentions they're Sacred Heart School alumni. He'll give us a tour after dealing with the other customers. He pours us generous tastes of the recent award-winning harvest.

When he returns, he begins with a bit of history: "After the closing of the school in 1985, it takes the Benedictine Order until 2003, to transform it into a working winery. Our first taste is the Revelation: A Bordeaux style blend, loaded with black currant and toasted American oak.

"There are more delicious wines in the warehouse, still in barrels, if you'd like to taste them," he offers.

"Yes, please when you're ready," I say eagerly. He signals for us to follow him through the back room to a large metal outbuilding. The wines are stored in oak barrels, stacked high in metal rack rows. He dips a siphon; also known as the thief, (plastic syringe) in the small opening of the barrel, dripping the wine, gently into each wine glass.

We sample a Cabernet Franc loaded with rich, red fruit flavors, with a hint of herbs, one of my favorite wines. Next, was an opulent Syrah—fruity and full-bodied. By now, we're feeling no pain, our bellies sloshing with high dollar wine. I ask Cha Cha for a Goddess reading for the traveler's journey ahead.

"Perfect timing, I received a message while basking in the Gregorian chant in the chapel. She came to me: Mary Magdalene, '*Love yourself, others and every situation—no matter what the outward appearances may be.*' Mary will see you all, safely home," Cha Cha assured them.

"Hallelujah! *Love is my religion!*" Oliver shouts from behind a barrel, where he's hiding, waiting to jump out and scare one of us. The Morgan sisters broke into a rendition of *Revival* by the Allman Brothers; "*People can you feel it? Love is everywhere,*" waving their hands Holy Roller style. Caleb looks at his watch; "Hey troops, we're running out of time for a visit to *The River*. Is everyone OK with that?" he asks. We nod in agreement. We got started too late while drinking too much.

"I'm off to Annapurna, Himalaya to lead an expedition. I'll be leading a group on horseback through the deepest gorge of the Himalayas. They get to participate in a Tiji festival. Pray for mild weather," Caleb requests.

"I'm moving from Seattle to Albuquerque. I sold my bookstore; I'm going to live with my sister, Eve. A new beginning for me, the rain in Seattle wore me down, so did the recession and Amazon," Scarlett said.

Sadie shrugged. "Same old shtick for me, raising kids, watching the days flitter by."

Martin is about to release a new album, begin a West Coast tour, and will visit me in the Sierra Nevada foothills.

Oliver has a whopper of a surprise: "I'm moving to Denver to start a novitiate program with the Denver Diocese." He clasped his hands over his mouth, holds his breath, and waits for our reaction. A huge galvanic roar erupts from the peanut gallery.

"*You wait till now, to tell us this ginormous news?* Come here; you deserve big, fat, noogies!" I scolded.

"The timing didn't work out, and this weekend wasn't about me but about connecting with old friends. I want to keep this on the down-low, in case I fall flat on my face. I've gotten a strange reaction from people—like I'm suddenly going to be a Bible thumper. That's not my style; holier-than-thou people, usually end up holier than nobody. I'll gather everyone's contact info from Rosie, expect me for a visit when it's least convenient," he jokes.

"Are you flying home tonight Rose?" Jack asks.

"So grateful I'm not with this hangover. I'm spending the week at Cha Cha's. She's helping me edit my book. Might dive in after you leave." I wink at her.

She rolls her eyes and clucks her tongue: "Oh no, you didn't just say that, we're chillin' when we get home." She bends over and rubs her sore knee.

I take my drink outside to admire the rows of grapes growing. It's why I Love living in northern California's wine country. The *perfect ending* to the reunion weekend.

We don't need to go to *The River—it is in our hearts and in our way of being.* We'll return when we need renewal. They've flights to catch and lives to resume.

The open wounds poked and prodded, time to tie-up the loose ends and frayed feelings. A tear rolls down my cheek. I can't stop it. Push it aside to be reabsorbed by my heart. I'm just another silly girl Love made a fool of. Jack never Loved me; *he Loved the way I Loved him.* Don't smother sorrow it dissipates once the underlying lessons are revealed. After letting go—God and Grace lead the way. Hard learned lessons of how relationships worked: a dance of mutual honesty, vulnerability, grace, and forgiveness. I release the ashes of the past, and *I'm free.*

We strive every day to make ourselves different and somehow, managed to remain the same person we were years ago.

The journey between who you once were and who you are be-coming *is where the dance of life really takes place.*

The Sacred Heart School students became *The Island of Lost Boys* whose shore I washed up on. *They were beacons of Love in my life.* Martin later emailed me: "Without knowing it at the time, we were all Lovingly, cradled in the silent hand of God." The people we Love most, become part of us physically, ingrained in our synapses, in our memories.

Aristotle believed that memory is the scribe of the soul. *The past is not dead until we learn its lessons good and bad, it changes by what we remember. Don't let its power steal the present.* We're given the gift of this short reunion. Bittersweet as the memories of high school. *Mysteries are created backward.*

There is no reason for regrets—*a huge relief,* things had to happen the way they did. Rolled out in imperfect patterns. We see each other differently, at first, until looking closer; we see *querencia,* where it all came together.

Our collective memories of *The River,* Red Cañon, Sacred Heart School, Love of music—the same soundtrack playing in the background, *was pure magic.* We shared a history that made us permanently connected and lived through such a tu-multuous transformation of society.

I'm standing at the intersection of past, present, and future. *Everything Belongs,* even the sad, futile, and hurtful parts. I close my eyes and retrace our steps throughout the weekend. I *lay yellow rose petals along the paths we walked.* I place a basket of pink roses at *The River* carried away by its bounding waves. I bless all the places we visited, every soul we came in contact with, *my friends, and this transformative experience.*

The cherished old friends stand on the shores of their magnificent immensity with this inspired reconnection for the next stages of our lives. *I believe in resurrection, reset, and second chances.* All are redeeming and reckoned with, everything absolved, caressed lovingly by the magic of new beginnings. I roll the luscious, deep purple elixir in my glass, and look out at the voluptuous vineyard dripping with plump grapes—*Mother Nature at her sexiest.* I inhale a fruity ancient breeze rolling gently off the Wet Mountains.

The hard work of Love is so essential to our unfolding; do we hold steady to its teaching tasks to be illuminated by its greatness? *I've come to trust infinite Love in finite stages.*

I recall with nostalgic radiance similar joyful weekends spent in high school. Experiencing the center of the universe with this band of bohemians, desperados, heroes, hooligans, trailblazers, underdogs, rapscallion rebels, radical non-conformists, renegades, rainmakers, rabble-rousers, Rainbow Riders, rogues, roustabouts, counterculture vagabonds, iconoclasts, free spirits, firebrands, groundbreakers, wanderers, Sages, Sojourners, Midnight Ramblers, and Mavericks.

My Beloved Band of Gypsies.

We are stardust (billion-year-old carbon)
We are golden (caught in the Devils bargain)
And we got to get ourselves
Back to the garden

ACKNOWLEDGMENTS

I want to thank you, the reader for choosing my story. To my sisters-in-arms Juliana Aragón Fatula—my North Star and Leslie M. Browning for her creative spirit, discerning taste, and kind heart. I am eternally grateful and thankful. To my mother—Emma Aragón Medina, Grandmothers—Barbara Vigil Medina and Genoveva Gallegos Aragón, sisters—Barb Medina and Jan DeCino, and aunties—Rose Solano and Susan Cruz. To my ancestors of strong women: *mujeres muy mujeres.*

Cheers to the three amigos muses-Michael Gulezian, Ralph Smith, and Ron Lopez (Michael Bergeman too). Mucho gracias to all the Holy Cross Abbey friends who generously shared their memories that helped fill in the gaps. I honor your friendship.

Thank you Patty Stephens for your beautiful familia, song, and a lifetime of friendship.

A heartfelt thank you to Father Richard Rohr for his constant inspiration and gift of the beautiful title.

My deepest gratitude and appreciation to my husband Chris who makes all this possible and has supported me in every way.

ABOUT THE AUTHOR

Aimée Medina Carr is a fifth-generation Indigenous Southern Colorado native, who lives in northern California in the foothills of the Sierra Nevada Mountains with her husband, two grown sons, two cats, and a Labradoodle.

She worked for ten years in film and television production. Her debut novel *River of Love* received Honorable Mention for the Landmark Prize for Fiction Award given by Homebound Publications in 2017.

Indigenous peoples' have survived by storytelling-a form of resistance. We're the ancestors of an age to come-a collective spirit through the centuries that work to make a difference, every generation has to move the boulder of good forward. If we don't tell our stories, who will?

Que Viva las Palabras!

You can visit Aimée at aimeemedinacarr.com.

HOMEBOUND PUBLICATIONS

Ensuring that the mainstream isn't the only stream.

AT HOMEBOUND PUBLICATIONS, we publish books written by independent voices for independent minds. Our books focus on a return to simplicity and balance, connection to the earth and each other, and the search for meaning and authenticity. We strive to ensure that the mainstream is not the only stream. In all our titles, our intention is to introduce new perspectives that will directly aid humankind in the trials we face at present as a global village.